continued . . .

"Sefton weaves yarn, fiber arts, and cooking into the mystery in ways that enhance it." —*Booklist*

"Very poignant and emotionally wringing." —*Gumshoe Review*

"A surprisingly entertaining story with a satisfactorily unexpected ending." —*Colorado Country Life*

Fleece Navidad

"Perfect for creating a warm, celebratory holiday atmosphere that readers will relish. [Do] drop in at the House of Lambspun and join its cozy knitting circle for excellent camaraderie and conversation." —*Mystery Scene*

"As feel-good a cozy as you can get . . . [A] perfect read either while waiting for Christmas to arrive or when snuggling down after the turkey dinner has been devoured." —*Mystery Books News*

"Visit Kelly Flynn and her friends for the holidays—it's never dull and will make you nostalgic for good friends and good times . . . You'll certainly enjoy these tasty recipes and the knitting projects." —*Gumshoe Review*

"A fun, quick read to curl up with when the stresses of the season get to be too much. Knitting and patterns and holiday recipes of the treats Kelly and her friends share complete the experience." —*The Mystery Reader*

"*Fleece Navidad* has it all: gift shopping, knitting Christmas gifts, baking—even a church pageant." —*Cozy Library*

"An enjoyable cozy mystery with a wonderful cast." —*MyShelf.com*

Dyer Consequences

"Make a glass of lemonade, find a porch swing, and cozy up to this cozy." —*Colorado Springs Independent*

"They just keep getting better . . . Each visit with Kelly and her friends becomes more enjoyable than the one before."
—*Gumshoe Review*

"Sure to please series fans." —*Publishers Weekly*

A Killer Stitch

"Plenty to enjoy . . . Settle back in front of a cracking fire and enjoy the company of Kelly and co." —*MyShelf.com*

"As light and fluffy as one of Kelly's balls of yarn . . . Readers may enjoy reading this book almost as much as they'll delight in knitting the cable knit scarf." —*Library Journal*

A Deadly Yarn

"A terrific series with a heroine who grows more and more likable with each investigation." —*The Mystery Reader*

"The whodunit is well crafted . . . A delightful mystery."
—*The Best Reviews*

Needled to Death

"Kelly is easy to like . . . A fun, quick read." —*The Mystery Reader*

"[A] tightly stitched tale." —*The Best Reviews*

Knit One, Kill Two

"Cozy up with a great new author . . . Well-drawn characters and a wickedly clever plot—you'll love unraveling this mystery!"
—*Laura Childs, New York Times bestselling author*

Unraveled

Maggie Sefton

BERKLEY PRIME CRIME, NEW YORK

THE BERKLEY PUBLISHING GROUP
Published by the Penguin Group
Penguin Group (USA) Inc.
375 Hudson Street, New York, New York 10014, USA

Penguin Group (Canada), 90 Eglinton Avenue East, Suite 700, Toronto, Ontario M4P 2Y3, Canada
(a division of Pearson Penguin Canada Inc.) • Penguin Books Ltd., 80 Strand, London WC2R 0RL,
England • Penguin Group Ireland, 25 St. Stephen's Green, Dublin 2, Ireland (a division of Penguin
Books Ltd.) • Penguin Group (Australia), 250 Camberwell Road, Camberwell, Victoria 3124, Australia
(a division of Pearson Australia Group Pty. Ltd.) • Penguin Books India Pvt. Ltd., 11 Community
Centre, Panchsheel Park, New Delhi—110 017, India • Penguin Group (NZ), 67 Apollo Drive,
Rosedale, Auckland 0632, New Zealand (a division of Pearson New Zealand Ltd.) • Penguin Books
(South Africa) (Pty.) Ltd., 24 Sturdee Avenue, Rosebank, Johannesburg 2196, South Africa

Penguin Books Ltd., Registered Offices: 80 Strand, London WC2R 0RL, England

This is a work of fiction. Names, characters, places, and incidents either are the product of the author's
imagination or are used fictitiously, and any resemblance to actual persons, living or dead, business
establishments, events, or locales is entirely coincidental. The publisher does not have any control over
and does not assume any responsibility for author or third-party websites or their content.

PUBLISHER'S NOTE: The recipes contained in this book are to be followed
exactly as written. The publisher is not responsible for your specific health or allergy needs
that may require medical supervision. The publisher is not responsible for any adverse
reactions to the recipes contained in this book.

UNRAVELED

A Berkley Prime Crime Book / published by arrangement with the author

PUBLISHING HISTORY
Berkley Prime Crime hardcover edition / June 2011
Berkley Prime Crime mass-market edition / June 2012

ISBN: 978-0-425-25128-7

BERKLEY® PRIME CRIME
Berkley Prime Crime Books are published by The Berkley Publishing Group,
a division of Penguin Group (USA) Inc.,
375 Hudson Street, New York, New York 10014.
BERKLEY® PRIME CRIME and the PRIME CRIME logo are trademarks of
Penguin Group (USA) Inc.

PRINTED IN THE UNITED STATES OF AMERICA

10 9 8 7 6 5 4 3 2 1

Acknowledgments

First, I want to thank Kristin Aamodt of Bellingham, Washington, for the novel's title, *Unraveled*. I had a "Name a Kelly Flynn Mystery" contest on my website last year and received many wonderful title suggestions, but Kristin's was a particularly apt description of what had happened in Kelly and Steve's relationship. Thank you again, Kristin.

Second, I want to thank my oldest daughter, Christine, for helping me describe in words what actually happens on the volleyball court. Christine was a star volleyball player in high school and in college years ago, playing in the SEC Division I. As a proud parent, I spent many a year on the bleachers watching the game as a spectator. Those skills come in handy when you're a novelist, and particularly when I wrote the "amateur" volleyball game scene that takes place in *Unraveled*. However, I did want to make sure I had the correct terminology when I tried to describe the action. Christine has coached secondary-school volleyball for years (in addition to a full-time business career *and* a mother of four) and is presently the Head Volleyball Coach for Fairfax High School in Fairfax, Virginia. If there are any mistakes in the description of the scene, please chalk it up to my note-taking.

Next, I want to thank Liesbeth Gren of Northern Colorado who sent me the recipe for the Yummy Chocolate Cake. I met Liesbeth briefly at a Bridal Show in Loveland, Colorado, two years ago when I was writing *Skein of the Crime*.

ACKNOWLEDGMENTS

That's the book where Kelly and her friends accompany Megan on a tour of several bridal shops in the search for the "perfect" wedding gown. Liesbeth told me about her yummy recipe then.

And last, I'd like to mention the exhibition that I attended in Chantilly, Virginia, in April 2010. I wanted to research particular scenes and found all the information I would need. The exhibition was organized and run by C & E Gun Shows and Showmasters of Blacksburg, Virginia.

Cast of Characters

Kelly Flynn—financial accountant and part-time sleuth, refugee from East Coast corporate CPA firm

Steve Townsend—architect and builder in Fort Connor, Colorado, and Kelly's ex-boyfriend

KELLY'S FRIENDS:

Jennifer Stroud—real estate agent, part-time waitress

Lisa Gerrard—physical therapist

Megan Smith—IT consultant, another corporate refugee

Marty Harrington—lawyer, Megan's fiancé

Greg Carruthers—university instructor, Lisa's boyfriend

Pete Wainwright—owner of Pete's café in the back of Kelly's favorite knitting shop, House of Lambspun

LAMBSPUN FAMILY AND REGULARS:

Mimi Shafer—Lambspun shop owner and knitting expert, known to Kelly and her friends as "Mother Mimi"

Burt Parker—retired Fort Connor police detective, Lambspun spinner-in-residence

Hilda and Lizzie von Steuben—spinster sisters, retired schoolteachers, and exquisite knitters

CAST OF CHARACTERS

Curt Stackhouse—Colorado rancher, Kelly's mentor and advisor

Jayleen Swinson—Alpaca rancher and Colorado Cowgirl

Connie and Rosa—Lambspun shop personnel

Unraveled

One

Kelly Flynn stepped out onto the wooden deck of Jayleen Swinson's rustic mountain log home. Clutching her ceramic mug of coffee against the cold, Kelly stood by the railing and gazed out at the snow-covered mountains in the distance. From this high up in Bellevue Canyon, north of Fort Connor, she could glimpse peaks of the Colorado Rockies behind the canyon ridges. A chilled early March breeze set the tall ponderosa pines to swaying and caused Kelly to shiver. Winter wasn't over yet, despite the sound of her friends' laughter coming from inside. They all knew their End of Winter, Welcome Spring Barbeque was premature. March was usually Colorado's snowiest month. But the gang never needed much excuse to gather for a party, especially when food was involved.

Jennifer Stroud stepped out onto the deck. "Hey, what're

you doing here in the cold? Come on in. Megan's going to slice that chocolate cake she made. I've gained three pounds just looking at it."

"I came out for some fresh air and a glimpse of the mountains. You know, a mountain fix." Kelly smiled at her friend.

Jennifer wrapped her shamrock green knitted wool shawl around herself and joined Kelly by the railing. "I know you love looking at these views, but aren't you glad you're not living up here in the canyons in the winter? Especially since you're having to work in Denver so often. Driving on these icy roads would get old pretty fast."

Kelly sipped her rapidly cooling coffee and snuggled into the bright blue sweater Megan had knitted her for Christmas. "You're right. My fascination with canyon properties extends to spring, summer, and fall. Sliding down those icy roads once was enough to change my mind."

Jennifer visibly shuddered. "Bad memories. Let's change the subject. Guess what? I've finally got a real estate client."

"Whoa, that's fantastic news, Jen," Kelly said, then leaned forward and gave her friend a hug. "I'm so happy for you. I know it's been hard these last months."

"Hard doesn't cover it. I was about to throw in the towel until this recession was over, but my broker came to the rescue. He gave me a new client. A real estate investor here in Fort Connor who's selling one of his mountain properties. It's up in Poudre Canyon."

"Boy, that was good of your broker to give you his client."

Jennifer gave her a crooked smile. "Well, it's not all kindheartedness. This guy, Fred Turner, has a reputation for being really disagreeable. My broker can't stand working with him.

So he practically begged me to take Turner off his hands. Of course, I knew about the bad rep, but hey . . . beggars can't be choosers, as they say."

Concerned about Jennifer's financial situation, Kelly added, "Remember, you promised you'd let me know if you needed money, okay?"

"I remember. Don't worry. Pete's catering jobs have picked up since February. Apparently some local businesses are weathering the downturn better than others."

The front door opened again, and sounds of laughter and conversation poured out. Lisa stood on the threshold and beckoned. "What're you guys doing out here in the cold?" she demanded in her familiar bossy tone. "Come on in so we can cut the cake. Marty and Greg are about to run out the back door with it."

"Lisa's in bossy mode. We'd better do what she wants," Jennifer said as she and Kelly followed their friend inside.

"My coffee's cold, anyway. I need a warm-up."

The warmth inside felt good, and Kelly rubbed her arms as she glanced at her friends scattered around the spacious great room with its wide glass windows and gorgeous views. The high vaulted ceiling allowed even more windows above the glass patio doors. Light poured into Jayleen's house even when the weather was cloudy. And the views of the sky were magnificent. Kelly wanted views like that someday.

Lisa's boyfriend, Greg, and Megan's fiancé, Marty, began one of their favorite pastimes—vying with each other for first crack at the dessert of choice. Suddenly red-haired Marty held up both hands and started to speak.

"Hey, guys. Before Greg and I start demolishing this chocolate cake, Megan and I wanted to say thank you again to Jayleen for offering to let us have our wedding and reception here on her ranch this fall."

Megan jumped from her chair to join Marty in the center of the room. Her face was flushed with excitement. "Thank you so much, Jayleen, for the very best wedding present ever. This is such a gorgeous setting. We can't thank you enough." She and Marty began to applaud, and the rest of Kelly's friends around the room joined in.

Jayleen saluted them all with her coffee mug and a big smile as she stood beside the bookcase with Lambspun shop owner Mimi Shafer. "It was my pleasure, folks. Indeed it was. And you'd better wait till you taste Curt's present before you start awarding prizes. It's hard to beat prime beef steaks."

"Whoa, I forgot about that!" Greg cried. "Sorry, Jayleen, I'm changing my vote."

Tall, silver-haired Colorado rancher Curt Stackhouse strode to the center of the great room and beckoned to a short, balding elderly man behind him. "While we've got everyone's attention, I wanted to introduce you all to my houseguest, Eustace Freemont," Curt said in his deep voice. "Some of you have already had a chance to speak with Eustace, but I wanted to make sure the rest of you met him. It's not every day that a famous writer comes to visit." Curt gestured to his guest. "Eustace here has written a series of bestselling history books on the Old West. In fact, I've got every book he's ever written. Let's show Eustace a Colorado welcome." He began applauding.

Kelly joined the rest of her friends in applause and watched the little man with the round happy face and big smile flush. Eustace held up his hands.

"Thank you so much for that warm welcome," he said. "Curt's introduction was a bit misleading, though. I'm certainly not famous. In fact, I'm probably only known to history teachers and lovers of American history."

"What books have you written?" retired detective Burt Parker asked as his wife, Mimi, settled on the sofa beside him. "I love reading histories. Maybe I've read one of yours."

"He's written the two best ones about the Old West that I know of," Curt said. "*Cowboys and Heroes of the Old West* and *Outlaws and Villains of the Old West*."

"You're kidding." Burt sat up straighter. "*Cowboys and Heroes* was the first book I had a chance to sink my teeth into once I retired from the police force. It was great."

"I told you folks he was good," Curt said. "I've been a fan since his first book. I wrote Eustace a letter a few years ago, and we've been corresponding ever since."

"Curt graciously extended his hospitality when I told him I was coming to Colorado to research a new book," Eustace said with a genial smile. Kelly thought Eustace looked like a clichéd movie version of a college professor, dressed with a vest over long-sleeved shirt, gold chain dangling from a watch stuffed into his vest pocket.

"Are you a gun collector like Curt?" café owner Pete asked as he walked up beside Jennifer. "He's got one of the best collections of Western revolvers and rifles I've ever seen."

"No, I've never owned a gun," Eustace replied. "But I've certainly admired Curt's collection. Those are some beautiful Colt .45s."

"What's your new book about, Eustace?" Greg asked as he perched on the chair arm beside Lisa. The better to pounce on the cake when it was time.

"More cowboys and outlaws?" Megan teased.

"Actually, yes. But I'm not researching personages from the past for this book. This time I'm writing about the cowboys and outlaws of the New West."

That answer sent a buzz around the room. "Well, in that case, you've got to include Uncle Curt," Marty said, gesturing toward the broad-shouldered rancher.

Curt held up his hands. "Count me out, folks. You're not pigeonholing me in some book."

"Aw, c'mon, Curt. You're a natural," Lisa persuaded.

Curt shook his head. "Nope. I value my privacy too much, folks."

Kelly recognized the familiar sign that her mentor and advisor on all things ranching had made up his mind. Even so, she couldn't resist cajoling. "Just think how excited your grandchildren would be to see your name in a history book, Curt."

That comment brought a general buzz of agreement from the group, but Curt simply continued to shake his head.

Eustace stepped up then. "Believe me, everyone, I tried my best to convince Curt to change his mind, but he's resolute."

"Can you convince him, Jayleen?" Jennifer suggested.

Jayleen shook her head, glancing toward her close friend. "Nope. I'm not one to argue with someone when his mind is made up. It's a waste of time."

Knitting shop owner Mimi asked, "I'm curious, Eustace. Who do you think are the cowboys and the outlaws today?"

"Actually, I've already started interviewing some real estate developers and energy developers who've become successful and managed to stay successful during this recession. That takes talent, hard work, and luck," Eustace replied, hands behind his back in teacher position. "They've had to use a cowboy's courage and sometimes, an outlaw's cunning."

Greg shook his head. "Well, Eustace, we used to have a whole lot more in that category. But several good people saw their businesses collapse last year."

Kelly noticed a subdued quiet momentarily fall over the group, and she knew the reason why. Everyone was thinking of Steve. Her former boyfriend Steve. Driven out of Fort Connor and out of business by the collapse of housing construction and development when the real estate bubble burst around the country. Even honest, hardworking, smart builders and architects like Steve Townsend went out of business. "Belly-up," as Curt called it.

Kelly also felt the surreptitious glances cast her way. She understood. It was impossible to separate Steve's business collapse and the breakup of their relationship. Steve had moved to Denver permanently six months ago. Right after he walked out on her.

Kelly decided she had to break the subdued mood herself. "If you're looking for successful real estate investors and developers, then you should interview both of my clients. Arthur Housemann and Don Warner. Housemann's in Fort Connor, and Warner's based in north Denver. They've both weathered this recession and prospered. So far." She held up crossed fingers.

Eustace's round face spread even more with his grin. "Why, thank you, young lady. You'll have to tell me how to contact these gentlemen."

Greg walked over beside Curt and Eustace. "I say this

sounds like a perfect time for a dessert break. Eustace and Kelly can confer on business, while our fantastic baker Megan cuts the cake."

"Please do," Pete added with a grin. "I can't wait to try that. If it tastes as good as it looks, I may add Megan's cake to the café menu."

"I call first piece," Marty said, jumping from his chair.

"No way, dude. I'm closer to the table. You have to get past me."

"But the cook is my fiancée," Marty complained.

"Too bad. You get this stuff all the time."

"Eustace, it's time for us to get out of the way of these two. They'll knock us down getting to the cake." Curt beckoned Eustace in Kelly's direction. "Kelly, I'd already suggested Eustace talk with you. Thanks to Warner, you're down in Denver so much you've probably met most of the guys he's planning to interview."

Kelly extended her hand. "Nice to meet you, Mr. Freemont. You sound like you have a heckuva more interesting job than most of us. Believe me, all those numbers start jumping around on the spreadsheet sometimes."

"Kelly here is a CPA and has become an integral part of both Housemann's and Warner's businesses," Curt said, smiling at Kelly with fatherly pride.

"So glad to meet you, Ms. Flynn," Eustace said, shaking Kelly's hand enthusiastically. "Curt has told me about your own success. I commend you. And I would definitely appreciate your giving my card to Mr. Housemann and Mr. Warner. They sound like excellent interview subjects."

"I'd be happy to," she said, spotting Lisa approach with two tempting slices of chocolate cake.

"I see cake, and that calls for coffee," Jennifer said, moving away. "Would you like some, Mr. Freemont?"

"Yes, thank you, and please call me Eustace."

"I'll help, Jen," Pete said, following after.

"This smells as delicious as it looks, so enjoy," Lisa said, offering plates to Kelly and Eustace.

The aroma of rich chocolate wafted up to Kelly's nostrils, and she inhaled the delectable scent. She took a bite and savored. *Heavenly*. Dark chocolate cake and rich, creamy chocolate frosting, all mixed together. Yum! "Ohhhh, this is scrumptious," she said before tasting another morsel.

"Oh, my," Eustace exclaimed, patting his mouth with a napkin. "That is wicked, indeed."

"I think Megan's outdone herself this time," Jennifer said as she approached with a coffeepot. Kelly held out her mug and let another delectable aroma fill her nostrils. Strong black coffee. *Caffeine*.

"If you ladies will excuse us, it looks like Burt's anxious to speak with Eustace," Curt said, beckoning Eustace to follow as he stepped away.

"Ms. Flynn—"

"Please, call me Kelly," she said behind a forkful of cake.

"I'll give you my card before we leave. Thank you so much for suggesting your employers." Eustace gave her a genial smile. "We'll talk later."

"Absolutely," Kelly said, then downed the tasty mouthful.

Pete came up to them, somehow balancing four slices of cake. "Here, you go." He expertly set all four plates on a nearby end table. "Now, either you guys dig in or I'll be taking seconds, and I sure don't need it." Pete patted his stomach before sampling the cake.

9

Kelly took a sip of Jayleen's strong coffee. *Ahhhh*. Just the way she liked it. She savored the last forkful of cake, then eyed the slices on the end table. "I'll have to run even more tomorrow morning. This is waaaay too good. I might have seconds."

Lisa glanced over her shoulder at Greg approaching, Megan and Marty not far behind. "Better claim it before those savages inhale it all."

"Hey, Kelly, it's good to see you," Greg said, sinking into a nearby armchair. "Your work schedule has you down in Denver so much we don't see you as often as we used to."

"I know, guys, but Warner has started working on a joint project with several different developers. A renovation deal the city of Thornton put together. So, I'm having to meet with a lot of different companies and coordinate with the project manager so I can integrate all the details into Warner's accounts." She took a sip of coffee. "I swear, he has so many irons in the fire it's hard to keep track. And of course, everyone has to have a meeting. There are huge meetings with all the developers. A mini mob scene."

"Death by meetings. I remember that," Megan said, lifting a forkful of cake. "That's what drove me out of corporate IT. There were so many meetings, I didn't have time to get my work done."

"Tell me about it," Kelly quipped behind her mug.

Greg snitched a crumb of Lisa's cake. She swatted his hand away. "The university specializes in meetings. You can lose half your day."

Marty settled on the arm of Megan's chair. "Do you ever see Steve at any of those mini mobs?" he asked quietly.

"Marty . . ." Megan turned to him with a concerned look.

"It's okay, Megan. You can talk about Steve in front of me. I know you guys see him whenever he comes into town," Kelly said, deliberately leaning against a desk.

She'd learned how to appear relaxed whenever one of her friends mentioned Steve. Inside, however, Kelly was anything but relaxed. An old familiar knotting started in her stomach. The tears had stopped months ago when anger briefly took their place. Beneath it all, the hurt remained. She'd learned to disguise it, but her friends knew her well. And they seldom mentioned Steve in front of her, except to subtly update her on what he was doing.

"He's started working full-time for that northern Colorado developer he was working nights for. Sam Kaufman," Greg offered. "Apparently this Sam raised his salary to more than that Denver architect firm was paying him, so Steve jumped at it."

Kelly let her surprise show. "That's a smart move. Tell him congratulations for me."

"So . . . have you ever seen Steve at these big meetings?" Lisa asked in a tentative voice.

"Yeah, maybe you could congratulate him yourself," Marty suggested, eyeing Kelly.

"Mar*teeee*," Megan shot him a disapproving look.

Kelly held up her hand. "Guys, I said it's okay. As a matter of fact, I have seen Steve at some of those meetings," she announced to her attentive friends. "But only at a distance, and he's never seen me." She gave them a crooked smile. "Life goes on, guys."

"Two ships passing in the night," Pete observed softly.

A pall of quiet dropped over the little group for a moment. Only the sound of forks clinking against plates. Kelly noticed Megan's expression had gone from concerned to sad to annoyed. A Megan eruption was due any second, Kelly could tell.

"I wanted to strangle him," Megan spouted, face screwed up in anger. There was no doubt as to who the "him" in that sentence was.

"Me*gaaaan*," Marty teased, imitating her scolding tone.

Too late. Megan's hand shot out in exasperation. "You know he didn't come to see us for a month after he left. He was afraid to."

"Jayleen said Curt called Steve on the phone and really chewed him out," Lisa offered. "She'd never heard Curt cuss like that before."

"We weren't sure he'd ever come back after Megan and Lisa took turns beating up on him. Even Jennifer went after him. Man, it was brutal." Greg gave a pretend shudder.

Kelly did her best to conceal her emotions. Despite herself, she couldn't keep from smiling inside when she heard that. But instead of answering "Serves him right," Kelly calmly asked, "How'd he take it?"

"Like a man," Marty said. "Kept his mouth shut and let them beat him up."

Greg glanced at Kelly. "Steve knows he screwed up bad."

Kelly could feel all her friends staring at her and couldn't resist a tart response. She also spotted Jayleen approach so she knew she wouldn't be pressured. "Good," was all she replied.

"Greg and Marty, you'd better go have thirds on that cake and save the rest of us from ourselves," Jayleen said as she approached Kelly and friends. "That was scrumptious, Megan. That's so good you should have it for your wedding."

Glad for the reprieve from further comments, Kelly quickly

followed up. "Yeah, Megan. Save a bill from the bakery and have this as your wedding cake."

Megan looked appalled. "Do you really think I'm about to bake cakes right before the wedding? You're crazy!"

"Thanks to Jayleen and Curt, we can afford to pay caterers," Marty said, his infectious grin returning. "Of course, Uncle Curt's steaks will take a big chunk out of that bill, too."

"You know, you'll have to hire someone to handle the grill as well as someone to tend bar," Pete reminded them. "I have names of people I've used you can trust to do a good job."

"I'll volunteer," Greg held up his hand.

Jayleen hooted. "I thought you were a vegetarian, Greg. I've noticed you falling off the wagon this last year."

"Blame it on Curt and his steaks." Greg shrugged.

"He's a weekday vegetarian. He can do it on weekends too unless we're going to Curt's or Jayleen's," Lisa said.

"Well, in that case, I wouldn't trust Greg around those steaks any more than I'd trust Kelly's dog Carl," Jayleen warned.

"Hey, maybe we could bring Carl to the reception so he could guard the grill and keep an eye on Greg," Pete joked.

At that, Kelly and all her friends joined Jayleen in laughter, picturing Kelly's Rottweiler chasing Greg away from the grill.

Two

Kelly looked across the mahogany library table at her client Arthur Housemann. Sunlight from the nearby window glinted off his silver-laced hair as he bent over the March expense estimates she'd prepared. "The business is doing well, Arthur. The vacancy rate for your rental properties is the lowest northern Colorado has seen in years. You're weathering this recession in fine shape." She took a deep drink from one of the Housemann company ceramic coffee mugs.

Housemann looked up from the documents spread out on the table. "So far, so good, Kelly. Cutting back on some of my expenses and putting off a couple of purchases helped, too." He peered over the top of his reading glasses. "When times get tough, you've gotta get tough, too. Only the strong survive these downturns."

Housemann returned his attention to the expense reports. He reminded Kelly of her late father in some ways. He was sixty-four, the same age her father would be had he lived. Housemann also had the same quiet, studious manner that her dad had. He spoke when he had something to say, and it usually counted for something.

That's why Housemann's comment caught her attention. Tough, good businessmen got swept away in this recession, too. So being tough and smart wasn't the whole story.

She felt compelled to add, "Well, a lot of smart, tough builders and developers went belly-up last year, too. So, I think there's more to it than toughness. Not having enough cash in the bank seems to me to be the deciding factor." She pointed to a column in another financial report that lay open on the table. "Now, you've been careful to keep a good cash position, Arthur. That's been the key difference."

Housemann started to smile. "You're right, Kelly. I sounded kind of flippant just then. Didn't mean to be." He dropped the reports to the table and removed his reading glasses. "I've been in this real estate business a long time, so I watched and learned how the survivors did it. Then, I patterned my rules after theirs. And whenever I didn't follow them, I lost big." He swung his glasses by the earpiece as he glanced out the sixth-floor office window, which looked across Fort Connor to the west. "And one of those rules was always have plenty of cash, to invest or to live on if necessary."

"Amen, to that," Kelly said with a smile, lifting her mug in salute. "Putting away cash takes a discipline that most people do not have, unfortunately."

"That being said, I am now about to dip into that cash pool," Housemann said, eyeing her. "I'll be withdrawing at least sixty thousand."

Kelly set her mug on the table. She couldn't hide her surprise. "That's serious money, Arthur. Are you sure you want to do that right now? What did I just hear you say?"

Housemann chuckled. "You have my permission to quote myself back to me, Kelly. But this is a once-in-a-lifetime purchase, and I simply cannot let it pass me by."

She leaned back in the upholstered chair and folded her arms. "Okay, I've gotta hear this. Tell me. What are you buying?"

"I've made an offer on a property in Poudre Canyon, right on the river. It's thirty acres of drop-dead beautiful. I've always wanted to have a property up there, but never could find the right one. I wanted river access and plenty of room to camp with my kids and grandkids." Housemann stared out the window again. "All these years, I'd think about scouting for properties to buy for my family, then another business deal would come along and take away the discretionary funds and my attention. Plus, a lot of the places just didn't strike my fancy. They had too much vertical, or they didn't have river access or not enough trees."

"Sounds like you wanted it all, Arthur," Kelly observed. "That's hard to find. Where is this jewel?"

"It's about ten miles up the canyon. I've driven past it all my life. You can tell how gorgeous it is from the road. And I've hiked some on the bordering trails over the years. There are stands of aspen and evergreens and ponds throughout. Deer graze there all the time. Nobody to chase them off. I never saw many people on the property. Some of my friends who live nearby said someone from out-of-state had owned it for years. I figured it was a family property of some kind and would stay that way." He turned to Kelly. "So, you can imagine my surprise when I heard about it coming on the market. Mark Dunham over at Northstar Real Estate keeps his eye out for me all the time, and he knows how I've always wanted a place on the Poudre River."

Housemann looked so happy Kelly had to laugh. The staid, conservative businessman looked like a kid who'd just stepped into a candy store and was told he could have whatever he wanted.

"It sounds like the stars aligned for you on this one, Arthur. As your CPA, I've already done my duty to warn you about depleting your much-treasured cash reserve. But I'm not about to rain on your parade. When do you plan to make an offer?"

"I already have. One of Mark's agents wrote up the offer and brought it over this morning," Housemann said with a kid-like grin. He was obviously already in the candy store. "In fact, here's my copy. I was planning to show it to you after we went through the expenses." He reached into a portfolio beside his elbow and drew out a sheaf of legal-size documents that Kelly recognized as a real estate contract.

"Take your time reading; I'll fill up our coffees," Housemann said, rising from the table. "I know you'll want some, Kelly."

"Yes, please," Kelly said, already immersed in the legalese. Reading past the purchase offer, Kelly read the name of the seller. "Fred Turner." Something sounded familiar about that name. "The seller's name sounds familiar. Have you done business with him before? I must have read that name somewhere."

Housemann gave a snort as he walked over to the table with the coffeepot. "I haven't done business with that bastard for years. Ever since he tried to cheat me out of some property I was buying in Denver. He's a real piece of work. Nobody in town wants to work with him unless he has a property they're hot to buy." He poured a dark stream into Kelly's mug.

Housemann's comment jogged Kelly's memory. "So, he has a bad reputation, huh?" she asked, paging through the contract.

"The worst. He'll use whatever he can to cheat someone out of their property and still be on legal grounds. Just barely." Housemann sank into his chair. "He'll jerk around anyone who'll let him. That's why I'm offering full purchase price with a significant cash down payment. I didn't bother to negotiate, because I don't have time or patience to play games with Turner, and I want that property." Housemann took a deep drink from his mug.

Kelly turned to the last page in the contract and read the names of the seller's real estate agency. It was Jennifer's company. She was right. Fred Turner was the "problem" client that Jennifer had described to her yesterday at Jayleen's barbeque.

"It looks like my friend Jennifer Stroud is the selling agent. She's very experienced. She's been working in real estate for years, so she should be able to keep Turner in line."

Housemann frowned. "I don't think anyone can keep Fred Turner in line. He's not afraid to make a scene when it serves his purpose. He loves to throw the other party off balance."

"Well, he shouldn't play any games with this offer. You're meeting his purchase price," Kelly declared, pointing to the contract.

"Even so, I won't relax until he's signed the contract, Kelly. I don't trust Turner as far as I can throw him."

• • •

"Hey, Kelly, good to see you drop in," Mimi said as Kelly walked into her favorite knitting shop, Lambspun. Mimi was hanging loops of fluffy spun yarns along the foyer wall. Cotton candy. "Most afternoons lately you've been in Denver."

"And I'll be there again tomorrow," Kelly said. "But I finished one client's account this morning, so I figured I deserved a break before going back to the other client this afternoon."

The entire foyer was alive with color. Yarns spilled out of the wooden bins lining one wall. An antique dry sink and a natural pine cabinet both bulged with colorful spring fibers. An open steamer trunk on the floor was piled high with inviting fluffy balls of mohair, silky loops of ribbon, and tidy balls of baby-soft cotton. Woven baskets were tucked in everywhere else. There wasn't an inch of the foyer that wasn't bursting with color. The skylight above allowed natural light to brighten the foyer and enhanced the various colors and textures.

"Well, we're glad to see you whenever you find the time." Mimi gave her a motherly smile as she hung the last loop of spun yarn on the wall with the others. A luscious lemon froth.

Kelly fingered the soft froth. "The spinners have been busy."

"Oh, yes. Why don't you follow me up front and fill me in on what you're doing? I need to catch up. I didn't get much time to chat with you at Jayleen's last night."

"Let me drop off my stuff first," Kelly said as she headed for the main knitting room. She set her knitting bag on the long library table where all the knitters and other fiber workers gathered regularly.

Bookshelves hugged the walls of this room. All the shelves were packed with books on every fiber subject imaginable— knitting, crocheting, spinning, weaving, dyeing, felting, tatting, and other stitchery. If yarns or threads were used in any form, there was a book on it. Kelly was always amazed at the fiber subjects she knew nothing about.

She walked through the central yarn room, where all four walls were lined with bins and shelves that overflowed with coils, balls, or skeins of different colors. Rainbows. Following Mimi's path toward the front of the shop, Kelly noticed there were no customers lined up at the counter.

Kelly couldn't help asking. "Wow, no customers. Has business dropped off or something?"

Mimi grinned at her as she picked up a ball of newly wound blue-and-gray wool. "You should have seen it this morning. We had loads of customers. You've started to forget how the traffic flows around here, Kelly. You haven't been in as often."

Kelly settled into a chair at the winding table and watched Mimi take one of the newly spun skeins of wool and loop it around the spindles of the yarn swift. Then, she started turning the swift's handle, slowly winding the yarn into a ball on a spindle at the other end of the table.

"You're probably right." Kelly stretched out her long jeans-clad legs. "I have business on the brain all the time now. That's why I grabbed this little slice of time and got out of my office clothes and headed over here for some relaxation. I need it."

Mimi wound slowly, glancing up at Kelly. "Yes, I have to admit you don't look as relaxed as you used to. It sounds like that Denver client has really started claiming a lot more of your time. You've even stayed down there overnight, I hear."

The Lambspun grapevine was as alive as ever. "That's right. When I have late night meetings or receptions and early morning meetings the next day, it's easier to stay. There are some nice hotels in the Cherry Creek area."

"Cherry Creek?" Mimi's brows shot up. "I should say."

"I figure after the long hours I put in with Warner's business, I deserve some luxury," Kelly said, grinning. "Believe me, I really appreciate sinking into that huge jetted tub in the bathroom. What a treat."

Jennifer popped around the corner of the hallway that led into Pete's café at the back of the knitting shop. "Hey, I didn't expect to see you here. Thanks for the congrats message on my voice mail. I went into a happy dance when I saw Housemann's offer on my desk this morning."

"Well, you deserve some good news," Kelly said.

"Did you sell your new client's mountain property? That's wonderful, Jennifer," Mimi said with a big smile.

"Thanks, guys. It came in at the right time, too. By the way, I'm going up there on Saturday, Kelly. You want to take a short trip into Poudre Canyon? You need to relax," Jennifer suggested.

"I might take you up on that offer," Kelly said, picturing the canyon's rock walls against the blue Colorado sky, the Poudre River running beside the road. Peaceful. Sometimes Kelly would escape up into the canyon all by herself just to think. She'd sit on a rock beside the river and clear her head. See what thoughts popped out.

"Who is that with Lizzie in the yarn room?" Mimi asked, glancing toward the adjoining room. "It looks like Curt's author friend, Eustace. Is he looking for yarns? I should go and help him." She started to push back her chair.

"No, no, don't," Jennifer admonished, holding up her hand. "Eustace came into the café this morning with Curt to have breakfast and decided to stay and work on his computer. Curt left to do errands." Jennifer leaned closer and lowered her voice. "After an hour, I noticed Eustace leave the table quickly and rush outside. I wondered what was up, because he'd left his computer open on the table. That's when I saw Lizzie outside, picking up several small packages she must have dropped on the flagstone path. Eustace obviously noticed and went out to help her."

"Well, that was gentlemanly of him," Mimi said, winding yarn again.

"But the best part is that he took Lizzie to his table and they've been sitting in the café all morning, chatting up a storm." Jennifer gave them both a Cheshire cat grin.

Kelly glanced into the adjoining yarn room. Sure enough, Lizzie was holding a skein of turquoise yarn and seemed to be explaining something, while Eustace stood attentively listening. *Well, well, well.*

"I'll be darned," Kelly said, returning her friend's conspiratorial smile.

"Oh, my goodness," Mimi said, eyes alight. "I'll have to tell Burt. Now, we should all act as if we haven't noticed a thing, understand?"

Kelly nodded. "Don't worry. After watching Megan slowly warm up to Marty a couple of years ago, Jennifer and I are pros at pretending not to notice."

"Well, time to get back to the café. I simply wanted to share my observations with you two. Give everyone a heads-up so they'll be on guard." Jennifer gave a wave and slipped around the corner.

Kelly watched Lizzie's round face, flushed now, and dimpling with her cheerful smile. Kelly noticed Eustace was smiling as well. Whatever they were talking about, yarns or the weather, they both looked very happy.

"They're so cute," Mimi observed as she continued winding.

Kelly couldn't resist. She turned to Mimi with a wicked grin. "That's exactly what we all said when we saw you and Burt flirting over the yarn bins."

Mimi's mouth dropped open, and she flushed scarlet. "You *didn't*!"

"Yeah, we did," Kelly teased. "You two were so cute together, and you never noticed us spying on you."

"You spied on us! How *could* you?" Mimi exclaimed, clearly shocked.

"We couldn't help it." Kelly laughed. "You two were in the shop and so were we. I'd go into the yarn room to get something, and you two would be giggling over the yarn bins."

"*Giggling!*" Mimi, clearly indignant. "We were not!"

"Yes, you were, and you were so *cute*, too." Kelly teased again.

This time, Mimi picked up a nearby ball of yarn and tossed it right at Kelly. Kelly simply cackled in reply and caught the yarn before it hit her face. First baseman's reflexes still razor sharp.

Steve pulled his big red truck into Greg and Lisa's driveway, behind their cars. Marty's car was parked on the street, he noticed. So was Jennifer's. Everyone was there. He stepped out of the truck and slammed the door, pausing only to check if any more FOR SALE signs had popped up since he'd been there last.

He felt that old familiar wrench in his gut as he counted every one. *Four.* Four that he could see down this street and around the corner. At least he hadn't heard about any other houses gone into foreclosure. Steve strode up the walk to the front door and rang the bell, a mixture of apprehension and anticipation running through him. He needed to relax with old friends, even if they couldn't resist ragging on him. Just to talk about something other than business. He needed *downtime.*

The door opened wide. Greg stood there with Steve's favorite amber ale. "C'mon in, buddy," he beckoned and handed Steve the brown bottle. "Pizza's on the coffee table. We left you some."

"That's a first," Steve joked as he entered the foyer. "You must miss me."

"Yeah, we do," Marty called from the great room where he sat on the love seat beside Megan. "Even Greg and I can't finish all this pizza."

"Here, Steve," Lisa said, pointing to the cocoa-colored armchair. "Sit down and dig in. There's more than enough."

Steve quickly scanned the circle of friends who'd gathered. "Hey, guys." He gave a crooked smile before he sat. "I grabbed a burger on the way out of town, but this sure smells good." He took a long drink of the Fat Tire ale.

"Your favorite, pepperoni and cheese," Megan said, pushing the box with several tempting slices toward him.

"Better watch those fast-food burger stops. They're deadly,"

Jennifer warned as she sipped her diet soda in a nearby love seat.

Pete sat beside her. "Ohhhh, yeah." He leaned over to grab a pizza slice. "Catch us up on what you've been doing since we last got together. Three weeks ago, I think."

"You said you were starting some new project with Sam's firm." Greg sank into the sofa on the other side of Lisa and took a drink of his beer.

"How's that going?" Marty asked as he snatched another pizza slice.

Steve savored the pizza before answering. *Yessss*. Now, he could feel himself start to relax. "It's going pretty good. Heating up, actually. Thornton city organized this group project to renovate one of the older industrial areas of the city, and they came up with the idea of letting several different firms collaborate on the project. Sam jumped on it as soon as he heard about it." Steve took a long drink of ale. "He'd wanted to diversify into renovating distressed properties, so this was perfect."

He snagged another pizza slice and practically inhaled it. So good. A helluva lot better than eating alone late at night in front of the television.

"That sounds like a pretty big project," Lisa said. "Is it just smaller construction companies or builders that are involved?"

Steve shook his head while he swallowed. "No, there are some pretty big developers, too. The city wanted to involve a lot of builders, so they've parceled out all of the specialty work. Even smaller firms are included." He grinned. "Smaller than Sam's, I mean."

Lisa shot a glance to the others, then back to Steve. "So there are big and little firms involved."

Steve tipped back his beer. "Yeah, that's right."

"Sounds like a lot of work," Marty said, twirling his beer bottle on his knee. "Is your boss gonna raise your salary again?"

Steve chuckled. "Well, kind of. He's put me in charge of handling the project and hinted there'd be some sort of promotion."

"Wow, that sounds good," Jennifer commented, snitching a sliver of pizza. "Sam must really be impressed with you, Steve."

"Yeah, I think he is. Sam's a straight-up guy. Easy to work for. Says what he means and doesn't jerk you around. Treats everybody fairly." He took another long drink. "And he also doesn't like to go to meetings," he added with a smile. "And there are a lot of meetings that go along with this project. So, guess who gets to go to those."

Megan looked around at her friends, then asked, "Is it only developers at the meetings or other people, too?"

Steve reached for another slice. "I wish it was just the developers; then it wouldn't be so crowded and we could move faster. But every company brings a whole boatload of staff. Those rooms are packed."

"Kind of a mini mob scene," Marty suggested with a little smile.

"Oh, yeah." Steve upended his ale and drained it this time.

"Here, I'll get you another," Greg offered, hopping off the sofa and heading for the kitchen.

"I wonder if any of the companies I've worked with in Denver are in that project," Jennifer said, staring off into the room. "Let's see . . . Hoffman Brothers, Warner Development, Ryker Builders. Any of them?"

Steve let himself sink into the sofa cushions, feeling more muscles let go. This is exactly what he needed. "Yeah, all three as a matter of fact."

"Here you go, buddy," Greg said, handing Steve another Fat Tire.

Steve took a long, deep drink, then let himself sink into the sofa even more. Glancing around the circle of his friends, he noticed they were all staring at him at the same time. *What was up with that?* Maybe it was his imagination. He was exhausted when he left Denver. And now, he felt sleepy. What was wrong with him? Two beers, and he was falling asleep.

"Warner Development is Kelly's client, you know," Lisa said, giving him a little smile.

All thoughts of sleep evaporated in the time it took to say her name. Every nerve cell went wide awake. Steve sat up straighter. "Yeah, I know." He stared at the ale in his bottle.

"You know, Kelly's been to those same meetings," Jennifer said.

Steve's head shot up. "What? How do you know?"

"Because she told us," Pete said, smiling at him. "In fact, she even said she saw you there."

Steve's mouth dropped open. He couldn't help it. *"What!"*

"But you didn't see her," Greg added, with a wry smile.

"Two ships passing in the night," Pete repeated his line to Kelly.

Steve stared at his friends, who were watching him and

smiling, sadly, he thought. *What the hell!* How could he have missed her? He was an idiot! Stupid, *stupid*!

"You gotta start looking around, buddy," Marty advised with a crooked smile.

His friends wanted to say more but were holding back, Steve could tell. But there was nothing his friends could say that could compete with the mental abuse he was inflicting on himself inside.

You idiot! What is the matter with you? You can't even take the time to look around a room? Are you stupid, or what? Jackass!

He rubbed his eyebrows. "Yeah, you're right. I . . . I can't believe I missed her."

Megan opened her mouth, but Lisa waved her silent. "Don't beat yourself up too bad, Steve. Kelly said you were on the other side of the room."

"Check out the next meeting," Megan said. "If you see her, just go up and say hi."

Steve gave Megan a jaundiced look. "Are you *kidding*? Just say hi? She probably wouldn't even speak to me." He swirled the ale in his bottle. "And I wouldn't blame Kelly. Not after what I did. I walked out on her, and . . . that hurt her bad."

The little circle fell silent. Steve drained his beer, and Greg got up to retrieve another.

"Here you go, buddy," Greg handed Steve the ale.

"I'd better not. Gotta drive back to Denver," Steve said.

"You're not getting on the highway, not tonight," Lisa announced in her best schoolmarm voice. "You're sleeping here on the sofa."

"Yeah, and come over to the café in the morning and

29

I'll make you pancakes," Pete promised, leaning back and draping his arm around the back of the love seat behind Jennifer.

Pete's pancakes. How long had it been since he devoured a stack? Too long. Steve could almost taste them now.

"Then we'll go out for a run," Greg added. "You gotta get back to working out. You look wiped every time we see you. Gotta get your mojo back."

Steve snorted. "I think it's lost in all those FOR SALE signs outside."

"That's it. We've gotta start meeting over at our place," Megan announced. "No signs around there."

"And speaking of signs," Jennifer said, leaning forward. "There will be one less FOR SALE sign outside. An agent in our office had a buyers' contract accepted. They're getting that three bedroom ranch around the corner the bank fore-closed on. And another agent has a couple interested in the two-story across the street. So, things are slowly starting to turn around, Steve."

Steve stared into Jennifer's warm brown gaze and felt another muscle deep inside his chest let go. *Whoa*. One house under contract and maybe another one. "Wow, Jen . . . that's the best news I've heard in a long time. Better than the new job, even."

"See, you're gonna get through this, buddy," Marty en-couraged. "So, start working out again. Start playing some basketball or something till baseball season starts. Get your mojo back."

"Yeah, Kelly can't stay mad forever," Greg said, twirling his empty bottle on his knee. "Can she?"

"Kelly's not so much mad. She's just . . . pissed," Lisa said.

"See, that's better," Marty said with a grin. "So, give it a shot."

"Yeah, ask her to give you a second chance," Greg advised.

Steve gave them a rueful smile as he sank back into the sofa. "Problem is, I'm not sure I deserve a second chance, guys. I destroyed the best thing I've ever had. And . . . and I don't know how to fix it. Or, if I even can." The ale had deadened the ache he carried around inside whenever he thought of Kelly. He'd tried to bury it, but it wouldn't stay buried.

"Man, you don't even sound like yourself, Steve. We gotta get you back."

"High noon. Basketball courts at the gym. Pickup game," Marty declared, pointing at them both.

"Done," Greg said, saluting Steve and Marty with his beer bottle. "You're gettin' back."

"Then you can give it another shot with Kelly," Pete said.

"Yeah, so you'll no longer be two ships passing . . ." Marty gestured until Megan punched him in the arm.

"Enough with those ships," she chided.

"Pete got to say it," Marty feigned petulance.

"Pete's got a certain . . . way with words," Megan gave a little shrug.

"I like that," Pete nodded.

"And I don't?" Marty said, aghast. "I'm a *lawyer*!"

"That's too many words," Greg shook his head.

"Waaaay too many." Lisa grinned, then upended her beer.

Steve felt his friends' good humor and laughter start to penetrate the black hole that he'd crawled into. He had to come back home more often. He missed this. No wonder he worked so late at night. Going back to his empty apartment was too sad.

"How's she doing?" he asked after a moment.

"She's in Denver most of the week," Greg said.

"Working all the time, like you," Marty added.

"She's doing great, actually," Lisa replied. "This Warner guy has involved her in everything he's doing, apparently. She was complaining about the meetings, too."

Steve rubbed his forehead. "Damn. I'm such an idiot."

"Yeah, we know." Lisa said. "But don't let that stop you from turning around and saying 'hello' at the next meeting."

Steve shook his head. "I don't know, guys. She probably doesn't want to talk to me. And . . . and I don't even know what I'd say to her."

"How about 'I'm sorry' for starters," Marty suggested quietly.

Steve snorted. "I don't think 'sorry' is gonna cut it. I don't know if I've got a chance."

"Steve, you gotta stop talking like that," Greg said, leaning his arms on his legs. "I've never seen you give up before."

Jennifer turned to Steve with a dramatic expression. "Yeah, Steve, *snap out of it!*" she ordered.

At that, everyone burst into laughter. Steve joined his friends, even though the laughter was directed at him. It still felt good.

Three

"So, you think your client Turner will accept Housemann's offer?" Kelly asked as she looked out the car window at the reddish brown walls of Poudre Canyon.

Jennifer steered her compact car around a curve. Snow was still on the ground here in the canyon. Snow always stayed longer in the canyons surrounding Fort Connor. Poudre Canyon and Bellevue Canyon both climbed higher than Fort Connor's five-thousand-feet altitude. The same was true for all the mountain towns west of Denver and Fort Connor. They were the high country, and they always got the snow first and kept it longer. That's why skiers and snowboarders flocked there when the first snowflakes arrived in the fall.

"Yeah, it sounds like it. I mean, Housemann met Turner's price. Nothing's involved that will slow things down. Thank God."

"That's good for you, Jen. You'll get your money faster.

When's the closing date? You should be able to close pretty quickly."

"The contract closing date is a couple of weeks from now, and I can't think of any reason Turner would want to delay. Housemann's met his price with no contingencies."

Jennifer's cell phone rang in her lap, and she slowed her car's speed. "Jennifer Stroud here," she answered. "Hi, Anita, what's up?"

Kelly stared out the window again, observing patches of brown grass where the sun had melted the snow along the sides of the road. The Poudre River, which ran alongside the road, had chunks of ice, but the rushing waters still flowed. The river followed one side of the road for a while, then it would disappear beneath and suddenly reappear on the other side, as they steadily climbed higher into the canyon.

She watched the traffic pass on the other side of the two-lane road. It was actually a state highway, which ran all the way from Fort Connor up into Poudre Canyon through the high peaks and across the high plains past the little town of Walden. Then it joined with Highway 40 and on into the beautiful resort town of Steamboat Springs.

Jennifer was right. Kelly needed this break. She'd been working way too many hours lately with Warner's new project. She needed to insist on having weekends free. Free for her to drive up here by herself sometime alone like she used to. Sit on a rock, stare at the Poudre, and think. She missed that.

"He *what?*" Jennifer exclaimed, startling Kelly out of her relaxed river reverie. "*Who* called?" Pause. "Birmingham? I don't remember talking to a Mr. Birmingham. What did he say again?"

Kelly turned to watch her friend's expression. Jennifer was clearly hearing something that concerned her.

"You're kidding. Turner's going to meet him? When? Where?" Pause. "Well, that's great. I'm on the way up there right now. In fact, we're only a couple of miles out." Jennifer exhaled an exasperated breath. "Okay, keep me posted if you hear anything else, Anita." She flipped off her phone and dropped it in her lap.

"What's up? Is there someone already at the property now?" Kelly asked.

"I cannot believe it." Jennifer let out a loud sigh. "Anita is Turner's assistant. She says that some guy with a British accent left a message on the voice mail last night saying he wanted to make an offer on the canyon property. He said he'd seen it listed and photos on the website, and it matched exactly what he's looking for. He wants to drive up and take a look and said he'd match or exceed any offer on the table."

"Whoa . . . that changes things. What happens now?"

"I won't know until I've spoken with Turner. Anita says this Birmingham guy was going to meet Turner this morning at eleven. So, maybe they'll still be there. It's only one twenty."

"Should we be barging in?" Kelly asked, slightly dubious.

Jennifer shot her a look. "I'm the listed agent in this transaction, and my client has just gone behind my back to meet with a potential buyer. You bet we should barge in. I need to know what's going on."

"Okaaaay." Kelly recognized that look. It was the "don't mess with me" look. "Man, that other guy must really want this property if he's willing to up the ante."

"Sounds that way. And I'm wondering if he's an agent

himself. Someone has to write up the contract offer. Maybe he's a lawyer." She slowed the car. "That's the turn up ahead to the right. Wait a minute, who's that?"

Kelly noticed a blue truck pulling out of the road up ahead. "Is that Turner's truck? Flag him down, then."

"No, Turner's got a big black one. Maybe that's Birmingham." Jennifer looked out the window as the blue truck drove past.

Kelly glimpsed a middle-aged woman driving the truck. "Guess not."

"That looks like Turner's wife. I recognize her from Turner's office. It's right down the hall from ours." Jennifer slowed down to turn onto the dirt road.

"Does she work with Turner or something?"

"No, but they're in the midst of a messy divorce. She's been coming into his office regularly to check on the properties Turner's been selling. Anita's told me about her. She grills Anita every time she comes in. Apparently she's convinced Turner is hiding money from her."

"Whoa, not good."

"You got that right. And it's really not good that she decided to drive up here while the new client is meeting with Turner. If she went into one of her tantrums, she could kill the deal. That is *so* not smart of her."

Kelly watched the river flow beneath the concrete bridge across the Poudre as the car drove over. "I love to watch that water." She looked out at the river winding around the bend in the distance. "This is truly gorgeous. Housemann wasn't exaggerating. No wonder he wants to buy it. Boy, he's going to be so disappointed if someone else gets it."

"Nothing will happen until we have a contract offer from

Birmingham. When we do, then I'll contact Housemann's agent and ask her if he'd like to make a counteroffer. These guys may get into a bidding war."

The car drove through a thick stand of aspens, their winter-bare branches crossing above. The road curved and turned into an open pasture setting. Up ahead sat a small rustic log cabin. "That's not as big as I thought. Is there a bedroom?"

"Two actually, but they're tiny," Jennifer answered as she angled the car into a space beside a black truck that was already parked. No other cars in sight.

"Well, I guess Birmingham has come and gone. Maybe Turner's wife drove him away."

Jennifer groaned. "Don't even think that."

Kelly stepped out of Jennifer's compact car and stretched, arms above her head, then down to the dirt beside her cowboy boots. She was used to more legroom for her long legs. Her sporty red car fit her just right. She turned in a circle, admiring the beautiful setting. Canyon walls rose up in the distance behind, the Poudre River flowed peacefully right beside the property, and aspen trees and evergreens were scattered everywhere.

"Now I know why Housemann fell in love with this place," Kelly said, following Jennifer toward the cabin's front porch.

"It's beautiful, all right," Jennifer agreed, glancing around as she walked to the door. "Listen, why don't you wait on the porch while I find out what's up with Turner and this Birmingham. Then, I can give you a tour."

"Take your time. I'm going to enjoy the view." Kelly stood by the split-log railing.

Jennifer knocked on the door once, then pushed it open.

"Mr. Turner? It's Jennifer Stroud," she said as she entered. "Anita called me and said a Mr. Birmingham had expressed interest in the listing."

Kelly watched a red-tailed hawk float on a wind current overhead, obviously searching for some tasty morsel in the brown grasses below.

"Mr. Turner, where are you?" Jennifer's voice came from inside.

The hawk floated for a second longer, then swooped lower, spying something. Kelly tracked the hawk, watching him swoop lower, then lower . . .

"Mr. Turner! *Oh, my God* . . . Kelly! *Kelly!*"

Kelly snapped out of her nature watch and ran inside the cabin. She could tell from the sound of Jennifer's voice that something had scared her. "Jen, what is it?" she cried as she rushed inside.

Jennifer stood beside a wooden table, her arm outstretched, pointing toward the floor. There was barely any furniture in the cabin. "He's . . . he's dead," Jennifer whispered. "Oh, my God . . . he shot himself."

Kelly rushed up to Jennifer and saw what had frightened her friend. There on the bare wooden cabin floor, a man lay on his side, a bloody wound on the side of his head. His eyes were open and stared vacantly. A gun lay on the floor beside his hand.

"That's Turner?" Kelly asked, feeling her body and mind react to seeing death up close and personal, yet another time.

"God, yes . . ." Jennifer whispered, her face drained of all color. Chalk white. "I . . . I think I'm gonna be sick . . . I can't look at this. . . ."

"Go outside, Jen, now," Kelly instructed, pointing to the door. "I'll check for a pulse."

"Oh, God . . ." Jennifer turned away, hand to her mouth, and ran through the door to the porch.

Kelly approached Turner and slowly knelt beside him, making sure she didn't disturb his body. She steeled herself and placed two fingers on the spot on his neck where she should have felt a pulse. Nothing. Turner was dead.

As she knelt beside the body, Kelly looked at the gun more closely. It was a pistol, not a revolver. And it looked different from the other pistols Kelly was used to seeing at Curt's and Jayleen's houses and had fired herself on their properties at target practice. There were a lot of guns in Colorado. But this gun didn't look like any she'd ever seen. It looked older than the other guns.

Kelly dug into her jeans pocket and pulled out her smartphone, touched the camera option, and snapped two photos of the gun. One close-up and one showing Turner's hand beside it.

"Is he still alive?" Jennifer asked, peeking around the corner.

Kelly stood up. "No, he's gone. It looks like he did shoot himself, Jen."

Jennifer walked away from the doorway. "I don't understand. I talked with him yesterday. He was fine. He was fine."

Kelly was about to join her frightened friend, then turned and studied the body on the floor again, then the cabin's open room. There was little furniture and nothing else looked disturbed. Only the chair where Turner had obviously been sitting was sideways on the floor.

She pulled out her phone again and snapped another photo, then shoved the smartphone back into her pocket as she returned to the porch.

"Had he ever acted or sounded depressed to you?" Kelly asked.

"Never. He was one of the most driven real estate guys I've ever met. I cannot imagine what would make him shoot himself." Jennifer paced the porch. "We've gotta call the police, Kelly. We'd better call them now." She pulled her phone from her jacket pocket. "Does nine-one-one work up here?"

"It should. It worked years ago when you and I walked in and found Vickie Claymore dead." Kelly said wryly.

Jennifer looked up, her brown eyes huge. "Oh, my gawd! I can't believe we've walked in on another corpse. Kelly . . . we can't come into the canyon together anymore. Not alone, anyway."

"Jen . . ."

Jennifer's hand flew up. "No. I'm making a vow. No more driving into canyons alone with Kelly Flynn. There's something about the two of us together in canyons that is bringing bad juju or whatever Jayleen calls it."

Kelly didn't reply, because the police department answered, and Jennifer began to explain that they'd arrived and found the dead body of her real estate client lying on the floor, obviously shot in the head. Kelly stood by the railing again and searched for another hawk while Jennifer related all the details to the county police. That meant Lieutenant Peterson would be investigating. She wondered what he'd say when he learned that she and Jennifer had stumbled onto another death scene. Again.

A slight movement at the corner of her eye caused Kelly

to turn ever so slightly to the right. Brush and heavy bush grew between the aspens there at the side of the clearing. She searched to see what had caught her eye. Then, she saw it. A brief glimpse. A man's dark blue plaid shirt. Kelly stood absolutely still, so as not to draw attention to herself. Jennifer's voice was loud enough to carry on the breeze, so whoever was listening could hear every word.

Another slight movement and more of the plaid shirt came into view. Then a man's face. A bearded face. Shaggy brown hair down to his shoulders. And something else. A shotgun lay in his arms. That got Kelly's attention.

The man suddenly looked straight at Kelly. She stared back at him, and he disappeared behind the bushes again as quickly as he'd appeared. Quick as a rabbit.

Kelly glanced at Jennifer and decided not to share the bearded stranger sighting right now. Her friend had been spooked enough already. She'd wait until Lieutenant Peterson arrived.

"The dispatcher said police should be here in twenty minutes," Jennifer said, slipping the phone back into her jacket again.

"That's good. Why don't we wait in the car, okay?" Kelly suggested, glancing over her shoulder toward the bushes again.

"Good idea. The farther I get from that cabin the better."

Amen to that, Kelly thought.

Four

Kelly leaned against Jennifer's car door and watched a county police officer lead the ambulance crew into the cabin. One man pushed a gurney-type stretcher. Kelly recognized it from watching similar scenes before. First, there were questions, while others went to check the body. Then, there were more questions. Meanwhile, several officers wandered around the property and the outside perimeter of the cabin.

The ambulance crew had arrived right behind Peterson and his officers and had rushed inside as soon as the ambulance rocked to a stop in the bumpy dirt roadway. The siren's wail still echoed on the canyon's breeze. Peterson had been inside with the medical crew ever since. Meanwhile, a younger officer interviewed both Kelly and Jennifer. Now, another police officer wrapped bright yellow police tape around the porch railing.

"Oh, brother, I remember seeing that last year," Jennifer said, her expression changing. "The sight of that yellow tape brings up some baaaad memories."

Kelly glanced over at her friend, who'd dramatically transformed her life since the traumatic events from last year when Kelly, Jennifer, and others were in this canyon for a special retreat. A man died while they were there. Murdered.

"Let it slide off, Jen. That was last year and another life ago. It's dust in the wind now."

Jennifer nodded. "You're right. It seems like another life long ago."

Lieutenant Peterson came out of the cabin and onto the porch. He glanced over at Kelly and Jennifer briefly, then approached an officer on the porch.

"Isn't Peterson going to talk with us?" Jennifer asked. "I'm going to have to get back to the office and talk with my broker before he leaves. I probably should have called him before the cops arrived."

"He'll be over in a minute. I can tell," Kelly said, watching Peterson talk with the young officer who interviewed them. "See, he's writing in his notepad. That's his procedure. I swear, I have it memorized by now."

"Well, this is the last time for me," Jennifer declared. "Even if that means I don't take any more canyon properties. I swear, I'm not gonna go through this again." Jennifer gave a finalized motion with her hand.

Kelly couldn't help but laugh. "C'mon, Jen, you know that doesn't make sense. Besides, the statistical probability of something like this happening again is—"

Jennifer's hand cut her off. "You know what they say about statistics, don't you? They're liars, or some such thing."

Kelly didn't bother to correct Jennifer's memory about the famous quote. Besides, true to form, Detective Peterson was headed their way, trusty notepad in hand.

"Hello, Ms. Flynn, Ms. Stroud," Peterson said, a grin spreading. "Imagine my surprise to find the two of you up here in the canyon at yet another death scene. Perhaps you both should reconsider visiting the canyons for a while, in the interest of public safety, you understand."

Kelly spotted the twinkle in Peterson's eye, but Jennifer jumped right in. "I told Kelly I'm not driving up here again with her. In fact, I'm not sure I want to list any more canyon properties."

"Well, it is a recession, Ms. Stroud," Peterson advised sagely. "You might not want to be hasty. Just leave Ms. Flynn at home."

"You got that right."

"Hey, I simply came along for the ride," Kelly joined in the teasing. "Jennifer promised pretty views. Nothing was said about dead bodies."

Peterson flipped through his notepad, all business again. "Ms. Stroud, you said you'd met your client Fred Turner about a week ago and had spoken to him several times, both in person and on the phone. And he had never said anything that sounded like he wanted to end his life, correct?"

Jennifer nodded. "Yes, sir. Turner was all business all the time. He's been buying and selling properties for years, and he's quite successful. He likes . . . uh, liked to buy low and sell higher, if he could." She gestured to the cabin. "This was a property he acquired through a defaulted loan, and he wanted to make a good deal on it because of the location. As you can see, it's a beautiful setting."

Peterson glanced around. "Yes, it is. Did you have a buyer yet?"

"As a matter of fact, we did. That's another reason I invited Kelly up here, because it was one of her business clients who gave us a purchase offer only three days ago. Arthur Housemann of Fort Connor."

Peterson scribbled in his notepad, then glanced up at Kelly. "Had your client mentioned he was making an offer, Ms. Flynn?"

"Yes, he had. He said he'd been looking for mountain properties when this came on the market." Kelly deliberately didn't add Housemann's long-term fascination with the property. She didn't feel obligated to reveal everything that was said in their conversation.

"Had you spoken with Turner today, Ms. Stroud?"

"No, I hadn't," Jennifer answered. "I was simply driving up here to put a SALE PENDING banner across the sign, and I thought Kelly would enjoy the drive." Jennifer paused, then continued. "On the way up here, however, I had a call from Turner's assistant who told me that Turner had an appointment scheduled here this morning with a Mr. Birmingham who wanted to make an offer on the property. Apparently this man left a message on the office voice mail."

Peterson peered at Jennifer. "You mean he didn't contact you? Earlier you'd said you were Turner's real estate agent. Why didn't this Birmingham contact you through your agency?"

Jennifer gave him a wry smile. "That's what I'd like to know. And why Turner would meet with a new client without letting me know. The property is clearly listed by my company, and I'm the selling agent."

Kelly decided to jump in at this point. "That's exactly right, Detective Peterson. We drove up here and saw Turner's truck. I waited on the front porch and Jennifer walked in and found him dead."

"And there was no one else here?" Peterson asked Jennifer.

Jennifer hesitated. "No, sir, but as Kelly and I drove along the canyon road, we saw a blue truck come out of this driveway and turn in the direction of Fort Connor. I think I recognized the woman driving the truck. It was Turner's wife, Renee."

Peterson stared at Jennifer with interest but said nothing. He simply wrote in his notepad. "Had you met her before, Ms. Stroud? You said you recognized her."

Jennifer glanced away, and Kelly could tell her friend was uncomfortable. "Yes, I'd seen Mrs. Turner come into her husband's office while I was there going over the listing contract. She'd . . . she'd been showing up at the office several times recently. Our real estate offices are on the same floor as Turner's office, so I've seen her several times. And, Turner's assistant, Anita, told me that Turner and his wife are in the midst of a divorce right now."

Again, Peterson watched Jennifer, then scribbled down everything she said. "I see," was his only comment.

But Kelly spotted Peterson's unmistakable signs of the detective's piqued interest. After watching Peterson in action for three separate investigations, Kelly had begun to recognize his body language. Not so, the formidable and less friendly Lieutenant Morrison of the Fort Connor Police Department. He and Kelly seemed to square off whenever they met.

"Turner never mentioned the divorce to me," Jennifer said earnestly.

Kelly decided to venture in again, even though it was none of her business. Simply to shift Peterson's focus away from Jennifer for a minute. Let her catch her breath. "You know, that gun he used looked kind of old to me, Detective," she said. "I'm not an expert on guns or anything, but I've never seen a pistol that looked exactly like that before. What kind is it? Did you recognize it?"

Peterson gave Kelly a slow smile. "Well, you're right about it being old, Ms. Flynn. I'm not sure exactly how old yet, but our forensics people will be able to tell once they take a look at it." Then, he eyed Kelly. "You made sure you didn't touch anything or disturb the body, correct?"

She shook her head. "Absolutely not, Lieutenant. I know better than that."

Peterson actually chuckled. "Well, considering this is the third time you've been present when we've come to investigate a death, I imagine you have paid attention to our procedures, Ms. Flynn. Plus, your track record for conducting your own investigations into past cases is quite good."

"Thank you, Detective. That's high praise coming from you," Kelly said with a grin.

"I don't sense the same interest on your part, Ms. Stroud," Peterson said.

Jennifer shook her head vehemently. "No, sir. I try to block all of that out. Kelly's the one who likes to poke around in crimes. We call it 'sleuthing.'"

This time, Peterson laughed out loud, glancing to Kelly, who shrugged good-naturedly. She was used to her friends' teasing. "That's a sensible attitude, Ms. Stroud." His expression softened, and he looked at Jennifer with a fatherly expression.

"I'm glad to see you doing well, Jennifer. I'm sure your friends were there to support you last year."

"You bet we were," Kelly added.

Jennifer glanced to Kelly with a smile. "I couldn't have done it without them, Detective. Or without Dr. Norcross. She was a lifesaver. Talking with her helped me more than you know."

Peterson nodded. "Believe me, Jennifer, I'm well aware of how good Dr. Norcross is. She's counseled several young women I've heard. She's a jewel."

Kelly was about to agree when the ambulance crew started backing out of the cabin door with Turner's body wrapped in a white covering on top of the gurney-stretcher.

"Okay, you two, you know the drill," Peterson continued. "We may contact you again for further questions, so stay in town."

"Wait a minute, Lieutenant," Kelly said as he turned to walk away. "I almost forgot. While Jennifer was calling you guys to report, I was standing by the corner railing, and I saw a bearded man in a blue plaid shirt hiding in the bushes, listening."

"*What!* And you didn't tell me?" Jennifer cried aghast.

"I figured you'd been spooked enough."

Peterson flipped open his trusty notepad and began to scribble. "Can you describe the man?"

"He was obscured by the bushes, and I only had a fleeting glimpse of him. He had a light brown beard about three or four inches long and his brown hair was long and shaggy to his shoulders. And he clearly didn't want to be seen, because once he noticed me looking at him, he bolted."

Peterson scribbled. "Anything else, Ms. Flynn?"

Kelly paused for full effect. "Oh, yes. He was carrying a shotgun draped across his arm."

Peterson looked up at that, while Jennifer gasped.

Kelly walked into Lambspun's foyer. It was nearly five o'clock on a Saturday afternoon, and customers were still browsing the yarn bins, choosing yarns and fibers for their next projects. She glanced toward the room with the counter and registers and spied customers lining up with their selections. Only a few minutes left until the shop closed.

Hoping to spot Burt, she turned the corner into the main room. There seated at the long library table was Lizzie, contentedly knitting away on a lemon yellow afghan. Beside her sat Eustace, pounding away on his laptop computer. Kelly couldn't help but notice that Eustace looked as contented as Lizzie.

"Well, hello, you two," Kelly said as she pulled out a chair. "You both look busy. That's a beautiful shade of yellow, Lizzie."

"Why, thank you, dear," Lizzie said, her smile showing her dimple.

Kelly couldn't help noticing that Lizzie's color was heightened, her normally rosy cheeks even rosier.

"I take it you're working on your book, right, Eustace?" Kelly asked. "Have you conducted any more interviews?"

Eustace looked up at Kelly, his round face spreading with a smile. "Goodness, yes. I interviewed four gentlemen this week and have four more scheduled for next week. Oh, and while I remember, let me take down your clients' names and phone numbers. I plan to call them for appointments, too."

Kelly settled back in the wooden chair, feeling strange because she didn't have her knitting with her. Usually when she sat in these chairs, she was knitting with her friends or simply by herself, relaxing in the shop's tranquil environment.

"Of course. I'll give both Housemann and Warner a heads-up that you may be calling. That way you'll get past the receptionist." She then recited the phone numbers for both men while Eustace scribbled them down in his notebook. It was larger than Peterson's, Kelly noticed.

"He's been in Greeley and Loveland in addition to Fort Connor," Lizzie affirmed, her bright blue eyes alight.

"Whom did you interview in Greeley? Macafée? He's a nice guy and has been able to stay in business through this whole downturn."

"As a matter of fact, I did speak with him. It turns out he and I share some distant relatives in Oklahoma and Texas." Eustace chuckled. "He was also more than forthcoming about some of the, uh, outlaws in the business. Several have been driven out, but others have thrived, according to Macafée."

"I've met him at a couple of those large developer meetings. He seems to know everybody in the real estate and development world here in northern Colorado," Kelly said.

"He was a great source of information. And, thanks to Curt's influence, I've made appointments with several energy developers as well."

Eustace removed his rimless glasses and started cleaning them with his white shirt. Kelly had observed Eustace always wore a dress shirt with cuff links. Even when he was at Jayleen's barbeque. An old-fashioned gentleman.

"Everyone I've spoken to so far has been so very cooperative," Eustace continued. "They've found time in their schedules for me to interview them. Some have even taken me out to see their properties, which provided me a chance to take pictures." Eustace picked up the larger spiral-bound notebook beside his laptop. "I take copious notes. They've all been most forthcoming."

Lizzie looked at Eustace with what looked to Kelly to be an adoring gaze. "Yes, he's been very busy with his book."

Kelly couldn't resist. "Well, it seems Eustace hasn't been too busy to see you, Lizzie," she said with a smile. "I've noticed you two working here at the shop several times."

Lizzie flushed a deep rose at Kelly's comment, dimpling both cheeks. Eustace, however, looked over at Lizzie with a fond expression on his round face. His cheeks a little pink, too, Kelly noticed. That accentuated the silver hair that ringed his head in fringe and gave Eustace a cherubic look.

"Visiting with Lizzie is the perfect accompaniment to my day spent with hard-driving, profit-focused businessmen," Eustace said, reaching over to pat Lizzie's hand. "Who knew I'd find such a delightful and charming companion in the midst of a yarn shop." He chuckled. "Life has surprises for us, doesn't it?"

"Indeed, so, Eustace," Kelly agreed, unable to miss his use of the word "companion." Kelly noticed Lizzie hadn't missed it, either. Her adoring expression turned more rapturous. Life definitely held surprises, and Kelly was glad a good one landed in the lap of such a sweet spinster and retired schoolteacher.

She was about to add something when Burt entered the room. "All right, everyone. It's five minutes to closing time tonight. If there's anything you want to purchase, you'd better go up front to the counter now," Burt said, gathering some of the stray balls of yarns that customers had left on the table. "How're those interviews going, Eustace?"

"Quite well, actually. I've got several scheduled this next week, and Kelly has shared her contacts, too." Eustace closed his laptop.

On seeing Burt, Kelly remembered why she'd stopped in Lambspun right before closing time. Chatting with the adorable senior couple had momentarily caused her to forget. However, Kelly decided to modify her comments until she was alone with Burt.

"Burt, I wanted to tell you that Jennifer has learned one of her real estate clients shot himself at his property in Poudre Canyon today."

"What? That's dreadful!" Lizzie looked horrified, knitting dropped to her lap.

Burt's cop expression fell into place. "What? Who was it?"

"Indeed, that is distressing to hear," Eustace said, clearly concerned. "Was the client depressed about the property not selling, do you think?"

"Actually, no," Kelly replied. "The property already had a purchase offer on it. So, who knows who made Fred Turner kill himself."

Eustace's eyes went huge. "Did you say Fred Turner? That's *awful*! I interviewed him this last week. He . . . he was so helpful . . . and interesting." He shook his head. "I cannot believe it."

"His name sounds familiar. Let me find out what I can and get back to you, Kelly. How's Jennifer handling it?"

"Pretty well, considering. She's had more than her share of walking in on traumatic scenes."

"This is simply tragic," Eustace said, shaking his silver-fringed head. "So sad to take one's life."

This time, Lizzie reached over and patted Eustace's hand. "I know, Eustace. It's incomprehensible. Shall we go to church and say a prayer?"

Eustace placed his hand atop Lizzie's. "Yes, let us do that. Then, we can go to dinner in that nice English pub Jennifer recommended. It won't be noisy with Saturday-night revelers."

"That's a wonderful idea," Lizzie concurred, gathering her knitting into its bag.

"Enjoy dinner, you two. If it's the same English pub I'm thinking of, the food is delicious," Kelly said as Eustace slipped on his suit jacket then held Lizzie's shawl for her.

"Thank you, I'm sure we will." Eustace gave them a big smile as he escorted Lizzie out of the room.

"Say a prayer for me," Burt called over his shoulder after them. "Aren't they a pair?"

"They're adorable. And I cannot believe how well they get along. From the start. Jennifer said they started talking from the first time they met and haven't stopped yet." Kelly paused. "How is Hilda taking this? I haven't been around to see her."

"Hilda hasn't been able to get out as much as she used to. Her arthritis is really giving her problems. So, I don't know how much Lizzie has shared about her, uh . . . budding relationship with Eustace." He grinned.

"Well, now that the 'older' lovebirds have left, I wanted to share some more details. Jennifer and I must have some strange energy thing going on whenever we drive into the canyons, because we walked in on Fred Turner's dead body today." Kelly retrieved her cell phone from her jeans pocket.

"Jennifer and I planned to hike around that gorgeous property. So we pulled up to the cabin in Poudre Canyon, and I waited outside while she went to talk with Turner. Then Jennifer cried out for me to come inside. I walked in and found him lying on the floor with blood coming from the side of his head. And a gun lying beside his hand." She accessed the photos on her smartphone. "I took a photo of the gun, Burt. It looked like some old-fashioned pistol. What do you think? I've never seen a gun like that." She handed the phone to Burt.

Burt stared at the photo, his brows furrowing. "You're right, Kelly. It does look like an older pistol. It'll be interesting to see what the crime lab determines it to be."

"Click on the arrow and you'll see another photo."

Burt clicked and stared at the photos Kelly had taken. "Looks like Turner wanted a quiet setting to end his life." He glanced up at Kelly with a little smile. "You've gotten kind of used to walking in on dead bodies if you're snapping photos. Better save it, in case the guys want to see it. You understand."

"No problem. I'm not even sure why I took it." She shrugged.

"Just part of being a good sleuth, Kelly," Burt teased.

Five

"Run, Carl, he's got a head start on you," Kelly called to her Rottweiler, who was dashing across the cottage backyard. Brazen Squirrel sprinted across the top rail of the chain-link fence separating Kelly's backyard from the adjoining city golf course.

Carl barked while in pursuit but trailed the fleet-footed squirrel, who leaped from the fence corner directly into a conveniently drooping cottonwood branch. Brazen scrambled up the still-barren limbs to safety.

Kelly watched her dog charge the chain-link anyway, barking ferocious doggie threats. *Next time*. Or, *I'll get you yet*. Riiiight, Kelly thought as she slid the glass patio door shut. Brazen had his highway down pat. He had dozens of squirrelly escape routes. There he was now, chattering and fussing at Carl, which only spurred Carl to more barking. While Brazen shook his tail and scampered to another branch.

Refilling her coffee mug, Kelly grabbed her knitting bag, pocketed her cell phone, and left her cozy cottage. The cottage that seemed less roomy these last six months even though Steve no longer lived with her. That was because of the new furniture. Kelly had bought a new chocolate-colored sofa and matching armchair for the living room. Even though both pieces took up more room, she loved the soft feel of the upholstery. Kelly had also bought a new bedroom set. A beautiful bed and dresser in rich cherry wood.

Kelly slammed the door and walked down the path to the wide driveway that separated her snug little beige-stucco, red-tile-roofed cottage from the identical but larger version that housed Lambspun. Once the Spanish colonial farmhouse for Aunt Helen and Uncle Jim's sheep farm, it was now turned into the knitting shop. The sheep were still there—simply in another form. Instead of grazing in the pastures outside, their fleeces filled the bins and shelves in an array of colors.

Walking toward Lambspun's front patio, Kelly checked the angle of the afternoon sun. It was late afternoon, and the sun was on the downward path but still in the middle of the sky, blazing bright. Early March, and the sun was setting a little bit later every day and rising earlier. Bit by bit, minute by minute, creeping toward the spring equinox. Twelve hours of daylight and twelve hours of darkness. Kelly loved the spring equinox that came each March because it always signaled that spring weather was near. On the horizon, inching closer.

Right now, she hoped to get in some relaxing time knitting and talking with whomever sat around the table. After a full day of balancing complex accounts and solving financial problems, Kelly figured she deserved a break. Tomorrow, she'd be in Denver all day with Warner's group. Right now, she could still sit in her jeans and sweater. No business suits or stylish outfits.

A familiar car turned into the driveway and pulled into a parking space. Jennifer. Kelly waited on the sidewalk beneath a huge black walnut tree for her friend.

"Hey, there, how're you doing?" Kelly greeted.

"Hanging in there," Jennifer said as she clicked her door lock and walked over to Kelly. "Glad you're here this afternoon. Now I've got someone to complain to."

"You're talking about the Turner property, right?" Kelly said, as they followed the brick walk that led to Lambspun's front door.

"Ohhhh, yeah." Jennifer shook her head sadly. "That deal is as dead as Turner." She pulled the heavy oak door open and sailed through, Kelly following.

"I'm sorry, Jen," Kelly commiserated. "Listen, if you need money—"

"Yeah, I know, and I appreciate the offer," Jennifer said, as she walked into the main knitting room. She dropped her knitting bag on the table. "It's just we were so close . . . it's so frustrating." She sank into a chair.

Kelly pulled out the chair beside her. "What's happening now? Is it in legal limbo, or is the contract invalid since the seller is no longer alive to execute the transaction."

Jennifer pulled circular needles and a peach-colored yarn out of her knitting bag. "Actually, there is a possibility that Turner's widow might want to sell the property eventually. After all, their divorce wasn't final, so she's still his wife and inherits everything. Anita says they had no children." Jennifer examined the two inches of completed stitches on her needles. "But, that doesn't help me now. That's why I'm actually picking up some additional catering jobs at the university."

"Jen, you don't have to do that. I'll loan you the money," Kelly offered, taking out a ball of multicolored yarn. About an inch of scarf hung on the wooden needles.

Jennifer held up her hand. "I know, but I'd much rather earn it myself, Kelly. If I really get into a bind, I'll let you know. But right now, I'm hanging on. These extra catering jobs hopefully will see me through. And, I was working phone duty this afternoon, and I have a couple wanting to go out and look at some short-sale houses, so that's promising."

"Fingers crossed." Kelly held hers up. "Meanwhile, I feel sorry for those short sellers. How much under market value are they offering the property?"

"Twenty thousand."

Kelly visibly flinched. "Wow, that's brutal."

"Tell me about it." Jennifer sighed as her needles picked up speed. "That's what this housing crash has done to people. If they're laid off or their jobs are cut to part time, they're forced to sell. It's awful to watch. They literally break down in tears when I show them how much money they'll have to bring to the closing. *If* the house sells, and that's a big 'if.' There're scores of marked-down properties on the market right now."

Kelly couldn't help but think of Steve's Wellesley development where Lisa and Greg were renting one of the houses. The last time she'd met her friends there, she counted the same number of houses for sale she'd seen the month before. Kelly couldn't help counting. She was an accountant. That's what she did.

"At least one of the Wellesley houses is now under contract. It's finally worked through the foreclosure process, and one of the agents in my office had the buyers. Plus, another agent may have a buyer for one of the Wellesley two-stories that's a short sale."

Wondering if Jennifer read her mind, Kelly deliberately tried to sound nonchalant. "That's good."

"Yeah, Steve was pretty happy to hear that last Friday night when he came over to Lisa and Greg's," Jennifer continued, without looking up from her busy needles. "He's looking pretty beat. Working too hard. His boss apparently is participating in the joint project Warner's working on in Denver. That's why you saw Steve at that meeting. His boss put him in charge."

Kelly concentrated on the multicolored stitches forming on her needle and didn't answer. This recycled silk yarn was different. She didn't know if it would tighten up on the needles or not.

Jennifer kept on anyway, as if Kelly was interested in the conversation. Which she wasn't. Not a bit. Steve's work was his business.

"We told Steve you saw him at the meeting," Jennifer continued blithely, still focusing on her knitting. Stitches forming. "He nearly fell off the couch, kicking himself."

Kelly couldn't keep her smile in check. The image of Steve trying to sit on Lisa and Greg's couch while kicking himself was funny. "I think that's physiologically impossible, Jennifer."

Jennifer finally glanced up at Kelly and spotted her smile. "Yeah, but I wanted to make you smile. Steve's lower than a snake's belly right now."

Kelly deliberately didn't reply, she just kept knitting increasingly tighter stitches onto her needles. Finally she said, "That's a great shade for you. Is it another sweater?"

"No, I'm making a short-sleeve top from the pattern hanging in the central room. I figure it'll start getting warmer by April. I hope." Jennifer's fingers worked the yarn and glanced over at Kelly's needles. "Is that the recycled silk yarn?"

"Yes, it is. It's been sitting in my stash basket for over two years, and I finally decided I was going to make something with it."

"Didn't you try a scarf with it before? I vaguely remember that."

Kelly nodded. "I'd tried three different times and never liked the look of it when I got it on the needles. Everyone said to combine it with another yarn, and I tried three different ones. Didn't like any of them, so I dumped it back into the basket."

"It's such a pretty yarn," Jennifer said, reaching over and fingering the nubbly silk. "All those different colors. It's hard to imagine women unraveled their saris and then spun the silk into yarn. That's got to be a ton of work."

Kelly rubbed the colorful fibers between her fingers. "I know. That's probably why the yarn is so uneven. I finally got the idea of knitting with double strands of it and voila! That made all the difference. It's going to be a really warm scarf."

"Well, I'm glad you didn't give up on the yarn. You know, once you finish with that, you should make this top. It's easy and it would look great with your business outfits."

Kelly reached over and fingered the pale peach color. Soft, yet springy. "Cotton?" she asked.

"Cotton and bamboo. It should be pretty."

Kelly returned to her stitches, glad she'd diverted Jennifer's attention and changed the conversation. She didn't want to talk about Steve and his lower-than-a-snake's-belly mood. He'd been in a bad mood the last six months they'd been together.

"You know, Steve wants to apologize, but he doesn't think you want to talk to him."

Clearly, Jennifer was determined to continue this train of conversation. *We'll see about that,* thought Kelly. "He's right. I don't. Tell him to e-mail."

Jennifer looked up at Kelly again. "E-mail?"

Kelly gave a nonchalant shrug. "It's fast and easy. Or, he can send a text."

Jennifer eyed her. "Okaaaay, I'll tell him next time he comes. Actually we suggested he just walk up at one of those meetings and say he's sorry."

Kelly looked at Jennifer, startled. "*What?* Are you nuts? I'm . . . I'm up to my ears with work at those things. I don't have time to talk to Steve. Don't be crazy."

"How about if he just says 'hello'? Or, maybe gives you a wave?"

"That's okay, I guess," Kelly said, unsure what to reply.

"Good, I'll tell him the next time I see him. Of course, I don't know when that'll be." Jennifer said, returning to her stitches.

Unsettled now by the scene Jennifer had painted, Kelly felt the silken yarn tighten up even more. She had to force her needle through the left stitch. Dropping it into her lap, she asked, "Did Pete put any coffee in the fridge?"

Jennifer looked up solicitously. "Do you need some caffeine?"

Annoyed by Jennifer's question and the meaning behind it, Kelly retorted, "No, I don't *need* any caffeine right now. I would simply like to have some."

"Wait a second, I'll check," Jennifer said, springing from her chair much faster than she used to before she and Pete began running every morning. She was back with a foam cup of coffee before Kelly could knit more than two tight stitches.

"I always forget how fast you can move when you want to," Kelly said, hoping to deflect Jennifer's train of thought. "You could join our team as a base runner. Someone else could bat and you'd run the bases. What do you think?"

"Nah, the key in that sentence is when I 'want' to. Running around bases and sweating in the hot sun isn't my thing."

Confident she'd deflected Jennifer's train of thought, Kelly returned to the recycled silk, trying to loosen the stitches so the needle could slide beneath them.

No such luck. With the needles or the conversation.

"Would you talk to him if Steve apologized?"

Kelly threw back her head. "*Arrrgh!* Enough about Steve, already! Tell him he should have apologized six months ago."

Jennifer didn't miss a beat. Still focusing on her needles. "He knows that. That's the main reason he's so depressed. He knows he screwed it up good between the two of you."

"Yeah, he did," Kelly shot back, trying to force the needle beneath another stitch. She didn't want to think about it.

"And he doesn't know how to make it better," Jennifer said quietly, watching Kelly's face.

Kelly didn't say a word. She didn't want to. She had nothing to suggest. Maybe it was too late for Steve and her. They had their time, and now it was over.

Just then, a familiar presence blew into the Lambspun shop, spotted Kelly and Jennifer, and headed toward them. "Hey, I couldn't have planned it better. I was hoping to find you two here," Jayleen declared as she charged into the room.

"Hey, Jayleen, how're you doing?" Kelly greeted the alpaca rancher cheerfully, glad for the interruption.

Jayleen grabbed a chair and straddled it backward in her Colorado Cowgirl fashion. She dropped her Stetson onto the table and fixed Kelly with a serious look. "I'm fair to middling. But I'm not here to talk about me. I hear that last Saturday you two went up to that Poudre Canyon property and found Fred Turner dead."

Kelly recalled yesterday's local newspaper article reporting Turner's death. "Well, not too much to say, Jayleen. Jennifer and I went up to the property to look around and found Turner shot dead, lying on the floor. Not pleasant."

"That's an understatement," Jennifer agreed, needles moving faster. "I think Kelly and I create bad juju when we drive into the canyons. People die and we find them. Awful." She shivered.

"Eustace told Curt and me. Says that Turner shot himself. Is that right?"

"Yeah. Gun was lying beside his hand on the floor. He shot himself in the head. Did you know him, Jayleen?"

"Yeah, I knew him. I've known both Fred and Renee Turner for years. Renee's a close friend of mine. I met her when I first moved up here from Colorado Springs." She shook her head. "Damn, I can't picture Turner killing himself."

"I'm sorry you lost your friend," Kelly started to offer sympathy.

Jayleen cut her off with a wave of her hand. "Hell, I'm not

sorry that bastard is dead. He was nothing but a crook. Even Curt says so. And you know, Curt doesn't bad-mouth anyone unless it's true. Turner cheated lots of folks out of their land. No-good conniving so-and-so. He was miserable to Renee when they were married and had been trying to cheat her in the divorce. It had gotten real ugly." Jayleen made a face. "Turner was hiding assets from her. Shifting money into other accounts, trying to hide property transactions, all sorts of stuff."

Jennifer let her knitting sit in her lap. "Renee came up to Turner's office one time when I was there, and she looked furious. She started yelling at him and accusing him of all that same stuff. It was ugly. I got out of there fast."

Jayleen nodded. "Yeah, Renee had watched Fred cheat other people out of their land and money, so she knew he'd try to cheat her, too. Even more so. He even sold off a piece of land that she'd picked out twenty years ago. Up in Redstone Canyon. Renee always talked about building a house there. It had great views of the Buckhorn Creek and valley. That bastard sold it last year. Did it on purpose because he knew she loved it." She scowled. "He was one mean son of a gun. I'm surprised one of those clients he cheated over the years didn't do him in. Even Renee said she wanted to plug him."

"Well, she's got all his assets now," Kelly said. "Turner's dead and they're still married. No divorce."

Jennifer looked pensive for a minute. "You know, I've been thinking about that. I didn't want to say anything before because it sounded so insensitive. I mean, the woman just lost her husband. But maybe Renee Turner really would be interested in selling that Poudre Canyon property to Housemann."

"Hell, nobody is gonna grieve Fred Turner. Least of all, Renee," Jayleen declared. "I wouldn't be surprised if she does sell it. Let's hope so."

"That would be great," Jennifer said, returning to the peach fiber. "Nothing can happen until after the estate is settled, but it would be good to know that a deal could eventually go through."

"Well, I'm sure my client Housemann would like to know," Kelly added. "He's really interested in that property."

Burt appeared in the doorway of the adjoining classroom, holding a white plastic bag. Creamy white fleece protruded over the top of the bag. "Hey, is there room for me and my wheel?" he asked with a smile.

"Sure, Burt, come and join us," Kelly invited, beckoning him over.

"Hey, Burt. You and that bag remind me. I've gotta ask Mimi about some fleeces I promised her." Jayleen effortlessly swung her jeans-clad leg over the chair as she rose.

"Well, you'd better get up front because she's there now, and it's nearly closing time." Burt pulled his spinning wheel from the corner and plopped the plastic bag beside. Settling into a chair, he pulled the wheel toward him.

"I'll talk to you folks another time," Jayleen said as she headed for the foyer.

"Bye, Jayleen, and thanks," Jennifer called after her, as she shoved the peach wool and needles into her bag. "I lost track of time. I've gotta go home and change and get over to the university for that banquet going on tonight."

"Sorry you had to go through that again, Jennifer," Burt said with a fatherly smile. "Walking in on a death scene. Not good."

"Well, it won't happen again, Burt," Jennifer said as she rose to leave. "Kelly and I aren't driving together into canyons anymore. She'll explain. Gotta go, guys." She gave a wave and headed toward the foyer.

"What was that all about?" Burt asked, clearly confused.

"Oh, Jen's convinced we have bad canyon juju." Kelly returned to her yarn and discovered the stitches had loosened. Strange. Maybe recycled silk was one of those temperamental yarns. She knitted several stitches easily and regained her rhythm.

Burt began drafting some of the fleece in his lap, pulling the fibers apart with his fingers, stretching them, to make them easier to spin. His feet began the treadle's steady rhythm while Burt started feeding the drafted fleece, or roving, onto the wheel. Smoothly the roving slid through his partially separated fingers and onto the strand of yarn that wound around the wheel and onto the spindle.

Kelly loved watching Burt spin. It was peaceful and calming. Kelly sat and knitted two entire rows, the only sound the hum of the wheel.

Finally, Burt spoke. "I heard from Paul Graves, an old friend with the county police. I'd left him a message last week after we talked. Paul said it appears Fred Turner committed suicide, but they're waiting for the medical examiner's report."

"It certainly looked that way," Kelly said, still focusing on her stitches.

"As you know, sometimes things aren't as they appear." Burt gave her a wry smile. "You've seen that yourself."

Kelly did, indeed. When they found their friend Tracy floating in the dye tub downstairs at Lambspun over a year ago, everyone assumed it was an accidental drowning. But it turned out it wasn't. It was murder.

Kelly remembered something. "Did your friend Paul have any idea how old the gun is?"

"He and I both guessed it to be at least fifty years old. The crime lab guys will give us a better idea when they finish. You still have the photos?"

"Sure."

"Don't you love technology? What would we do without it?" Burt smiled.

"Well, for one thing, people wouldn't expect us to be available electronically twenty-four/seven," Kelly replied. "We're all dragging around an invisible electronic tether. We have to be all the time. Computer and smartphone, now."

"I'm glad you convinced me to get one of those. I'm totally addicted to it now," Burt said with a laugh.

"Told you."

Mimi strode into the room then. "Oh, you've started spinning. I've closed up the shop and was about to turn off the lights."

"Sit down and knit with us for a few minutes, Mimi," Kelly suggested. "It's so peaceful with everyone gone except us."

"Well, normally I would, but I put a pot roast on in the Crock-Pot cooking slowly, and it should be ready about now." Mimi checked her watch.

Burt immediately slowed the wheel's turning. "Mimi's pot roast. That does it. Spinning can wait." He shoved the rest of the roving into the white plastic bag.

"Would you like to join us, Kelly?" Mimi invited with her maternal smile. "It'll be a nice change of pace from pizza or conference food. You've been working so much in Denver, we'll enjoy having some time with you."

Kelly pictured Mimi's pot roast and her stomach growled. "You don't have to ask me twice," she said, shoving the re-cycled silk into her bag.

Six

Kelly shifted in the wooden chair, trying to get comfortable. The morning meeting at Warner Development's north Denver office was in full swing. The speaker at the end of the long conference table was winding down his presentation. The last chart was on the screen. Kelly hoped there would be a short break before the next speaker took over. She needed coffee badly. And judging from the looks on the faces of some of Warner's staff, she wasn't the only one.

Most presenters brought pages of drawings and plans and reports to help explain whatever they were talking about. Whether it was current mortgage interest rates in northern Colorado or housing foreclosures spreading throughout the Denver metro and northern Colorado areas. Consequently, Kelly and everyone else in the crowded meeting room had a sheaf of papers to shuffle through for each speaker.

Kelly managed to stifle a yawn as she rested her chin on

her hand. Glancing to the side, she saw Dave Germaine give her a quick smile. He'd obviously noticed her yawn. Kelly sent him a little smile in return. Warner had brought Dave on board to head up the joint project in Thornton with all the assorted project developers. According to Warner, Germaine had made a name for himself among Denver's developers as someone who could guide a project through any number of minefields to successful conclusion, all while keeping costs under control. Not an easy task, especially in the present economic climate. Considering Dave Germaine had only been on the Denver development scene for eight years, it was quite an accomplishment. Tall with rugged good looks and in his late thirties, Germaine was a rising star on metro Denver's real estate and development scene.

Kelly recalled how pleased Warner had been to entice Dave Germaine to join his company and had bragged about Germaine's commitment to service. Apparently Germaine had gone for his architect degree after he returned from his military service. That was a definite plus with Warner, whose own son was serving overseas in the armed forces.

"Thank you, Bill," Warner's voice came loud in the quiet room. "What do you say we take a coffee break right about now, okay?"

Kelly eagerly rose from her chair and stealthily stretched muscles that were tired of sitting for two and a half hours. Meanwhile, she made a mental note to drink two cups so she wouldn't be tempted to yawn again.

Dave Germaine approached Kelly as she joined the flow of eager meeting goers escaping from the conference room. "Coffee isn't coming a minute too soon, right, Kelly?"

"Oh, yeah. I hope you were the only one who spotted my yawn. I couldn't help it."

"I'd already swallowed mine down. I learned how to do that when I was on night watch in the military. You fall asleep, you're in the brig." he said with a laugh.

"Whoa, don't tell Warner," she joked as the person in front of her finished with the coffee machine. Kelly turned the nozzle and watched a dark stream pour into her ceramic Warner Development coffee mug. "Sometimes those charts make my eyes cross, and I'm an accountant." She stepped away and took a long, deep drink, felt the familiar harsh burn on her throat. Caffeine. *Yessss.* Brain cells lulled to sleep were coming back online.

Dave chuckled as Kelly drank nearly the entire mug of coffee standing there. "You remind me of the army sergeant who led my platoon. He could drink coffee straight from the pot like that. Didn't even bother to blow on it."

"Sounds like a man after my own heart," Kelly joked as they walked into the main room where several architects were working on computers and drafting tables, drawing up building plans. That sparked Kelly's curiosity. "Did you start out like this?" She indicated the men and women busily designing. "Designing projects for Overby Associates?"

Dave nodded and sipped his coffee as he looked out over the heads bent in concentration. "Yeah, at first. But it wasn't Overby. I started with a smaller firm that Overby took over right after I signed on. That was a stroke of luck, because old man Overby liked to develop talent. And I was hungry and a hard worker. So, I grabbed every chance he threw my way. Worked my head off, and it paid off."

"I should say. Weren't you in charge of Overby's Lake-wood mall renovation? That was quite a coup." Kelly lifted her mug in salute.

Dave smiled. "Yeah, that did turn out pretty well. I was proud of that."

He had a nice smile, and Kelly could tell Dave wanted to say something else, but Warner was headed their way.

"Glad I found you two together," Warner said with his trademark wide grin. Silver edged the black hair at Don Warner's temples, his face suntanned even in winter. "Dave, I'd like you to go over those estimates you showed me on the Thornton project with Kelly. She needs to be up to speed with the latest numbers."

"Absolutely," Dave said. "When are we breaking for lunch? We could go over it then. Or, at least start."

Warner scanned the rest of his staff and associates, who were milling about, talking on cell phones or checking e-mail on their smartphones. "You know, the rest of this meeting isn't essential for either of you. Joe and Bruce will be talking about finishing some long-running project in Brighton. Why don't you two take a long lunch on me and go over this information. How's that?" His sharp brown eyes darted from Germaine to Kelly.

"Works for me," Kelly offered. "I've been anxious to see some figures anyway. So, this sounds like a great time. And, it means I won't have to work late." She gave Warner her own signature grin.

"That's my girl," Warner said with a laugh, patting Kelly's shoulder. "I depend on you for those numbers, Kelly. You keep me on track."

"I do my best."

"That's a great suggestion," Dave added. "Otherwise we'd be grabbing burgers and fries from the fast food down the street."

"Excellent, excellent. Pick up the card for my club at the front desk. Martha keeps it," Warner said, clapping his hands together. He started to turn away then stopped, his smile faded. "By the way, Kelly, I saw a notice in yesterday's *Denver Post* about Fred Turner dying in Fort Connor over the weekend. The newspaper hinted it might have been a suicide. Did you hear anything about that?"

Kelly paused, choosing her words carefully. "Yes, I did. One of my friends was the real estate agent who listed Turner's land for sale in the Poudre Canyon. Apparently, that's where he was found." She sipped her coffee and didn't say more.

Warner looked shocked. "Damn! I can't picture Fred Turner killing himself. He was hell-bent on amassing a real estate fortune and was well on the way, the last I heard it."

"Yeah, I can't picture it, either," Dave added. "When I first met him eight years ago, Turner was gobbling up properties right and left. And he'd use whatever tactics he could on an unsuspecting client. He was a crook if you ask me." Dave gave a disgusted look.

Warner gave a wry smile. "Well, Fred was never known for his honesty, I'll say that."

"Got that right," Dave said, taking a long drink of coffee.

Kelly debated adding anything and decided to register a moderate comment. "You know, my friend did mention Turner had a rather unsavory reputation. Now, I know what she meant."

Warner let out a hooting laugh. "Unsavory? *Ha!* That's

putting it mildly. Fred's deals smelled so bad, nobody I know wanted to work with him. On anything."

"The only good skunk is a dead skunk," Dave said grimly and drained his coffee.

"Hey, Kelly, we saved some pizza for you," Greg said as he opened the front door for Kelly later that evening.

"No, thanks, I grabbed some chicken salad and soup after I worked out at the gym." She smiled at her friends who were scattered about Lisa and Greg's living room. "Hey, guys. How's it going?"

"Better now that you're here," Lisa said. "We need an impartial third party to help Megan and Marty decide on the caterers for the wedding. They've got it narrowed down to two. We've all voted, and it's a tie. Three for the Downtown Grill and three of us voted for the Sunflower Café. So, you can break the tie." Lisa tipped back her brown bottle of ale.

Kelly sank into the free spot on the sofa beside Jennifer and Pete. "Ohhhh, pressure, pressure. I've got enough of that on the job," she teased. "Let's see . . . the Sunflower has great salads and desserts, and the Downtown has great barbequed chicken and beef. But, you don't need their meat because Curt's donating all those steaks. Hmmmm." She pretended to ponder.

"Here, this will help," Greg said, handing Kelly a Fat Tire ale before he rejoined Lisa on the love seat.

"You can't go wrong with either one," Pete said. "And if you can't decide, why don't you order the salads from Sunflower and have the Downtown bring their barbequed chicken. You're already hiring someone to grill the steaks."

Everyone turned to Pete and stared for one brief second. Then exploded in affirmations.

"Fantastic idea!"

"Why didn't we think of that?"

"Love it!"

"Perfect, just perfect. Thanks, Pete."

"See, you didn't need me," Kelly teased and took a long, cool drink of ale.

"He's the man," Jennifer said with a sly grin, tipping her cola can to Pete, who was taking mock bows.

Lisa asked. "So, how was the workout?"

"Good. I'd been ramping up my entire weight routine with the machines and free weights, and it feels really good. I've gotten a lot stronger, too. I can even heft around Carl's forty-pound bags of dog food with one arm now." She reached for a stray tomato on the side of the salad plate.

"That reminds me, I've gotta get back to that," Greg said, making a weight-lifting motion with his right arm. "I think I pulled a muscle when Marty and Steve and I were shooting hoops last weekend."

Kelly decided to deflect that conversational direction before it even started. She didn't doubt that Jennifer had already told the gang about Kelly's reaction to news about Steve. She wasn't in the mood to listen to everyone rag on her. It had been a long day in Denver. She just wanted to relax.

"You know, Warner asked me about Fred Turner's death," she said to Jennifer. "I acted like I didn't know much but it looked to be suicide. Warner said no one in Denver wanted to work with Turner because he was such a crook. Looks like Turner cheated people all over northern Colorado. Even Dave had a run-in with him. Called him a crook and a skunk." She took another drink.

"Who's Dave?" Jennifer asked.

"Dave Germaine. Warner's hired him to head up Warner's part of the Thornton joint project."

Jennifer's brow lifted. "Dave Germaine? I remember him. He gave a presentation for Overby Associates at last year's state real estate convention. Smart guy."

Kelly snagged half a chocolate chip cookie and settled back into the sofa. "Yeah. He's one of the few who can actually make sense when he's talking to a whole group."

"Good looking, too," Jennifer added, then sipped from her cola can.

Kelly couldn't help smiling. She knew where Jennifer was headed with this, but Kelly wasn't about to fall into Jennifer's trap. "Yeah, that, too."

Jennifer took another sip from her cola can, while Kelly watched the rest of her friends focus on the two of them. "Has he asked you out yet? If not, he will." Jennifer said nonchalantly.

Kelly wasn't expecting that. She'd been expecting Jennifer to beat around the "good-looking" bush for a little bit while Kelly danced away. Nope. Jennifer went straight as an arrow to the bull's-eye. Kelly should have known better. She should have said Dave Germaine was ugly and awful. *When would she learn she couldn't outwit Jennifer in these matters?*

Kelly felt all her friends' eyes on her. And, a slight color creeping up her face. "How'd you know?" she demanded.

Jennifer raised both hands and smiled. "Hey, I'm an expert

in those matters. Or used to be. Ted the bartender used to call me the doctor of love. Plus, I've got really good antennae."

Kelly used that as an escape and chimed in. "That's right, they called you the Love Doctor at the Empire Bar."

"Hey, do you have a license?" Marty teased. "If so, there're a couple of guys in my office who're in serious need of guidance."

"Doctor of love, huh?" Greg picked up the thread. "Listen, do you take appointments? Lisa's doing this thing that really annoys me, and I need to—*ow*!"

Lisa punched Greg in the rib while everyone cackled. Kelly took the reprieve to regain her footing. "In answer to your question, yes, Dave did ask me out to dinner, but I declined."

She took another drink of the tasty ale and could almost hear the collective sigh of relief from her friends.

All except Jennifer, who turned to Kelly with that relaxed expression. "Why didn't you say yes? Don't you like him?"

Kelly wasn't expecting to be grilled, so she shrugged. "Sure. He's a great guy. I—I just didn't want to stay late in Denver again. I've had to do that so many times. It gets old."

"You've gotta be kidding," Jennifer scoffed. "You stay overnight in Denver regularly because of late night meetings. You could do it for a late night date."

"Yeah, I suppose." Kelly shrugged again because she didn't know what else to say. She was uncomfortable with everyone hanging on her every word.

"Plus, you stay at the Cherry Creek Inn. How hard is that? Luxury at your fingertips."

"Wow, I wouldn't mind staying there," Lisa said, reaching for a cookie. "Why don't you give Dave my number. I'll drive down for a date. Greg's gotten *really* annoying lately."

Kelly joined her friends' laughter as Greg looked sheepish. She was hoping Jennifer might drop the subject now.

No such luck. Jennifer picked it up again. "You stay in Denver regularly, so that can't be the reason. Did he do something really annoying like belching really loud in the middle of lunch?"

"I hate it when someone does that," Greg said, then belched loudly to his friends' laughter.

"That does it. Give Dave my card, will ya?" Lisa said.

"Please don't give Marty any ideas," Megan said, pointing to her fiancé beside her. But it was too late. Marty was already hitting his stomach with his fist and produced an even louder noise.

Kelly laughed loudly at her friends' schoolyard antics, particularly watching Megan look horrified, then roll her eyes at her fiancé's behavior. Marty was having too much fun laughing to care.

"Okay, Love Doctor, I need one of those appointments," Megan said when the laughter died down. "I don't know if I can live with that forever. We may have to cancel the wedding."

"Too late. You've ordered a cake."

"I haven't got a gown yet, so it's still open."

"You can cancel but say good-bye to Curt's steaks."

"Good point."

Good-natured teasing went around the circle, making Kelly relax even more. Good friends and shared laughter. Good times. She needed her friends.

Not a minute passed before Jennifer picked up the thread once again. "Well, aside from possibly lacking social skills, is there any other reason you didn't want to go out with him? Dave Germaine is a nice guy."

Kelly released a long sigh and surrendered. Jennifer wasn't going to stop until Kelly told the truth. "Yes, he is. But I'm not sure I want to get involved with anyone."

"Going out to dinner is not getting involved," Jennifer countered gently.

"Yeah, well . . ." Kelly demurred.

"Jennifer, if she doesn't want to go out with him, leave her alone," Megan protested quietly.

Jennifer turned to Megan and the entire circle with a smile, hand to her chest. "Please, the Love Doctor is in the midst of a consultation. Do not interrupt."

The slight tension that Kelly felt building was dissipated right away. So, she responded honestly. "I'm just hesitant, that's all."

"It's been six months, Kelly. You've gotta get back out there. Or else, you'll lose your nerve. And you don't wanta lose that, Kelly. It's one of the things we love about you." Jennifer gave her a sympathetic smile. "It's like when you fall off a horse, you've gotta get back on and ride. Or you'll be scared of horses forever."

Kelly glanced around the circle of friends and saw their expressions. Pete and Jennifer looked sympathetic. Lisa looked sad. Megan frowned, while Greg and Marty looked resigned. Kelly threw in the towel. Time for this drama to stop before it went any further.

"Okay, okay, I'll say yes the next time he asks me. So, now can we change the subject, Doctor?"

"Absolutely," Jennifer said with an encouraging grin.

"Who's interested in joining the Lambspun Wedding Dress pool? We're all taking bets on what Megan will wear to the wedding. I have my money on the white sheet. Kelly's betting on softball jerseys and cleats. We've got three bets on lace and another three on jeans and tee shirt. Who's in?"

Seven

Kelly walked across the gravel driveway in the lightly falling snow. Instead of heading toward the knitting shop's front door, she chose to take the winding path through the garden patio behind Pete's Porch Café. March was usually Colorado's snowiest month, so there were a few inches of snow remaining on the ground from last week's storm. Still, March meant spring was only a month away. And the hope of spring was alive inside every bud. The promise of warm weather, plants pushing upward through the soil, flowers bursting into bloom. And what was best—spring led to summer. Kelly's favorite season.

She fingered some of the tightly wrapped buds on the adjacent bushes in the garden. Spring was inside. She pushed a snowy tree branch to the side as she walked, and it shook snowflakes over her bright red ski jacket. That reminded her. She had only gone skiing with her friends once this winter.

Increased client demands on her time had kept Kelly working on several winter weekends, while her friends took off for the mountains.

Kelly missed going with them, but skiing would also bring back a lot of memories, too. Memories of Steve and her on the slopes together, skiing together, relaxing in the lodge afterward, clumping around on their ski boots, poking through ski resort towns, finding great cafés, and simply being together. Kelly wasn't sure she wanted to have all those memories reinvade her mind. She'd worked very hard to cordon off all those painful bittersweet images and keep them in the very back of her mind, where they wouldn't bother her—too much.

She hurried up the stairs to the front door of Pete's café, stamping snow from her boots once she was inside the warmth. Customers were scattered at practically every table. Windows surrounded the café on all three sides so that even on cloudy days Pete's café was bright inside.

The tempting aroma of breakfast food lingered in the air. Bacon, sausage, eggs, pancakes, all versions of yummy. All of it inviting Kelly to taste. Breakfast food was one of her many weaknesses.

"Morning, Kelly," one of the waitresses greeted. "Sit down, and I'll get you some coffee after I've served this table." She balanced a tray with four plates of temptation.

"Thanks, Julie. You could read my mind." Kelly dug her coffee mug from her knitting bag. Noticing Burt waving at her from across the café, Kelly headed his way.

"Hey, Kelly, c'mon over here and keep me company," Burt said. "Maybe you can share this last pancake with me so I won't eat it all myself."

Kelly laughed as she tossed her jacket on the back of a chair and sat down. "Oh, no, Burt. I've already had breakfast. I'm not going to save you from those pancakes."

"Darn . . ." Burt frowned at the temptation on his plate. "I really hate to leave food on the plate. It's not right."

"I know. But it's better on the plate than on you," she teased. "I allow myself pancakes on the weekends only. The rest of the time it's lots of fruit, yogurt, and nuts for me."

Burt shook his head and dropped his paper napkin to his plate. "Okay, you convinced me. Or made me feel guilty, whatever. You can take it away, Julie. Kelly's persuaded me to be good. For today."

Julie poured a black stream of the café's black nectar into Kelly's mug. The grill cook, Eduardo, made coffee the same way Kelly did. Strong and dark. Not for the weakhearted, this brew. Only the brave dared drink it. "Can I get you anything else, Kelly?" Julie asked.

"No, I'm good, thanks anyway." Kelly glanced around the café. "Jennifer still here or left for her office already?"

"I think she had to go in and talk with her broker about that listing up in the canyon. You know, the one where the guy died." Julie made a face. "I don't know if it'll sell now. Who'd want a place where a guy blew his brains out?"

Watching the young waitress move to another table, Kelly had to agree with her. "Julie's got a point, Burt. I'm wondering if my client Housemann will change his mind about the deal. He hasn't had much to say since it happened. In fact, he acted like he didn't want to talk about it when I mentioned hearing about Turner's death. He went all quiet on the phone, so I didn't ask again."

"Did you mention that you and Jennifer are the ones who found Turner dead?"

"Lord, no," Kelly replied, before taking a deep drink of Eduardo's steaming-hot brew.

Burt sipped his own coffee, then leaned over the table. "You know, I heard from my friend Paul on Tuesday. The medical examiner finished his report, and it was a surprise to say the least. Turns out that Fred Turner may not have blown his brains out after all. Someone may have done it for him."

Kelly's mug stopped at her lips. She stared at Burt over the rim. "What? Dan thinks someone *killed* Turner?"

Burt nodded. "The examination found injuries to the back of his head that they believe came from Turner being hit from behind by a hard object, maybe the gun or even a rock. It doesn't look like suicide anymore. Peterson and the guys will investigate it as a possible homicide now."

Kelly leaned back in the chair, holding the mug against her chest. The warmth penetrated even her knitted wool winter sweater. "Did the gun have any prints?"

"Nary a one."

"So that means the killer probably wore gloves."

Burt nodded, then sipped his coffee.

"Whoa . . . Fred Turner had a whole bunch of enemies from what I've heard this last week. I was down in Denver yesterday and the developers said they couldn't stand him. Sounds like Turner had enemies all over northern Colorado." She wagged her head. "Boy, the cops are going to have their hands full trying to weed through all the people who had a grudge against him."

Another little thought buzzed in the back of Kelly's mind,

insistent. It hadn't come into focus yet. She took a long drink of coffee and let it buzz.

"Paul said they've already started interviewing people. Colleagues, business associates, what friends the man had."

"It didn't sound like he had any friends, only enemies. Peterson will be interviewing for days. I wonder if my client Housemann will be interviewed. After all, they were in a contract together."

"I imagine Housemann will be interviewed, too. Along with anyone who was in a contract with him recently."

Kelly took a deep sip of coffee while the insistent little thought buzzed closer. Finally, it focused in the front of her mind. "I just remembered something, Burt. Jennifer got a call from Turner's office when we were driving up into the canyon. His assistant told Jennifer that some British guy had called and left a message about the property. Name of Birmingham. Apparently he was really anxious to see it and said he'd top any offer on the table. The assistant said Turner made an appointment to see him at the property that same morning."

Burt's eyebrows raised. "Really? Well, I'll mention it to Paul. Peterson can ask the assistant when he interviews her. For all we know, he may have already learned about this guy."

"I'll be interested in hearing what he finds out." Kelly drained her mug.

"Don't worry, Kelly. I'll keep you informed. Oh, and Paul said the scary guy you spotted in the bushes was the neighbor, Benjamin Marlow. He owns the property beside Turner's and has lived in the canyon for years. Kind of closemouthed and didn't have much to say, according to Paul."

"That's strange. He certainly looked nosy when I saw him."

"Well, Paul said he was a recluse and tries to keep to himself. Apparently he didn't see anything." Burt looked across the café and waved. "Hey, Jayleen. C'mon over." He beckoned her over as he rose from his chair.

Jayleen strode to the table and doffed her Stetson. "Hey, folks, glad to see you. I was hoping Kelly would be here. How're you doing, Burt?" she asked with a smile.

"I'm doing good, Jayleen. You take my chair because I've got to go out front and help Mimi. Rosa couldn't come in this morning."

"Thanks, Burt. Tell Mimi I'll stop by and say hi in a few minutes," Jayleen said as she settled into the chair Burt offered.

Burt hurried from the café and toward the hallway that led to the knitting shop. Kelly signaled Julie and the coffeepot. "You want some coffee, Jayleen? You look like you've got a lot on your mind." She couldn't help noticing her friend's worried expression.

"Thanks, Julie." Jayleen held out her cup as the waitress poured the coffee. "You're right, Kelly. I've got a whole lot on my mind." She paused until Julie headed to another table. "I'm worried about my friend, Renee Turner."

Kelly took a long drink. *Oh, brother.* Someone else who did not wish Turner well. That guy had enemies on all sides. "Yeah, I remember your telling me about her. Burt just said the cops are now investigating Turner's death as a homicide. Apparently they found injuries on the back of his head. He must have been hit from behind."

Jayleen shook her head sadly. "That's what Renee told me. She called me this morning. The cops came over to question her late yesterday evening. She's a wreck. Turns out she went up to that cabin right before you gals came and found Fred dead on the floor. Renee said she panicked and ran outta there. Problem is, someone must have seen her driving away from the place and told the police."

Kelly didn't volunteer anything, only saying, "Uh-oh. That's not good. Did the police tell her she was seen?"

"Not at first. They asked her where she was at that time last Saturday. And Renee, fool that she was, told them she was at home on the computer. Alone." Jayleen gave a disgusted look. "That's when they told Renee they had a witness who saw her driving her car out of the driveway back onto the canyon road at that time."

"Ohhhh, boy. They caught her in a lie," Kelly said. "That is definitely not good."

"You're tellin' me. Of course, Renee got all frightened and flustered after that. She told the cops she panicked when they first asked her because she'd been to the cabin and found Fred. And she drove away as fast as she could."

"I'm sure they asked her why she went up there." Kelly was curious about Renee's answer.

"You bet. They wanted to know why she went and how she found out he was there. And that opened up a whole new can of worms." Jayleen looked at the floor. "Renee said she asked Fred's assistant where he was. Then she tried to explain to the cops that she'd heard about some new buyer who was interested in the property, and she went up there to make sure Fred knew that she was keeping track of the sale."

Kelly couldn't believe what she was hearing. "So, Renee basically admitted she went up to the canyon to confront Turner. That makes her look even guiltier. What was that woman thinking?"

"She wasn't," Jayleen said with a grimace. "That's why she called me first thing this morning. Renee's scared to death the cops are gonna suspect her in Fred's death. She lied about her whereabouts, and the cops can prove she was there around the time he was shot. And everybody in town knows the two of them have been fightin' like cats and dogs over money and the divorce."

"Boy, Jayleen, I've got to be honest. It doesn't sound good for your friend."

"Don't I know it." Jayleen stared out into the café. "I wish I knew how to help her. If she'd called me over the weekend, I would've been able to talk to her, get her to go to the police, and report Fred's death. Get on top of the situation."

Kelly hated to say it, but she had to. "You know, Jayleen. There may be good reason why Renee didn't call you. She may have actually killed her husband. Accidentally, of course. Who knows? Maybe she went up there with a gun to threaten him, and things got out of hand." Kelly shrugged. She knew that scenario didn't really make sense, but it was the only reason she could offer Jayleen. Lame, though it was.

Jayleen looked Kelly straight in the eye. "I know how it looks, Kelly. But I've known Renee for over ten years. She's hotheaded, sure, but so was Fred. They had a stormy marriage. But Renee couldn't kill Fred, no matter how mad she got at him."

"Didn't you tell me that Renee had threatened to 'plug' him, meaning Fred? Now, you're not the only one who heard that most probably. So, the police are going to find out about that as well. It's a verbal threat. She even made it in front of other people." This time Kelly shook her head. "I tell you,

Jayleen, it doesn't look good for Renee. She's bound to make it to the top of Lieutenant Peterson's list of suspects."

Jayleen flinched. "I hear what you're sayin' Kelly, but I just cannot for the life of me believe that Renee would kill Fred. She wouldn't cold-bloodedly knock him on the head then shoot him while he lay there. That's cowardly, and Renee's not a coward."

Kelly gave her a rueful smile of her own. "I'm not sure that's a good defense, Jayleen."

"I know, I know. . . ." Jayleen stared off into the café again.

Kelly debated for a long minute, then decided she had to tell Jayleen the whole story. She was a friend, and you were always honest with your friends.

"You know about the witness who saw Renee drive away from the property last Saturday?" she said. "Well, there were actually two witnesses."

"What?" Jayleen looked up in surprise. "How do you know? Did Peterson tell you?"

"Jennifer and I were the two witnesses, Jayleen. We saw a blue truck pulling out of the property's driveway as we were driving down the canyon road. Jennifer recognized Renee Turner as the truck drove past us. Jennifer said she'd seen Renee at Turner's office. Her real estate office is in the same building as Turner's. She said Renee came over there several times and had loud confrontations with him." Kelly watched the shock register on Jayleen's face. "So, we were the ones who told Detective Peterson about Renee. I wanted you to know."

Jayleen's shock turned to a mixture of sorrowful resignation as she put her head in her hand. "Oh, Lord. What'd she look like? I mean, as she drove past your car?"

"We only caught a glimpse. She looked like someone in a hurry." Kelly shrugged. There was nothing else she could say.

Jayleen closed her eyes. "Lord, Lord," she whispered.

Steve pulled his truck into an empty space along the street bordering a strip mall and got out. A white-and-gray Samuel Kaufman Construction truck sat parked behind him. He spotted several of his company's construction workers carrying a cart filled with wallboard into the front door of a sprawling fitness center. Steve could see one of the electricians inside, while another worker motioned the cart inside. Both glass entry doors to Fit 4 Life were propped open, so workers and materials could move in and out of the beige stone building in north Denver. Steve waited for the men to safely push the heavy cart through the doorway, then he followed them inside the building.

Carpenters, electricians, and construction workers were scattered around a huge, high-ceilinged space. Electricians balanced on ladders, surrounded by colorful cables and wires that dangled from the ceiling. Most of the ceiling was open, Steve noticed, which told him that the electrical wiring was yet to be completed.

Steve passed a carpenter who was nailing a panel of drywall into place as a smaller side room took shape. Carved out of the open space. Another worker was applying a grainy gray compound over the seams between the drywall sheets. Steve noticed two other side rooms had already been framed in. Carpenters appeared to be on schedule, he noted as he walked through the crowded fitness center, looking for his boss Sam Kaufman.

Gym goers were everywhere—running and walking on treadmills and elliptical machines, cycling on stationary bikes, and pulling, pushing, or stretching on weight machines. Exercise equipment was wedged into every spare corner of the large space, shoved cheek-by-jowl beside other equipment. Practically every machine was being used. The gym goers didn't seem to mind all the hammering and the dangling wires, or the shrill whirr of the electric saws. In fact, they seemed to barely notice, so intent were they on completing their exercise routine in the prescribed time period. Lunchtime was always busy.

Steve spotted several men playing basketball on one of the renovated courts. Remembering how much he'd enjoyed getting back into the gym with Greg and Marty last weekend, Steve paused for a moment and watched the pickup game. Five guys lunged and dove for the ball, fighting for it. When one grabbed it, he'd dribble down the floor, heading for the basket while fending off guys who were trying to steal the ball. All of them slammed together under the basket, leaping and blocking shots.

He was going back to the gym this week. He had to. He'd forgotten how good it made him feel. Plus, he slept like a rock afterward. No worries and no disturbing memories kept him awake. One of the guys he'd met at the developers' meetings had invited him to join a group of guys for some pickup games with other developers. Blow off the pressure from the project. There was a gym near the Thornton project. Steve had declined at first, but after last weekend, he was going to give the guy a call. He was in.

Steve turned in a slow circle, trying to spot his boss amidst all the people crowded in the huge space, working out and just plain working. As he walked toward the area with the free weights and benches, Steve saw short, silver-haired Sam Kaufman talking with one of his workers. Beside them was a middle-aged man who was flat on his back, bench pressing a formidable amount of weight on the barbells. Steve watched him slowly raise the barbell above his head, his face flushed with the effort.

"Hey, Sam," Steve said as he walked up to his boss.

Kaufman turned and acknowledged Steve with a smile. "Steve, I was just about to call you."

"I'll tell Johnny you want to see him, Sam," the construction worker said as he walked away.

"Thanks, Alfredo," Sam called after him before turning his attention to Steve.

"I wanted to stop by and see if you had any more instructions," Steve said. "They've scheduled another meeting for tomorrow afternoon and thrown in a dinner speaker, so I'll be gone all day."

"Yeah, I want you to talk to Bill Daniels if you see him and ask if he's got some extra drywall. I swear he said he had some in stock that he was not using and wanted to sell it. We'll need it out here." Sam gestured toward the rooms taking shape.

Steve looked around with an experienced eye, grown even more discerning thanks to all the varied projects he'd worked on at Sam Kaufman's company. "Looks like it's coming along pretty well."

"Better than expected. Everybody's working their tails

off, so we're a little ahead of schedule." Sam's sun-creased face frowned. "Wish I could hire more guys, but I can't. Not and stay on budget."

Steve fell in step with Sam as he walked around a cluster of weight machines. "You're doing good, Sam. This project is on target and will come in a little under budget if we're lucky." He glanced up into the ceiling where several panels were gone and wires dangled. "Working inside helps, too. No snow in here," he joked.

"Ain't that the truth," Sam said with a laugh. "Listen, Steve, while you're there tomorrow, keep your ear to the ground and find out if there are any medium-sized remodeling projects in the planning stages. If so, we're gonna bid on them. See if we can snag any from the bigger guys."

"Will do. I've been grilling some of the guys I've met there to see what their companies have got in the pipeline. They're a good group of guys. A couple of them from Overby Associates asked me to join them in a basketball league a couple of nights a week. I may take them up on that."

"You should, Steve. You've been putting in some pretty long hours these last few months. You need to relax more. I don't want you burning out. I've got plans for you," Sam added with a laugh as he slapped Steve on the back.

Steve felt Sam's praise wash over him and allowed himself to bask in it for a few seconds. "I appreciate that, Sam. You're a good man to work for."

Sam paused beside a ladder with a man on top. "How's it going, Rudy?"

"Goin' good, Sam," the man answered, still concentrating on the wires above his head.

"You heading back to the office?" Steve asked as they continued weaving a path through the exercise machines. One middle-aged woman was slowly pulling down the curved bar on the lateral pull down. Judging from her closed eyes and clenched face, Steve figured she was getting a really good workout.

"No, I have to meet with the plumber this afternoon. Lots of things to oversee." Sam's bright blue gaze swept the huge room.

Steve could tell Sam loved every minute of the "overseeing." Steve understood. He still felt a sharp jab inside whenever he went to a building site to confer with contractors. He'd spent his entire career tracking across building sites, overseeing his men while they built houses. The smell of lumber, freshly sawed. The sound of nails hammered into two-by-fours as rooms took shape. There was nothing like that feeling of satisfaction when he stood and watched a completed house rise from the dirt. He wondered if he would ever get to feel that again. The renovations on this fitness center had some of the same sense of accomplishment connected to it. But this project was Sam's to oversee. Steve only hoped the Thornton renovation project would be more compelling once they started knocking out walls.

"Okay, I'd better head back to the office and get some work done. Tomorrow will be another Denver day. And night."

Sam clapped him on the shoulder. "I know you want to be out digging in the dirt somewhere, Steve, but we just have to hunker down and get through this downtime. It'll get better. Meanwhile, this Thornton project will really help. For us, and for these guys too."

"Yeah." Steve allowed himself a sigh. "You're right. I've actually started to get ideas about some unique remodeling projects. Particularly with older homes. That's happening more and more. According to one of Overby's guys, they've done a couple of those projects, and they are really lucrative. A lot of specialty consulting involved."

Sam looked over in surprise. "Overby has been doing that? Those are smaller jobs. Sounds like they're scrambling, too."

"Well, this guy Vic suggested the idea to Overby and they went for it. Old man Overby even sent Vic to an institute in San Francisco for some special seminars."

"Hmmmm, that bears watching. Good work, Steve. Looks like you're keeping your ear to the ground at those meetings."

Sam slowed as they approached the entry doors. "Plus, you get to spend all day listening to some guy or gal drone on, so I can stay back here and enjoy myself." Sam let loose a guffaw.

"You got that right," Steve said with a grin as he turned to leave.

Eight

Kelly sipped the mediocre white wine as she stood outside the hotel banquet room doorway. Two small bars had been set up in the hotel's circular atrium, and both had long lines of people waiting to order drinks. After an entire afternoon of presentations and charts and panel discussions and charts and more talking followed by even more charts, the entire mini mob of developers, builders, and staff were beyond thirsty.

She slowly strolled away from the crowds around the two bars. There were less people in the plant-filled atrium, so Kelly headed toward the greenery.

White-jacketed hotel staff pushed carts with large closed metal serving dishes. Kelly sniffed the air, trying to guess what the hotel caterers were serving. She couldn't tell, which she figured was a bad sign. Two more carts followed, also carrying metal servings dishes. Another rubber chicken banquet, Kelly thought ruefully.

She'd had way too many banquet meals lately. Since Warner started including Kelly in his top echelon of staff, she'd lost count of the bland meeting meals she'd consumed. With the recession putting a squeeze on companies' costs, hotel kitchens had clearly cut back on whatever expenses they could and not risk losing their clientele. Consequently, Chicken Served a Thousand Ways was usually the main feature.

Kelly touched the bright red hibiscus plant blooming inside the atrium, safe from Colorado's snows and winter cold. The large bugle-shaped blossom opened wide beneath the protective bright lights. Hibiscus was a tropical plant. Only a protected setting allowed it to bloom in its vibrant splendor. It would be May before temperatures were warm enough to allow planting equally vibrant annual flowering plants outside. Mid-May was actually safer, Kelly had found. And even then, there were no guarantees. Light snows on Memorial Day had happened more than once at Colorado altitudes.

But soon, April would be here and would bring its own special spring colors that were hardy enough to push through snow-covered ground. The spring perennials—tulips and jonquils, larkspur and daffodils. Kelly never had been able to tell the difference between daffodils and jonquils. They were both bright yellow and had those cheerful trumpet-like heads that braved Colorado's chilly early spring temperatures. Mimi had persuaded her to plant some of the yellow sunshine last fall in the flower boxes and containers bordering her front walk. They would be Kelly's first sign that spring was coming, despite the snow's capricious behavior.

"Hey, Kelly, I've been looking for you," one of her Warner colleagues said as he walked up, beer bottle in hand.

"Hey, Ralph. You ready for Chicken Surprise?"

The older man chuckled. "You got that right. Listen, I heard that Fred Turner didn't kill himself. Someone did it for him. Is that true?" He took a long sip of beer.

Kelly nodded. "That's what the newspapers say. Did you know Turner?"

Ralph's mouth twisted. "Hell, yes. If you were involved in real estate in any form in northern Colorado, sooner or later you ran into Fred. Later, if you were lucky."

"It sounds like you weren't a fan. I didn't know him."

"You were lucky. I ran into him when I was working with some guys up in Northglenn on an apartment development years ago. We were trying to get a piece of land that bordered the parcel we had, but that bastard Turner wanted to gouge us on price. After he jerked us around for six months." Ralph drained his beer.

Curious, Kelly probed some more. "Up in Northglenn. Was Arthur Housemann involved in that project? He's another of my clients, and he told me he helped with a large Northglenn apartment complex years ago."

"That was the one. Art was involved, all right. In fact, he tried to persuade us not to try dealing with Turner. Said he'd had a run in with him and didn't trust Turner."

Intrigued, Kelly pressed. "That's funny. Did he ever say what it involved?"

Ralph shook his head. "Naw. But I always had the feeling there was some bad blood between Turner and Art."

Kelly was about to follow up on that until Ralph's cell phone rang. Insistent, jangling.

"Excuse me, Kelly," Ralph said as he dug his phone from his pocket and turned away.

Curious as to Ralph's "bad blood" comment, Kelly looked

across the atrium and noticed more of her Warner colleagues clustering near the banquet room doors. That meant it was almost time to go inside and see what Chicken Surprise the chefs had prepared tonight. Kelly drained her glass and slowly strolled to the edge of the atrium, ready to rejoin her colleagues and enter the banquet room. Then, she stopped. Held in place by the sight of a familiar face.

Steve stood near one of the bars, holding a bottle of what she guessed was his favorite ale. He was smiling and talking to a very pretty blonde woman Kelly had seen at these meetings before. The woman was smiling back at Steve as she talked. Only twenty feet away.

An old ache started deep in her gut. A forgotten ache. One she hadn't felt for a while. The last time she'd seen Steve, it was a fleeting glimpse as she and her colleagues were leaving one of the early joint project meetings. He was all the way across the room. Farther away.

Apparently proximity made a difference. Kelly felt old memories dig their way out of the sands at the back of her mind. They danced in front of her eyes again, bringing their sharp sting. Bittersweet. Steve and her together. Kelly pushed the images away again, back to their hidden corners. They were the past. They weren't real. Not anymore.

She watched Steve take a drink from his ale, then nod and smile at the woman. A blonde, of course, Kelly thought wryly. She'd always suspected Steve had a weakness for blondes. Probing her computer-file memory, Kelly thought the woman worked for a large Denver development firm, like Overby Associates. Steve worked for Sam Kaufman's smaller company.

Just then, the blonde gave Steve a nod and a smile, then

turned and walked away. At that moment, Steve tipped back his ale and turned toward Kelly. Kelly held still, wondering if he would even notice her in the crowd. She was curious as to his reaction, if any.

She didn't have to wait long. Steve looked toward the atrium and spotted her. Kelly could tell the moment he did. She could feel it. Steve stared at her, not moving. Kelly held her ground and stared back. Steve opened his mouth, then closed it again, but he didn't move.

Curious, Kelly held his gaze, wondering what he'd do. Would Steve turn away? Follow the blonde? Wave at her like old friends in passing? What was that Pete said? "Two ships passing in the night."

Or, would he try to talk to her? Actually walk across the room and say hello? Didn't her friends say Steve wanted to apologize? Well, here was his chance, standing right in front of him. Kelly continued to hold her gaze, waiting for Steve to make the first move. She certainly wasn't. He walked out on her, for Pete's sake.

Steve continued to stare, then opened his mouth again. But it was too late. Kelly heard her name being called. Her Warner colleagues beckoned. She broke her gaze at last and saw Dave Germaine walk up to her.

"Hey, Kelly. Some of us can't take chicken anymore, so we're going over to Landry's Steakhouse. Want to join us?" Dave asked with a friendly smile. "You know, it's over on Sixteenth Street."

Kelly welcomed the suggestion, not only for the promise of prime beef but also as a way to break the uncomfortable connection with Steve. "That's a fantastic idea. I don't think I can stand another Chicken Surprise."

"Me, either. C'mon, let's get out of here." Dave beckoned her toward the hotel's front lobby and exit, placing his hand on Kelly's back as they walked. "Some of us are going to leave our cars here for now. Want to share a cab?"

Kelly checked her watch. Waiting for other people to wind down might take a lot longer than she wanted. Her regular room was waiting for her at the Cherry Creek Inn . . . and so was the Jacuzzi tub in the luxurious bathroom. She would need that relaxation even more tonight.

"I think I'll go ahead and take my car, Dave. I may have to leave earlier than everyone else."

Dave grimaced as they neared the revolving door. "Don't tell me you're going to work tonight. I was hoping you'd go out with me for a drink after dinner."

Kelly pushed through the doorway and waited for Dave. She had promised herself she'd accept the next time he asked her to join him. After-dinner drinks wasn't a bad idea, and it was an easy way to gradually reenter the dating world. She'd promised Jennifer that she would, and Kelly always kept her promises. Plus, she didn't want to lose her nerve.

"You know, the Cherry Creek Inn has a really nice quiet bar. I stay there regularly whenever I'm in Denver late. Why don't you drive over after the dinner, and I'll meet you in the bar." Kelly said with a friendly smile. Not too friendly, though. She didn't want Dave to get any ideas. Not those kind of ideas, at least. Not now. The future, well, that was something else.

Dave's grin spread, and he wiped pretend sweat from his forehead. "Whew! I thought you were going to shoot me down again. Cherry Creek Inn bar, it is."

Kelly turned toward the parking lot. "Save a seat for me at the table, okay? I'll be there as soon as traffic allows."

"You got it," Dave said, snapping out a quick salute as he turned toward the Warner folk already assembling at the hotel entrance while taxis lined up.

Steve stood there and watched Kelly walk away . . . with another guy. He felt like a mule kicked him in the gut. *Hard.* He hadn't seen Kelly in six months, then suddenly, there she was. Several feet away. Standing there looking at him. And all he could do was stare back and say nothing. He didn't know what to say. He couldn't yell his apology across the hotel bar. So, he just stared at her. Like an idiot. He couldn't even make himself move. It was like he was struck dumb by the sight of her.

He was worse than dumb. He was a *total* idiot. There she was, standing only twenty feet away, and he couldn't do anything. He couldn't even move. *What the hell was wrong with him?* He stood there and watched while another guy walked away with her. And she never even looked back at him. Not once.

That invisible mule kicked Steve in the gut again, harder this time. *Damn!* He was stupid beyond belief. No wonder Kelly walked away with that other guy. Steve was standing there like a moron, unable to say anything to the woman he loved. Still loved. Still ached for. *What the hell was wrong with him?* He must be losing his mind.

Who was that guy anyway? He looked familiar. Damn, Kelly looked fantastic. She'd changed her hair. Not much, but a little. It looked great all the same. She looked great. *Damn!* He was a fool.

That mule kick must have loosened those old memories he tried to hide, because they washed over Steve in a torrent now. A tsunami. Memories of Steve and Kelly together, laughing with friends, running in the mornings by the Poudre River, playing ball, lying in bed, making love. . . .

"Steve, I called Bill, our construction manager," the blonde woman said as she walked up to him. "He said he had a gross more of those drywall sheets in the warehouse and would be grateful if you and Sam could take them off his books."

Steve shook off the memories, giving thanks for a welcome respite. "Uhhh, thanks, Cathy. I'll tell Sam tomorrow. We'll send one of the guys over."

The blonde looked over Steve's shoulder. "Hey, it looks like everyone's heading into dinner. I'll see you at the next meeting, okay? My husband's picking me up out front in five minutes, and we're going to my little girl's school concert." She shoved her cell phone into her purse.

"Thanks, again, Cathy. Have fun with your family," Steve said. Then he turned and hurried to join his colleagues and the banquet dinner. Anything to keep those memories away.

Kelly dug into her purse looking for car keys as she walked through the hotel's outside parking lot. Spitty light snow had started falling. Little flakes, but steady. She was glad she'd decided to stay over at the hotel tonight. Colorado's light snows had a habit of turning heavier late at night, which made for slick highways and more treacherous drives especially over a distance like that to Fort Connor.

She flicked the car lock and watched her car's lights flash up ahead through the snowflakes. As she approached her car, she heard the throaty rumble of a truck engine revving up. Bright red taillights flashed on as a big black truck backed out of a space a few yards ahead. That sound always caught Kelly's attention. It sounded exactly like Steve's truck, the same big engine revving . . . and it always brought back memories.

The truck backed out of its parking place, turned, and lumbered in the other direction. Then, something caught her eye. The color red. In the space next to the now-empty parking spot sat a big red truck. Exactly like Steve's. Kelly stared at the truck. Maybe it was Steve's. After all, he was inside the hotel.

Kelly started to approach her car again, then stopped. For some reason she wanted to know if it was Steve's truck. She flipped up the hood on her black belted raincoat and walked down the parking lane. She checked the license plate. It was Steve's truck, all right. Kelly walked around to the driver's side. She didn't know why. She just felt like it. Looking through the window she saw Steve's briefcase on the passenger seat. Empty coffee mugs in the cup holder. Lots of clutter was scattered around. Steve had gotten messier these last few months, she noticed. He used to keep his truck neater.

Feeling the tug of old memories wanting her to indulge them, Kelly pushed them away. Then, another memory floated up. A musical memory. The lyrics of a popular country pop song that rode the charts a while back. The woman's strong voice sang in Kelly's mind, lyrics that suddenly seemed to apply now.

I dug my key into the side of his pretty little souped-up four-wheel drive . . . a Louisville Slugger to both headlights . . .

Staring at Steve's truck as the singer's voice sounded inside her head, Kelly had to smile. She kept a Louisville Slugger baseball bat in her car trunk all the time. You never knew when a pickup game would happen. Would she do it?

Kelly trailed her finger through the snow on the side of the red truck. Was she tempted? Maybe . . . a little. But no. She wasn't going to trash Steve's truck. She turned back to her own sporty red car and flicked the lights again.

That was the thing about country music. All those songs about love lost and found, thrown away, or wasted chances. Once in everybody's lifetime, they seemed to apply. She guessed it was her turn.

Nine

Kelly balanced her coffee mug in one hand while she dug her phone out of her jeans pocket. She thought she'd heard its distinctive beep. No hands left, she shoved Lambspun's heavy front door open with her hip.

Kelly stamped the slight snow from her boots on the coarse mat in the knit shop foyer, then stopped and took in the color. Green, green, everywhere. Saint Patrick's Day was coming and Lambspun was awash in green of every hue and shade. Lambspun's shop elves must have turned into leprechauns overnight.

Kelly paused beside an open straw basket with a pink stuffed rabbit standing beside it. Inside the basket, mixed in with the variegated green yarns, were several bright yellow plastic eggs.

There were baskets and bins filled with every shade of green. Lining the walls, sitting on top of chests and dressers, spread on the maple center table, and peeking out from the antique dry sink. Early spring grass. Snow still may be on the ground outside, but inside the shop, spring had sprung. Kelly fingered the various green yarns, feeling the delicious caress of silk, the luscious brush of mohair.

She wandered into the central yarn room ahead where shelves and yarn bins lined every wall. Spring colors spilled forth from every opening. Cottons, crispy and springy. Cottons spun with bamboo, softer yet still crisp. Mohair and silk, spun together into luscious violets and pinks. Kelly took turns stroking each yarn, enjoying the sensuous feel of the fibers. Glancing toward the main room, Kelly noticed Lisa was already at the table knitting. Lizzie sat beside her, and at the end of the table was Eustace, typing away on his laptop.

Trailing her fingers past bins of hand-dyed silk, Kelly indulged herself a moment longer, then remembered her phone. Sure enough, the little green light was blinking. She touched the menu bar of her smartphone to check the recent message. Megan had called a few moments ago. Kelly touched the message on the screen to return the call. Megan picked up quickly.

"Hey, there, I saw you called. What's up?" Kelly said, fondling a ball of soft pink-and-white mohair.

"Are you working at home or at the shop by any chance? I can't remember your schedule," Megan asked.

"Actually, I've been at home all morning on the computer, and I stepped into the shop this minute to take a short break before returning to my accounts. Do you need something?"

"Yes. Please grab two skeins of that shamrock green Lamb's Pride wool in the other room. I'll need it to finish this sweater, and I don't want to risk the shop running out, especially now with the Saint Paddy's Day sale going on."

"Will do, let me check to see if it's there. I've gotta dump my things first." Kelly plopped her knitting bag and mug on the library table, then gave a little wave to her friends seated there before approaching the bins of Lamb's Pride wools. The shamrock green stood out. Three skeins left. "Perfect timing," she told Megan as she grabbed two soft skeins. "I'll leave them up front, okay? Are you coming in?"

"Maybe. I'm swamped with a report my client wants by tomorrow. And I'm pushing to get work done ahead, so I can grab some time to go shopping again."

That didn't sound like Megan. She wasn't much of a shopper. "What are you shopping for?" Kelly asked as she headed through the adjacent yarn rooms toward the front of the shop and the counters.

"Three guesses, and they all begin with white or lace or satin. Gauzy stuff."

"Ohhhh, you must mean wedding gowns. That's right, you're coming up on that six-month deadline. Remember, the wedding shop lady said you needed six months or more to have a gown delivered," Kelly said.

"Yeah, yeah, yeah," Megan said. Kelly could hear the frown in Megan's voice.

"It's crunch time," Kelly couldn't resist. "You've gotta pick something."

"I know, I know. But I'm so busy, I don't want to take the time to go. Plus, you guys are way too busy to come with me. Jennifer's working more hours at the café, and Lisa's got tight class and work schedules, and you . . . you're in Denver all the time anyway."

"That's right, you haven't checked out those Denver shops yet," Kelly reminded. "Better do it soon, Megan. They'll surely have something you like."

"I've heard that before. We'll see."

"When are you thinking of going?"

"I can't this weekend, because Marty and I are going over to his parents'. And I can't afford time off from working, so maybe next weekend. Listen, another call is coming in. Talk to you later. Thanks, Kelly."

"Sure thing," Kelly said, then clicked off her phone as she reached the front counter. Longtime shop assistant Connie was alone at the register, and—magically—there wasn't a line of customers. "Hey, Connie, Megan wants you to hold these two skeins for her. She'll be in tomorrow maybe."

"No problem," middle-aged Connie said as she took the yarns. "I'll put them in a bag with Megan's name on it. She's smart to save some. The greens are disappearing. How're you doing, Kelly? You still working a lot in Denver?"

"Yeah, at least twice a week, sometimes more. Often I stay over at night, especially if there's an evening function or meetings. That way I don't have to drag myself back late at night."

Connie gave Kelly a sympathetic smile. "That's a smart idea, especially while we've still got snowstorms in the picture. You don't want to be sliding on that ice."

Kelly grimaced. She had bad memories of that. "You're absolutely right, Connie. Once was enough for me. I don't have time for broken ankles or whatever." Changing the subject, she leaned over the counter and lowered her voice. "I noticed Lizzie and Eustace are at the table again. Are they here every day?"

Connie nodded, a twinkle in her eye. "They sure are. Eustace told me that he and Lizzie take a walk every day near the river or the trails. Then, he gets to work. Either he goes to interviews, or he's here with Lizzie working on his book while she knits." She grinned. "Doncha love it? Lizzie finally found a 'beau' after all these years."

Kelly smiled. "I think it's great. But I wondered how Hilda's taking it. Have you seen her much? Burt says her arthritis is keeping her at home more."

"I'm afraid you're right. Hilda's slowed down a lot from what I see." Connie's smile vanished.

"I wonder how she's adjusting to Lizzie's new relationship. Has Hilda ever said anything?"

Connie shook her head. "Not a word. My guess is she's as surprised as everyone else. She probably doesn't know what to say."

Kelly noticed a customer holding a ball of yarn nearby and backed away from the counter so Connie could focus on business. She returned to the main room to pick up the silk scarf she'd started knitting and chat with friends before she had to return to her cozy cottage and accounts. It was Friday, and that meant Lisa and Greg were having everyone over for takeout and DVDs.

Pausing by the large loom in the adjacent room, Kelly fingered the soft green and blue yarns that some weaver was using to create the pattern. Beautiful, she thought as she passed by.

"Hello, dear, it's so nice to see you," Lizzie greeted as Kelly pulled out a chair across the knitting table from the others. "We miss seeing you here more often."

"I miss being able to drop in, but my Denver client has

big plans and he wants me to keep track of them." She pulled out the multicolored yarn and needles from her bag.

"Ahhh, that reminds me." Eustace paused over his keyboard and looked at Kelly. "I must make an appointment with both of your clients for interviews, Kelly. Arthur Housemann and Don Warner."

Kelly returned to her stitches. The rows of nubbly silk yarn were growing. "I think you'll enjoy both men. They've each weathered several Colorado recessions in real estate. None has been as deep as this one, but they're doing much better than so many others. Too many of our builders and developers went belly-up last year. Have you interviewed any of them? I know Curt was giving you names."

"Indeed, I have." Eustace removed his glasses and cleaned them with his tailored blue shirt. "All of the builders I've interviewed in Denver were most forthcoming. I've also interviewed more builders who haven't weathered this recession well. Alas, they've lost their businesses. So sad. I've decided to expand the book to include some of their stories. To counterbalance the success and survival of the other subjects. Unfortunately, I still haven't found a replacement for Fred Turner." He pursed his mouth. "He was going to be my lead character in the 'up and coming' New West cowboys section."

"From what I've heard it sounds like he should be in your outlaw category," Kelly remarked. Another row of stitching formed on her needles.

Lizzie gave a little giggle. "Goodness, that man sounds like a schemer."

"I only wish I could interview more people who knew the

man. Surely he had a more generous side," Eustace said, swinging his spectacles by the earpiece.

"Maybe not," Kelly said. "Money blinds some people to everything else. They'll do anything to get it."

Lizzie sighed dramatically. "So true, so true."

"I have an idea," Lisa piped up. "Why don't you interview Steve Townsend? He's the young builder we told you about. He's watched his entire business go down the drain in this recession. But he's been working two jobs in Denver for months now, clawing his way back to success." Lisa's chin lifted proudly, Kelly noticed. As if she was a mother hen parading her chicks.

"Ohhhh, yes, I forgot about that young man," Eustace said, scribbling on a notepad beside his elbow. "I'll be sure to contact him. Perhaps I can expand that section, too."

Kelly decided to change the subject before Lizzie had a chance to ask about Steve. Kelly noticed the elderly knitter casting worried looks her way every time Steve's name had come up in conversation during these six months she and Steve had been apart. She might as well deflect conversation now.

"Are you and Greg hosting the gang tonight, or are we going to Megan and Marty's?" she asked Lisa.

"Are you youngsters going out to dinner?" Eustace asked, peering over his rimless glasses at them.

"We'll be dining in and ordering Italian," Lisa replied with a smile. "Jennifer and Pete are working a banquet, but Marty and Megan are coming. Are you in, Kelly?"

"I'll be there for sure," Kelly said. "Italian's one of my favorites."

"That way we can all watch a movie together," Lisa continued. "Everyone's schedules have gotten so busy we have to grab whatever time we can."

Kelly finished another row of stitches. Glancing at Eustace and Lizzie, she couldn't resist asking, "What are you two planning for this evening? It's Friday night, date night."

Lizzie blushed a rosier red and concentrated on her knitting while Eustace reached over and patted her hand. She looked up at him with an adoring expression.

"Unlike you youngsters, Lizzie and I enjoy dining in your fair city's fine restaurants. I must say, Fort Connor has quite a vibrant café scene. I'm quite impressed. Houston is such a huge city, I find it difficult to explore nowadays. Too much traffic and too many people. And all of them seem to be driving at the same time. Fort Connor's traffic is much more manageable." Eustace smiled at Lizzie and kept his hand over hers.

Kelly kept her smile hidden with great effort. "Well, make sure you two try one of my favorite cafés, the Jazz Bistro. The food is delicious, the martinis are cold, and the jazz is hot." She gave Eustace a wink.

"Ohhhh, we *have* been there, dear," Lizzie spoke up, her cheeks still rosy. "It's so . . . so lively! I can understand why you and your young man enjoy it so." Suddenly, Lizzie's eyes popped wide and her hand flew to her mouth. "Ohhh, I'm so sorry, dear. I didn't mean to . . . to mention Steve! It simply came out."

At that, Kelly had to smile. Lizzie looked so contrite. This time, Kelly reached over and patted Lizzie's other hand. "That's okay, Lizzie. No one's died. It's all right."

Lizzie still looked guilty, and Kelly was about to find

something else reassuring to say when her cell phone rang. Thus rescuing her from the conversation.

"Excuse me, folks," she said as she rose from her chair and dug into her jeans pocket. Recognizing Jayleen's name and number flash on the phone screen, Kelly hastened over to the adjacent yarn room, which was currently empty of customers. "Hey, Jayleen, how're you doing?"

"Not good, Kelly. I'm worried about Renee," Jayleen answered. "The cops went out to question her again this morning."

"Uh-oh, that doesn't sound good." Kelly was familiar with Lieutenant Peterson's investigative procedures. He didn't question someone a second time unless he had a reason.

"Don't I know it," Jayleen said with a short exhaled breath. "Renee called me a few minutes ago, and I tell you, Kelly, she's scared. She said that Detective Peterson was real intimidating."

That aroused Kelly's curiosity. "He can be. Particularly if he's learned something that makes him suspicious. Renee's already in his crosshairs, Jayleen. She came up to the cabin alone to confront Turner. And there's no witness to prove she walked in and found his dead body."

"I know, I know. . . ."

"You have to admit, Jayleen, your friend looks like the main suspect. They were in the midst of a nasty divorce, and she was convinced he was cheating her." Kelly pushed open the shop front door to remove herself and the conversation from the earshot of nearby customers.

Jayleen exhaled a loud sigh on the other end. "You're right, I know. It looks bad. And getting worse. Renee just told me that the cops learned she'd been paying Fred's assistant to tell her what deals he was working and the money involved and who the clients were. Stuff like that."

"Oh, brother, that makes her look even guiltier," Kelly said, waving to Lisa, who was leaving the shop and walking to her parked car.

"Don't I know it. *Damn!* Why'd Renee do that? It was stupid."

"People do stupid things when they're scared, Jayleen. And I can't think of anything scarier than being on Detective Peterson's radar screen in a murder investigation."

"Listen, Kelly, do you think you could do Renee a favor? For my sake, please? Could you ask Burt if his old pal at the department has told him anything about the investigation? Renee keeps talking about some British guy who called Fred. Name of Birmingham. Turner's assistant told her the guy, Birmingham, was going to meet Fred in the canyon that Saturday morning. Maybe Burt can find out if the cops have learned anything about this guy. I mean, maybe he was up there and saw something."

Kelly felt that insistent little buzz inside at Jayleen's suggestion. Burt hadn't said anything, so she'd assumed Peterson and his guys were still investigating Birmingham. "Sure, Jayleen. I'll ask Burt. Jennifer told me about that guy, so I'm curious, too."

"Fred's assistant Anita played the voice mail for Renee, and she says this Birmingham sounded like he was hot to buy the place. So, you'd think the cops would be looking into the guy."

Kelly yanked the heavy wooden front door open. "I'm sure they are, Jayleen. Burt will find out for us."

"All I know is that Fred Turner had a whole passel of

enemies all over northern Colorado. And I wouldn't be the least surprised if one of them did him in. But I know for sure that Renee couldn't do it. I know that woman. She's as good as the day is long. Rough around the edges like I am, but she sure ain't a killer."

Kelly kept her mouth shut. Renee was Jayleen's friend. But Kelly had learned long ago that good people often did bad things. Very bad things, sometimes. Sometimes they even killed. An idea came to her then. "Hey, Jayleen, I'd like to meet Renee. Can you bring her over to the shop for lunch sometime?"

Jayleen's voice brightened. "Sure thing, Kelly. I think that's a good idea. You need to meet her yourself. You'll see what I mean. I'll call her and get back to you, okay? Listen, I've got another call coming in. Talk to you soon, Kelly girl."

"Bye, Jayleen." Kelly clicked off and returned to the main room and her abandoned knitting on the long table. Glad to be back inside the shop's warmth, Kelly settled into her chair and picked up her stitches where she'd left off.

The long table was empty now. Lisa had left and Lizzie and Eustace were nowhere to be seen. Lizzie's knitting was sitting atop her embroidered knitting bag, and Eustace's laptop computer was closed on the table as well.

Kelly knitted a row, enjoying the peaceful quiet. That was one of the things she continually enjoyed about knitting. You didn't need company to enjoy doing it. It was a satisfying, yet contemplative activity that allowed her mind to roam free while her hands were busy creating with color and texture.

"Oh, good. I'm glad you're here," Jennifer's voice came through the quiet. She pulled out a chair beside Kelly. "I thought I'd take my break now before the lunch crowd picks up. Lizzie and Eustace are at their favorite table. I won't get to see you guys tonight, so let's catch up now. How're things going in the Denver development fast lane?"

"Well, I'm not in the fast lane, but Warner sure is. He's got more ideas for projects. Only this recession is holding him back. Once things start to settle he'll be shifting into high gear."

"Sounds like Don Warner." Jennifer worked the coral stitches on the top she was knitting. Half finished. "How's Housemann doing? Has he said anything to you about this dead deal with Turner? Has he lost all interest?"

"You know, I've barely had a chance to talk with him. Every time I called last week, I always got his voice mail. I finally touched base with him on the phone a few days ago, but I didn't get a chance to ask him because he was in a hurry. Sounded preoccupied, too. His answers were real short. Not like him."

Jennifer frowned. "Oh, darn. I was hoping he talked to you about the canyon deal falling through. I spoke with his agent Bethany, and she hasn't heard anything from him, either. I mean, if he still wants the property, he could let Bethany know he's interested, and she can notify us. Turner's wife will own all the property once the estate is settled. I sure hope Renee Turner wants to continue using me as an agent."

"I don't know if that would be a good idea right now," Kelly countered. "Jayleen told me Lieutenant Peterson questioned Turner's wife a second time. You and I know that means she's in Peterson's crosshairs. So, I don't think it would be a good idea for Renee Turner to talk about selling the property so soon after her husband's death."

Jennifer's fingers moved faster, which happened whenever she was worrying about something, Kelly noticed. "Oh, brother. I was hoping that deal could eventually be salvaged. I guess not."

Kelly recognized the concern in her friend's voice and repeated her earlier offer. "Remember, Jen. I'm happy to float you a loan to help tide you over this rough period."

Jennifer smiled at Kelly. "I remember. Thank you. And let's hope it doesn't come to that. Those catering jobs are really helping to fill in. I'm okay, so far. I just think it's such a waste when a willing seller and a willing buyer are unable to get together. After all these years in real estate, that's frustrating to watch."

"I understand. But right now, Renee Turner seems to be standing on shaky ground." Kelly shrugged. "Maybe Jayleen is right. Maybe Renee didn't kill her husband. Maybe Turner was killed by someone he'd burned in a bad real estate deal. Who knows? Maybe that mysterious guy Birmingham is someone from Turner's past."

Jennifer let her stitches drop to her lap and stared out into the empty room, lined with yarn bins and bookshelves. "I told the cops everything I knew about that phone call when they questioned me. It wasn't much because I never spoke with Birmingham. I wonder what they found out about him."

"Well, Jayleen says Renee is wondering, too. Jayleen asked me to find out what Burt has heard from his county cop friend Paul. I have to admit I'm curious, too."

"Uh-oh. That sounds like sleuthing to me."

"Can't help it, Jen. It's in my nature," Kelly teased.

Jennifer's head jerked up from her knitting. "Oooo, what

about that spooky guy you saw lurking around the cabin. Did the cops ever find out who he was?"

"Yes, Burt told me he was the owner of the property right next to Turner's and has lived in the canyon a long time. Kind of a recluse. Apparently he didn't have too much to say when police questioned him."

Jennifer gave a little shiver. "Well, I'm glad he never came over while I was out there all by myself. He would have scared the bejeezus out of me."

Kelly laughed out loud at that and decided to change the subject. There was something else she was curious about. "You know, I saw Steve the other night. It was at one of those Denver project's mini mob scenes. We had a speaker then a dinner. We were all out in the lobby bar before dinner, and I saw him drinking a beer and talking with some woman. A blonde, of course." Kelly deliberately used a lighthearted tone.

Jennifer looked over at her, busy fingers stopped their movements. "Oh, really? Did he see you? Did he come over and talk to you, I hope?"

"Yes and no. Steve turned and spotted me. I swear he was so shocked his mouth dropped open." Kelly said in a wry voice. "But he didn't say anything or do anything. He just stood there and stared at me."

"And what did you do?"

"I stood there and stared back. Didn't blink. I was half expecting him to walk over and say something. After all, you guys told me Steve wanted to apologize. That would have been the perfect time. But he just stood there." Kelly said, concentrating on her stitches.

"I thought you said you didn't want Steve to come over

and apologize when you were at a meeting. Did you change your mind?"

Kelly shrugged. "Yeah, I guess. I mean, the meeting was over, and we were all standing around with drinks. It would have been the perfect time to do it if he wanted to. But he looked so surprised to see me, he just stood there. After a minute he kind of looked like he was going to say something, but Dave came up then and said they were ditching the rubber chicken for a steak house."

"Ahhhh, so you went with Dave, then?"

"Absolutely." Kelly gave her a sly grin. "Rubber chicken can't compete with steak."

"Good. I'm glad you did. And, I'm glad Steve got to see it."

"So am I," Kelly admitted. "In fact, I met Dave for drinks after dinner. I wanted you to know that I'm following your instructions, Doctor."

Jennifer returned to her knitting. "Good for you, Kelly. Maybe that will kick Steve into making a move."

"Hey, maybe I don't want Steve to make a move," Kelly felt compelled to reply. "He walked out on *me*, remember?"

Jennifer kept knitting. "I remember. And believe me, so does Steve."

Ten

"Stand still, Carl, I'm trying to dry you off," Kelly instructed her Rottweiler. Carl ignored her and kept wiggling, snowflakes on his nose. "Carl, sit," Kelly commanded in Alpha Dog voice.

Clearly, Carl didn't want to sit, he wanted to wiggle and jump around the kitchen. Kelly gave a little tug on his collar to ensure compliance. Carl sat, reluctantly, while Kelly wiped off the rest of the snowflakes.

"Okay," Kelly said, releasing Carl from his sit. Carl immediately raced around the kitchen, sniffing the floor. Just in case stray food crumbs were hiding. "What were you rooting around in the snow for?" Kelly asked her dog as she reached for her now-empty coffee mug. "Did you find Brazen Squirrel's cache of nuts?"

Carl didn't bother to look up but kept investigating the floor in hopes that food would miraculously appear, no doubt.

Kelly gave her dog a head rub and slipped on her winter jacket. March may have the first day of spring on its calendar, but it was still cold. And March snowstorms were often heavy and wet, causing all the evergreen branches to droop with snow.

Kelly grabbed her knitting bag and headed out the cottage front door. About five inches of soft snow crunched beneath her mountain boots as she made her way across the driveway and through the outside patio of Pete's café. She needed coffee. After spending an entire Saturday morning working on the computer spreadsheets of her two clients' accounts, Kelly needed Eduardo's strong brew. And maybe some lunch before she returned to number crunching and analysis.

Brushing aside a tree branch heavy with snow, she paused for a moment beside the canvas-covered tables and chairs. All the bushes had been painted with the same snowy brush. It was so quiet. Even the street traffic outside the stucco walls surrounding the Lambspun property was muffled. That was one of the things she loved about snow. It seemed to swallow noise as it fell and enveloped the world in white.

An icy breeze blew against Kelly's face and tousled her hair. Through the café's wide windows, she could see the waitresses serving lunch. Hitching her knitting bag up her shoulder, Kelly ended her short solitude and hurried inside where it was warm.

Wonderful aromas assaulted her nostrils the moment she stepped inside the café. Burgers, fries, soups. Lunchtime. Kelly's stomach growled as she stomped her snowy boots on the floor mat.

"Hey, Kelly, come and join me," Burt called from the corner table. He waved her over. "I need your help with this hamburger. I ordered it in a weak moment. I have no business eating the whole thing."

Kelly laughed as she slipped off her jacket and pulled out the chair across from him. "So, once again you want me to save you from yourself, is that it?"

Burt gave her a big grin. "Something like that. Here, I've already cut it in half. You can eat this, and it won't even show. You run three miles a day. Me, it'll show immediately."

Kelly looked at the tempting burger, and her stomach growled again. "First, it's pancakes. Now, it's a burger. Okay, Burt, you're lucky you caught me when I'm starving. I've been immersed in client accounts all morning."

"Thanks, Kelly. You're a lifesaver," he said with a chuckle as he placed the half burger in front of her.

Julie hastened over with her coffeepot in hand. "Need a refill, Kelly? Or should I even bother to ask?"

"You know me, Julie, I *always* need coffee." Julie snapped open the mug and poured a black stream inside, then returned to other customers.

The burger's tempting aroma teased Kelly again, and she succumbed. She took a bite and savored the flavorful meat and mayonnaise and tomatoes and condiments. *Yum.* She licked her lips afterward. "Boy, Eduardo makes a good burger, doesn't he? And you've got all my favorites on here. A classic burger."

"Don't I know it. That's one of the things that makes working in the shop so risky. Food smells. I swear they come floating out of here and find me all the way in front of the shop where I'm spinning."

"Keep running, Burt. You and Mimi are still working out, aren't you?" Kelly took another bite.

"Oh, yeah. Believe me, that's the second hardest thing I do every day, after staying away from temptation here."

Kelly savored the rich taste, then followed it with some of Eduardo's black gold. Strong and dark. The caffeine helped her remember the questions she had for Burt. "By the way, Burt, I was wondering how that investigation is going into Fred Turner's death. Do the police have any suspects?" she asked innocently.

"Well, it's proceeding, according to Paul," Burt said as he leaned back in the wooden chair and folded his arms across his chest. "They've been questioning Turner's wife and his acquaintances and the office assistant. It looks like the guy didn't have any friends to speak of. But Paul said Turner didn't lack for people who were not his friends."

Kelly licked a drop of mustard from her lip. "According to Jayleen, Turner had a lot of enemies around northern Colorado. People he'd either cheated in real estate deals or managed to steal property from them by using shady practices. Have they found any that raised their suspicions?"

Burt smiled over at her. "I'm afraid the only person who's raised any suspicions at all is Turner's wife. I know she's a friend of Jayleen's, but right now, she's not in a good spot. According to Paul, she went to confront Turner. They'd been wrangling over property in a nasty divorce." Burt wagged his head in a manner Kelly recognized. "Not good. And apparently she paid Turner's assistant to keep tabs on his real estate deals and the money involved."

Kelly swallowed the last bite of burger and grabbed her napkin. "I hear you, Burt. Jayleen updated me yesterday and asked if I'd try to find out what's happening in the investigation. Jayleen swears one of Fred's enemies did him in. And

Renee keeps asking about that British guy, Birmingham, who left a phone message at Turner's office. Apparently the office assistant played the message for Renee, so she knew the guy wanted to buy the property and was going to meet Turner at the site Saturday morning." She took a sip of coffee. "Has Peterson learned anything about this guy?"

"I asked Paul about it, and he said they knew about the phone message. They followed it up, but there was no way to trace the number. Apparently, the guy used one of those disposable phones that can't be traced to anything. And there's never been any contact since. Paul says there's no way to prove the guy ever drove up to the property to meet Turner. They followed up on Birmingham's name, but got nowhere. Since it's a total dead end, the guys let it go."

Kelly stared off into the café. She saw Jennifer standing in front of the grill counter, loading plates of luncheon specialties on a big brown tray. "That's frustrating. Maybe that guy did drive up there and saw something. Maybe—"

"And maybe he saw Turner's dead body and took off like a bat outta hell," Burt broke in. "There's no way we'll ever know, Kelly. We don't know who he is, where he lives, what he looks like, nothing. Trust me, it's a complete dead end."

Something about Burt's statement made Kelly's little buzzer go off inside, but she didn't pursue it. "So, that leaves Peterson with only one suspect to concentrate on. Renee Turner."

"Unfortunately, that's true."

Kelly sipped her coffee and another thought wiggled forward. "Did they ever question shaggy neighbor Benjamin again? Maybe he saw more than he's telling."

Burt smiled at Kelly, a twinkle in his eye. "That's a possibility, Sherlock. Sounds like you're getting interested in this case."

Kelly gave her friend and advisor a good-natured shrug. "Well, kind of. I promised Jayleen I'd ask questions. But what usually happens is whenever I ask questions, I wind up with even more questions. That's what sucks me in, Burt. Trying to figure out the questions and the answers. It's a puzzle. Kind of like accounting."

Burt laughed softly, then leaned his arms on the table and leaned forward. "You wouldn't be you, if you didn't have questions, Kelly. And for the record, an old acquaintance of yours from the canyon, Deputy Don, told Peterson he'd go and ask neighbor Benjamin some more questions. He's known this Benjamin guy for over fifteen years. Deputy Don says he's a real loner and can be pretty tight-lipped with strangers. Don thinks he may get more information out of him than Peterson's guys did. We'll see."

Kelly had fond memories of Deputy Don. He was the one who arrived in the nick of time two years ago when Kelly was holding a killer at bay. "Well, if Deputy Don is on the case, we don't have to worry, do we, Burt?" she said with a grin. "He'll get answers for sure. How is he doing? Isn't he nearing retirement age?"

"Don's doing fine. He's as ornery as ever," Burt said with a chuckle. "And don't ever mention retirement anywhere near him. Don loves his job, he loves those canyons he patrols, the Poudre and Bellevue, and he's as sharp as he's ever been. So, I think it's safe to say he'll be on the job for a while longer."

"Have you ever regretted retiring early, Burt?"

"I did for about the first year, but ever since I've come

here to Lambspun, I feel like I'm halfway back on the force. Thanks to you, Sherlock, and all your questions."

Kelly joined her friend in laughter.

"Hey, Kelly," Jayleen called as she stepped down from her gray truck parked outside the wrought-iron fence behind the café's patio.

Kelly stopped on the steps leading into Pete's café and waited for Jayleen to stride through the snow in the garden. "Where's Renee?" she asked when Jayleen approached.

"She'll be along in a few minutes. She was at a lawyer's office, I think." Jayleen bounded up the wooden steps beside Kelly. "Listen, thanks so much for agreeing to come over on such short notice. I figured I'd better grab Renee while you were still in town and not in Denver. I hope this doesn't mess up your work schedule, Kelly girl."

Kelly yanked the door open. "It's fine, Jayleen. I got a lot done this morning before I came over to the shop for lunch." She stepped inside and waved at Jennifer, who was cleaning tables. "Hey there, Jen. Is it okay if Jayleen and I take a back table and talk with a friend? She'll be here in a few minutes. I know you guys will be closing up soon, but you can ignore us."

"You two are kinda hard to ignore," Jennifer teased. "Go ahead and find a table. I'll bring you some coffee and leave a pot on the warmer when we leave."

"Thanks, Jennifer, you're a lifesaver," Jayleen said as she followed Kelly to a corner table. "I can use some strong coffee about now."

"Is there any other kind?" Kelly joked as she settled into

a chair at a table beside a window that looked out onto the still-frozen garden patio.

Jayleen sank into the chair across from Kelly and dropped her Stetson onto an adjacent chair. "I'll be curious to hear what that lawyer told Renee. I guess it's a good thing that she went to see him. John Skinner. Good man."

"I'm glad she did, Jayleen," Kelly said, leaning over the table. "I talked to Burt at lunch and it sounds like Renee is still on top of Peterson's suspect list."

Jayleen screwed up her face. "*Damn!* What about that British guy? Didn't they talk to him?"

"They would if they could find him. Burt said the guy used one of those disposable phones, and they can't trace anything. They even tracked his name, but it was a dead end."

"Damnation! Did they talk with anybody in Denver? I mean, Fred made enemies everywhere he went."

Kelly nodded. "It sounds like they did, but you and I both know, it's one thing to say you hate someone's guts, and it's another thing to go out and kill them. That's why Renee is on top of the list. She had both motive and the opportunity to do it."

Jennifer approached with a coffeepot and three mugs. "Here, you go," she said, setting everything on the table. "Enjoy yourselves. Close that door between the shop and café when you're finished. Oh, and please leave by Lambspun's front door. We're setting the door alarms out here."

"Will do, Jen," Kelly said, saluting her friend. "See you tomorrow, maybe. Do you and Pete want to go out to dinner or are you catering?"

"Catering, thank God," Jen said, untying her waitress apron with pockets full of order pads and pens. "Both tonight and Sunday night. Why don't you come in for breakfast tomorrow, and I'll steal some time."

"Deal," Kelly said, giving her a wave.

"Take care, Jennifer," Jayleen said, as Jennifer headed toward the hallway leading to the shop. "She's a working fool, trying to make ends meet, I imagine. When Fred died, that deal went south faster than a Canada goose in November."

Kelly poured a mugful of coffee and took a deep drink. *Ahhhh.* A memory fragment floated from the back of her brain. "There's something I want to show you, Jayleen, and I'm glad Renee isn't here." She dug out her smart phone from her jeans pocket. "I took a photo of the gun Fred Turner used. It was lying right beside his hand on the floor. And I wanted you to take a look at it."

Jayleen gave her a wry smile. "Whooeee, Kelly girl, you really have turned into a detective. Taking photos of a dead man."

Kelly pulled up her photo gallery on the phone's screen. "I didn't take a photo of Turner," she tried to explain. "I was simply curious about the gun. I think you will be too when you see it." She found the photo in her gallery file and touched the screen to increase its size.

"Curt keeps telling me I need one of those newfangled phones. But I don't want to have to learn something new all over again."

"You can do it, Jayleen," Kelly said, smiling. "You're smarter than most people I know. And once you get used to these, you're hooked. You can't do without it." She handed the phone to Jayleen. "Take a look at that gun. It looks pretty old to me. Burt thinks it could even be a World War Two pistol."

"Well, I'll be damned. . . ." Jayleen breathed. "That does look kind of like one of those from the War."

"Have you ever seen any guns like that?"

"Only at gun shows. Or in private collections. Lots of people collect old guns." She handed the phone back to Kelly.

"Burt told me the crime lab couldn't find any identifying serial numbers or anything on the gun, though. No prints, either. So it's impossible to trace."

"That's not surprising. Private dealers usually have those guns. That's probably where the killer bought the gun he used to shoot Fred."

Kelly peered at the photo again. "It makes me curious though. Why would someone use a collector's piece like that to kill Fred Turner? I mean, you see stuff on television about how criminals remove serial numbers off guns so they can't be traced. Why would he go to the trouble to use an old war pistol?"

Jayleen shrugged. "Hard to say, Kelly. Maybe he had it in his family or something."

Kelly felt her inner buzzer go off again. She clicked out of the photo screen. "Have you gone to many gun shows?"

"Oh, sure. Curt and I went to a really big one in Denver last year. In fact, it'll be in Denver next weekend, if you're interested in going and sleuthing around," Jayleen teased.

Kelly shoved the phone back into her pocket, choosing her next words carefully. "Maybe I will. By the way, you mentioned that Renee Turner was a hunter like you and Curt. So that means she's bound to have guns at her home, right?"

Jayleen's smile faded. "Yes, she does. Renee's a damn good hunter and teaches classes in marksmanship, too. Which I'm sure that Detective Peterson already knows by now."

"I'm sure he does, Jayleen. You see where I'm going with this."

"A blind man could see it with a cane," Jayleen said, frowning. "Renee's got guns, of course. Mostly hunting rifles and shotguns."

"Have you ever seen a pistol or revolver at her house?"

Jayleen shrugged. "No, but she probably has one for protection. I know I do."

"It all goes back to motive and opportunity, Jayleen," Kelly said, noticing a tall, slender woman dressed like Jayleen in jeans and denim jacket stride through the patio garden toward the café.

Kelly was about to jump up and wave her toward the front when Julie pushed open the café back door. "Are you looking for Jayleen? She's here inside." Julie beckoned Renee up the steps.

"Thanks, Julie," Kelly said. "You can lock up now. We'll go out through Lambspun."

Jayleen pulled out a chair at the table, gesturing her friend toward it. "Renee, have a seat. This is Kelly Flynn. Kelly, Renee Turner."

Renee Turner immediately shoved her hand toward Kelly. "Thanks so much for taking the time to meet me, Kelly."

"No problem, Renee," Kelly said, returning her firm handshake. Renee's palm felt calloused like Jayleen's, but Renee's face had a lot more sun wrinkles. Her short, brownish gray hair was close-cropped, and her green eyes stared right at Kelly.

"How was the lawyer meeting?" Jayleen asked as Renee sat down.

Renee clasped the mug of coffee Jayleen offered with both

hands. "Scary. He said I should not talk with the police anymore without him present. I swear, Jayleen, I came out of there more scared than I was when I went in." She took a deep drink from the mug.

Jayleen reached over and patted her friend's hand. "Hang in there, girl."

"I'm trying to, I swear, I am. But I'm gettin' this sinking feeling, Jayleen. I mean, even John Skinner told me it didn't look good. I mean . . . how can that happen?" She looked around the now-empty café. "He thinks the police will call me in for questioning downtown. And . . . and they might even file charges against me!" She ran her hand through her short hair. "Damn," she whispered. "I can't even believe this is happening. I didn't shoot Fred! Why aren't they out looking for that Birmingham guy on the phone?"

Jayleen glanced over at Kelly, then back to her friend. "Kelly found out today that police can't track that guy. He used one of those cheap phones you can throw away, and there's no way to find him. They don't have a name. Nothing."

Renee's green eyes turned huge, and she looked from Jayleen to Kelly then back again. Kelly saw panic.

Renee sank her head into her hand. "Oh, my God . . ." she whispered.

Jayleen looked across at Kelly with an imploring look of her own. Kelly leaned forward over the table and took a sip of coffee. "Renee, why don't you tell me everything that happened that Saturday. Start at the beginning."

Eleven

Kelly turned her car into the parking lot of a redbrick office complex. Grabbing her briefcase, Kelly exited her sporty red car and headed for the building with Arthur Housemann's office. Monday morning had dawned clear and cold, but Colorado's brilliant sun shone bright in the deep blue sky and had warmed the temperatures considerably. Kelly only needed her business suit. Her coat and scarf stayed in the car.

She hadn't spoken with Housemann in over a week. They continued playing phone tag. She'd leave a message, then another, and no answer. Finally Housemann left a cryptic message that said, he'd "try" to see her this week. Since Monday was the beginning of the week, Kelly figured she'd attempt to catch Housemann at his office. She'd wanted to give him the financial reports he asked for two weeks ago. He'd sounded like he was anxious to see them, so Kelly wondered why he hadn't asked for them. Arthur Housemann had never been hard to reach before, and Kelly was curious at his sudden unavailability.

Riding the elevator to the third floor, Kelly removed the portfolio from her briefcase, then headed down the hall to Housemann's corner office. When she stepped inside, she spotted Doris, Housemann's secretary, who'd been with him for four decades.

"Hi, Doris," Kelly greeted the older woman. "I was hoping to catch Mr. Housemann in, so I could show him these reports. Is he around?" She glanced toward Housemann's door. His office was dark. No computer was open atop the desk, which was a sure sign the boss wasn't there.

Doris shook her head, a concerned expression crossing her face. Her hair was short and curly in tight little curls. "No, he's not, Kelly. He left a little while ago, and he didn't say when he'd return."

That didn't sound like Housemann. In the year that Kelly had been doing his financial accounts, Arthur Housemann was almost as anal as she was about details. And every time she'd called the office, his faithful secretary Doris always knew exactly where Housemann was and when he would return.

"Darn it. I've been trying to get in touch with him for over a week, and he doesn't return my phone calls. That's why I came over this morning, hoping to catch him. He'd acted really anxious to see these reports when I finished them." She glanced around the office. "It's kind of strange. He's never been hard to reach before."

"He seems to have a lot on his mind lately." Doris's worried expression intensified. "He's not as talkative as usual. And he's canceling appointments. This morning, a man from the county stopped by. He visited Mr. Housemann for a while, then when he left, Mr. Housemann cancelled all his appointments for the rest of the day." She glanced at the appointment book on her desk and her expresson softened. "Including an interview with that nice gentleman who writes historical books. Mr. Freemont. Such a pleasant man. I was looking forward to learning about his books."

"That's too bad. I've met Eustace Freemont, and he's an interesting man. In fact, I suggested he interview Arthur. Maybe they can reschedule."

"Well, I hope so. I was looking forward to meeting him."

"I'm curious, Doris. What did the man from the county want? Is he with zoning or something? Housemann always keeps me posted about any impending legal notifications."

Doris shook her head. "He didn't say. He just identified himself and asked to speak with Mr. Housemann."

More curious now, Kelly pressed. "What was his name? Do you remember?"

"Oh, yes. I wrote it down." Doris scanned the desk pad calendar on her immaculately neat desk. "Edward Peterson. And he said he was with Larimer County Justice Department. He was tall and very polite," she added.

Kelly tried not to show her surprise. She knew that would cause the elderly woman even more concern. "Really? That's interesting." She placed the portfolio of reports on Doris's desk. "Well, I'll leave these with you. Please ask Mr. Housemann to call me after he reads them if he has any questions. I hope he turns up soon so you can stop worrying about him." Kelly forced a smile.

"Thanks, Kelly," Doris said, taking the reports. "I hope so, too. Take care, now."

Kelly gave her a little wave as she hastened to the door. Edward Peterson with the Larimer County Justice Department had to be none other than Lieutenant Ed Peterson of the county police. Kelly wondered why Peterson visited Housemann himself. Usually he had his officers do those kinds of interviews. Then she remembered her Warner colleague Ralph's comment about there being "bad blood" between Housemann and Turner.

Kelly hastened down the stairs instead of the slower elevator, worrying that Peterson had heard the same rumor. She pulled out her phone and punched in Burt's phone number as she got into her car. Burt answered on the third ring. "Hey, Kelly, how're you doing?" his warm voice asked.

"I'm okay, Burt, but I've got a question."

Burt chuckled. "Not surprising. What is it?"

"I just left my client Arthur Housemann's office. He wasn't in, but his secretary told me Housemann had a visitor earlier this morning. An Edward Peterson from the Larimer County Justice Department. That has to be Detective Ed Peterson." She waited for Burt's reaction.

Burt paused before replying. "Really? That's interesting."

"Isn't it now? You can imagine how that aroused my curiosity. I'm wondering why Peterson visited Housemann. Peterson usually has his officers question people first, right?"

"That's been Peterson's standard procedure," Burt replied. "The only thing that comes to mind is Housemann and Turner were in the midst of negotiations on that Poudre Canyon property. Now you've made me curious, too."

"I was hoping that's the only reason. When I was in Denver the other day, one of my Warner colleagues told me he'd worked on a project years ago with both Housemann and

Turner. He said he got the impression there was some sort of 'bad blood' between the two of them. So, I wondered if Peterson had learned anything new."

"Well, Paul will know, Kelly. Let me check with him and get back to you, okay?"

"Thanks, Burt. That's what I was hoping you'd say. I'll wait for your call."

Kelly clicked off, then tossed her smartphone onto the adjacent car seat and started her car. Backing out of the southeast Fort Connor office complex, Kelly turned toward the main highway that headed west toward the central part of the city.

Driving along this large east-west artery, Kelly always spotted new shops or stores, even new mini malls that weren't there six months before. She drove past a row of new restaurants; some were familiar chain restaurants, others were newer additions. Another shopping center came into view on the right side of the street. A "lifestyle mall," it was called. Large anchor stores with popular names, selling shoes, clothing, sporting goods. Another version of Big Box was there, and scores of smaller boutique shops dotted between the bigger stores.

Her phone rang as she turned onto a large avenue that would take her toward the knitting shop and cottage. She wanted a few minutes of quiet knitting before she returned to her accounts.

"Hey, Kelly, how're you doing?" Dave Germaine's cheerful voice came over the phone.

"Doing fine, Dave. What's up? Does Warner want something?" She turned north on Lemay Avenue.

Dave laughed. "Warner always wants something, but that's

another story. I'm calling to see if you're coming down for the joint project meeting this Friday? The mayor's going to speak at lunch." Dave laughed softly.

"Oh, joy. Rubber chicken and politicians," Kelly joked. "I guess I can't wiggle out of that."

"Glad to hear it. Listen, I wanted to ask if you'd come over to the Metropolitan gym later that evening and play in a mixed-league volleyball game. Some of us from the project got together and started playing basketball after the meetings. Jan and Carla from the office suggested we do a pickup volleyball game, too, so the women could join in. The companies will all be mixed up among the teams. And it's a fun way to blow off some recession frustration on the court. What do you say, Kelly? We could really use you."

Kelly considered his suggestion while she pulled behind another car at a traffic light. "Boy, Dave, I haven't played volleyball regularly since college. Just every now and then. I don't know how much help I'll be."

"Hey, you told me you run every day and play softball and tennis. That means you're better than ninety percent of the others on the court. Trust me."

"That's a slight exaggeration."

"Naw, you'll be great. Plus, we need another tall girl on the front line. Carla and Jan are athletic, but they're not real tall."

"Okay, I'll give it a shot. I hope you and your teammates aren't expecting a great performance. Have you got a good setter? Can the team pass?"

"Actually, we played at the gym last night, and we're not bad. Plus it was fun to release some of those recession bad vibes."

"Isn't that the truth," Kelly said as she drove past residences followed by grocery stores and shops. Hearing Dave's voice caused her to remember something. Something Dave had said.

"We'll all go out to dinner afterward," he added.

"That sounds good. Listen, Dave, do you remember our talking about Fred Turner a couple of weeks ago?"

"Sure. Why do you ask?"

"You know the police are investigating it as a murder now, did you know that?"

"Matter of fact, Warner mentioned it to me last week, I think. We were both wondering if Fred's cheating finally caught up with him. Do the cops have any leads on who might have done it?"

Kelly weighed her next words carefully. "Actually, Turner's ex-wife is at the top of that list right now. A close friend of mine says she's known Renee Turner for years and believes she's innocent. Unfortunately, Renee has no alibi. And she and Turner were in the midst of a bad divorce."

"Ouch. That doesn't sound good."

"Yeah, we know. My friend asked me to check out some of Turner's colleagues in Denver. She says Turner made a lot of enemies, and he did lots of deals in Denver. That's when I remembered your saying something about working a deal with Turner, and how he tried to cheat everyone."

"Yeah, he did. And your friend is right about Turner making enemies. I vowed I'd never work with the crook again. And so did Warner. You can ask him yourself. This town is filled with guys he tried to cheat."

"Remember any more names?"

"Ohhh, Devries, Carruthers, Simon Contractors, even old

man Overby got burned. And a few years ago, Art Housemann from up your way was working a deal with Bill Parosky
from Northglenn. They were going to develop a strip mall in
Brighton. They wanted to buy some land from Turner that
they needed for a parking lot. He screwed them over. I remember Bill talking about how mad Art Housemann was.
Parosky and I used to play ball at the gym and he told me
what happened. Parosky said Art was so mad, he swore he'd
get even with Fred one day."

"Wow, they really doesn't sound like Housemann at all,"
Kelly said, steering the car around a corner. Remembering
the comment from another Warner employee at the dinner
reception last week, Kelly asked. "Do you know if Housemann and Turner had any past history together? Maybe that
explains it."

"I don't know, Kelly. But Bill Parosky will know. He's
worked on deals with Art before. And Parosky should be at
the Friday meeting. I'll introduce you, and you can ask him
yourself."

"Hey, thanks, Dave. I appreciate it. I told my friend I'd
see what I could find out this week, even though she's grasping at straws. No matter how many people Fred Turner has
cheated over the years, most people aren't going to kill a man
because he cheated them in a real estate deal, no matter
whether it was years ago or last week."

Dave paused on the other end of the line. "Don't be too
sure of that, Kelly. This is the West. People have been killing each other over land since the explorers first set foot on
these mountains."

* * *

"**Is** that one of those recycled silk yarns?" Megan asked, looking across the knitting table. "I haven't seen those for months."

Kelly leaned back in her chair and checked the rows of reds, blues, and greens on her needles. "Indeed it is. I got tired of seeing it sitting in my stash basket and decided to do something with it. It's a funny yarn and doesn't work with everything."

Jennifer looked up from the peach-colored top she was finishing. "It's coming along nicely, Kelly."

"Anything happening at the real estate office?" Megan asked.

"I wish it were, but buyers are few and far between. Except for investors. And they're scooping up most of those foreclosure properties at bank sales. They're getting some really sweet deals, too."

"Hang in there, Jen," Megan said, obviously worried.

"With the help of the extra university catering and my office broker, I'll be okay. He's been helping me out because the Turner deal fell through. He's even paying me to go to Denver for him this week. There's a real estate meeting on the mortgage loan modifications that are possible now. I'm going to take notes so I can make a presentation at the office next week."

Kelly looked up from her colorful yarn. "That's great he's paying you. What day is the meeting?"

"This Friday. I plan to get on the interstate really early in the morning so I'll have a fighting chance to be at the Denver Tech Center by eight thirty."

"I have to be in Denver for a meeting on Friday, too. I'd planned to go down on Thursday and check into that Cherry

Creek hotel, relax, and not have to fight the morning traffic. Why don't you join me? I've already charged the room, so there'd be no cost to you."

Jennifer looked up, clearly surprised. "That would be great. I've never been in that hotel because it's too pricey, but I've been dying to see it."

"You'll love it," Kelly said, returning to her stitches. "It's a huge suite. There's a heated Jacuzzi tub and fancy bathroom. Two double beds. Downy soft bedding to snuggle into at night. All sorts of goodies and stuff are in the fridge, and I have room service when I'm really dragged out from those meetings. Or, we can go out to dinner Thursday night. Lots of good cafés in Cherry Creek."

"Okay, that is way too tempting for me to pass up," Megan said, dropping her lime green yarn and the needles to her lap. "Can I invite myself along? I have to get to Denver to check out those last bridal shops or Mimi will have my head. I'd thought about going this weekend, but I didn't want to go alone. This way, I'll be with you guys Thursday night, then I can hit the shops all day Friday, while you're both in meetings."

"Sure, Megan. We'll make it a working road trip. There's plenty of room in that suite."

"Thanks, Kelly, that will make the odious bridal shop search more bearable. I'm only doing it for Mimi. I'm convinced I won't find anything I like. I'm about to take Lisa's suggestion of a seamstress seriously. I might have someone fix up a simple white dress and call it good."

Megan returned to her knitting while Kelly and Jennifer exchanged glances. "Don't count out those bridal shops yet,

Megan," Jennifer advised. "You may walk in there and find the perfect dress and fall in love with it."

Megan gave her a sardonic look. "Sure. When pigs fly."

Kelly laughed softly at her friend's stubbornness. It was hard to change Megan's mind once she had it set. "Well, even if you don't find a dress on Friday, I can promise you entertainment Friday night. Some of the Warner people are playing in a volleyball game with some of the other Denver project developers. Kind of a morale builder, to blow off recession stress. Whatever. Dave Germaine said they needed more women players, so I joined up. Sounds like they could use you, too. You up for it, Megan?"

Megan's head jerked up and the light of competitive fire Kelly was so used to seeing danced in Megan's blue eyes. "Absolutely! I haven't played volleyball since last year!"

Jennifer leaned toward Kelly, fingers still working the yarn. "She makes that sound like forever. I'll bet she was the star player."

"Don't be silly," Megan said, giving a dismissive wave. "It was a league. But I was just an all-star on my college team. In addition to softball and basketball."

Kelly stared at her friend. "Whoa! You really were a triple threat."

"Now you know why I'm scared of her," Jennifer teased. "She could beat me up three different ways."

Twelve

"Boy, I love this bathroom," Megan said, checking her face in the enormous mirror of the luxurious hotel bathroom. "A small army could put their makeup on in here."

Granite countertops with double sinks filled one entire wall. Stylish brushed metal shelving was filled with super-thick and fluffy towels. A huge Jacuzzi tub took up one whole end of the room. Brushed metal, mirrors, and green tinted glass—all gave the room a peaceful, tranquil look and feel. Perfect for relaxing in the tub.

"I don't think the army uses much makeup, but I could be wrong," Jennifer said from across the bathroom at another long granite counter with a large mirror. She gave her auburn hair another squirt of hairspray.

Kelly checked her image in the floor-to-ceiling mirror on the side wall—hair, makeup, chic business suit. All was in order. "I'm ready, Jen. How about you?"

"All set." Jennifer snapped her makeup case shut. "Let me get my briefcase, and we can join morning traffic."

Kelly checked her watch. "We're doing fine. With luck, I can drop you off at the Tech Center by seven thirty, then head downtown to the meeting. Shouldn't be a problem."

"With Denver traffic, there are never any guarantees," Jennifer said as she followed Kelly from the bathroom. "I can't thank you enough for letting us stay here, Kelly. You've saved me at least two hours of sleep."

"It was fun. Maybe you guys will join me again." Kelly picked up her shoulder briefcase from the armchair in the seating area of the suite. A flat-screen television and entertainment center dominated the space.

Megan grabbed her purse from an end table beside the bar. "This is one pretty place," she said, looking around the suite. "I will definitely come back if you'll have me."

"I'd love the company," Kelly said as she slid into her stylish black raincoat. "Plus, it was a treat to try that new restaurant in LoDo. Beats the heck out of those rubber chicken dinners."

Jennifer slid on her jacket. "Which bridal shops are you checking out first, Megan?" she asked as Kelly held the hotel room door open for them.

"I'm starting out nearby, actually. There's one here in Cherry Creek. But first, I'm going to find a restaurant that specializes in breakfasts and have a great big plate of huevos rancheros." Megan threw her jacket over her arm and sailed through the doorway.

"Oh, Lord, I don't want to hear about it," Jennifer groaned. "That used to be one of my favorites."

"You could still have it, if you stay away from the beans

and tortillas," Kelly joked as they walked down the carpeted corridor toward the elevator.

"What fun is that?" Megan teased. "Listen, guys, I'll probably be here when you return from your meetings. What time do we have to be at the gym tonight?"

"Eight o'clock for free play and then the game starts. But this is just casual, so I have a feeling they won't be holding a time clock on anyone." Kelly pushed the elevator button and watched the doors slide open.

"When are your meetings over?" Megan stepped inside first.

"Mine should be finished by five, I hope," Kelly said. "How about yours, Jen?"

"Oh, certainly by five. Real estate agents like to head back to their offices before they go home. I'll wait for you in the office building lobby. Call me when you're getting close, and I'll go outside."

The elevator hummed as it rode downward, then the doors slid open. "Sounds like a plan," Kelly said as she stepped out into the elegant hotel lobby.

"My car's parked in back, so I'll see you guys later," Megan said, turning toward another hallway.

"Good luck, Megan," Kelly said as she and Jennifer headed toward the glass revolving entry doors.

"Find something this time," Jennifer called over her shoulder.

"Let's hope," Kelly joked before she pushed through the doors.

Walking up to the uniformed attendant, she handed him her parking ticket. "Could you bring my car, please?" The man nodded and scurried away toward the garage doorway.

"Valet parking. I could get used to that," Jennifer said, zipping her briefcase.

"In this area, it's a necessity. Parking spaces in Cherry Creek are either metered or garage or restricted shopping centers."

"Oh, I wanted to tell you something before I forget. Bethany, the agent who wrote the contract offer for Arthur Housemann, called me yesterday. I'd left a message on her office voice mail a week ago asking if Housemann had mentioned if he was still interested in buying the canyon property after Turner's estate is settled."

Kelly looked at her friend with interest. "Did he say he was?"

"Bethany thinks he still wants the property, but that's not what caught my attention. She went on to say that Renee Turner had called her a couple of days after Turner died and said she'd be willing to go ahead with the sale, provided Housemann still wanted to buy." Jennifer caught Kelly's gaze. "I asked her what Housemann said when she told him. Bethany said he kind of hemmed and hawed on the phone and told her he wants the property, but he didn't want any trouble. Then, he hung up on her."

Kelly let Jennifer's comments race through her mind. "Brother, that doesn't sound good for Renee," she said, refraining from making a comment on Housemann's behavior. After all, his comments sounded completely straightforward considering the circumstances.

"I know, but they make sense once you've seen or heard Renee Turner in action. It's all about the money. She was totally obsessed with the idea that Turner was trying to cheat her." Jennifer shrugged. "And knowing Turner, he probably was. Still, it wasn't a smart move on Renee's part to tell Housmann's agent she'd sell the property so soon after Turner's death."

Kelly watched the attendant drive her red car out of the garage. "That's why you have to call Burt and tell him everything."

"I was afraid you'd say that." Jennifer frowned. "Damn. I don't want to get anyone in trouble."

"No one will know it came from you, Jennifer. The cops are talking to all sorts of people about Fred Turner. Call Burt and he'll tell Paul. Then the cops will decide if it's important information or not."

Kelly's red car pulled to a stop right in front of them. "Why don't you call Burt while we're driving down to the Tech Center. Once you get there, you'll be sucked up into business."

"Good idea," Jennifer said as she opened her purse. "I'll get the tip."

Kelly scanned the crowded banquet-turned-meeting-room, searching for the coffee urns. Morning meetings required constant caffeine intake to make them bearable. Afternoon meetings did, too, to be truthful.

Spotting a cluster of people beside some long tables covered in white cloths, Kelly zeroed in on the group. Food and coffee were the only things that enticed that much interest, especially at eight thirty in the morning. As Kelly got closer, she spotted a tray of pastries and—worst of all—donuts. Fresh donuts. The kind she loved. The hardest kind for her to resist.

Deliberately turning her head, Kelly aimed straight for the coffee urns at the other end of the table. Having to wait in line behind several others, she couldn't help noticing other people sampling the donuts. Sampling was a kind word. Grabbing and gobbling was more accurate. Munching hungrily, donut sugar sprinkled on their chins and down their shirt fronts.

If only rush-hour traffic hadn't been so congested, she could have grabbed some real food. Even fast food would be better than those tempting sugary pastries. She and Jennifer and Megan had set the alarm with no cushion for breakfast. Kelly pictured Megan sitting down right now, chowing down on a huge plate of huevos rancheros. Only Megan could get away with that. Kelly's stomach growled just as she reached the coffee urn.

Quickly filling her cup, Kelly tried to get away from the platters of temptation, then she spotted a lonely apple sitting forgotten and ignored beside the donuts. Kelly glanced over her shoulder and grabbed it, then shoved the apple into her briefcase. She'd have it as a midmorning snack. Or maybe now. Maybe she . . .

"Hey, good morning," Dave's voice came over her shoulder. "You look bright and cheerful for so early."

"It's a ruse, I assure you," Kelly said, grateful for the distraction. "I'm trying to ignore the donuts. I didn't have time for breakfast, so it's coffee." She took a large gulp and felt the hunger pangs recede.

"I caved. Gave in to temptation." Dave grinned. "Those blueberry ones are my weakness. Then, of course the cinnamon sugar ones—"

"Stop!" Kelly ordered, holding up her hand. "Those are my favorites, too. I don't wanta hear about it."

Dave chuckled. "Okay, I'll stop. Say, I wanted to tell you I talked with Bill Parosky yesterday, and I asked him about Art Housemann."

Noticing several people aiming for the coffee urns, Kelly motioned Dave back into the main room, which continued to fill with people. Most of the chairs were already taken, she noticed. A raised platform with a podium and several chairs graced the end of the room.

"Really? You didn't have to. I was going to talk to him today," Kelly said, curious that Dave would take it upon himself to address her concerns.

Dave shrugged. "I wasn't trying to intrude or anything. It simply occurred to me that if you walked up to Bill and started asking him questions about an old friend of his, Bill would shut down. He's kind of a private person, if you know what I mean."

"That makes sense," Kelly replied. "So, what did Parosky say about Housemann and Turner?"

"He said Art was pretty hot after the land deal fell apart." Dave looked out into the crowded room. "He called Turner every name in the book on the phone one day."

"Did Housemann make any threats?"

Dave looked back at her with a smile. "Now, that's the kind of question that would spook Bill. He didn't use the word 'threat' exactly, but he did mention Housemann saying he thought Turner wanted to get even. But he didn't explain. That's all Bill said."

Kelly let that comment work through her mind. *Get even.*

That could mean a lot of things. And, it could refer to the "bad blood" between Housemann and Turner the other developer mentioned. "That's interesting," Kelly said, then took a large drink of coffee, deliberately not saying more.

"I can see the wheels inside your head spinning right now," Dave teased. "Do you really think Art Housemann could be involved in Turner's death? He's such a straight arrow."

"Hey, I'm not thinking anything," Kelly said, looking Dave square in the eye. "I'm simply asking questions for my friend and relaying the answers. That's all." She took another big sip.

Dave eyed her skeptically. "Why do I get the feeling you're dodging the question?"

An expert dodger, Kelly gave him a sly smile. "I think you've had too much sugar already."

Dave's cell phone rang then, and he reached into his jacket. "The Warner crew has settled in chairs near the front," he said as he walked away.

Kelly noticed several Warner staff had filled the front two rows of chairs. She checked her watch. The first speaker was due on deck in less than ten minutes. Enough time to freshen her coffee. She headed toward the coffee urns again and filled her cup to the rim.

As she walked away from the urns and into the room again, she spotted someone walking toward her. Someone else she recognized. *Steve*. Kelly took a big gulp of coffee as he approached. Steve had obviously found his tongue.

Steve stopped about six feet in front of her. Keeping his distance, she imagined. "Hi," he said with a little smile.

Kelly could feel Steve's hesitation as he stood there, so she decided to take the lead. They were adults, for Pete's sake. "Hi, yourself. I thought you were going to come over and say something at the last meeting, but you just stood there. Did you think I was going to bite your head off or something?"

Steve's easy grin suddenly appeared, like sunshine. Then, it was gone. A self-conscious smile replaced it. "Yeah, I kinda did."

Kelly watched him, old feelings bubbling up from inside, conflicted feelings. Old memories, good memories, and hurt. She glanced toward the front rows where her colleagues gathered. "We're adults, Steve. We move on, right?"

"I guess." Steve's smile disappeared. "You changed your hair. It looks good."

Surprised that he noticed, Kelly glanced back to him. "Thanks." She deliberately didn't say anything more.

Steve paused and looked into her eyes. "You look great, Kelly."

Regret radiated off Steve. Kelly could feel it. She stared back into his dark eyes, which had turned sad. Kelly didn't know what to say. "Thank you" sounded lame, so she looked into her coffee cup and changed the subject.

"I heard that you're working full-time for Sam Kaufman now. So you gave up the architect firm?"

Steve stared at his shoes. "Yeah, Sam promoted me. He needed the help. That's why I'm handling this joint project for the company. Sam likes to stay on the worksite, getting dirty." A little smile returned.

Kelly remembered when Steve spent all day walking around his worksites, mud on his work boots. That's what he loved. A poignant fragment of memory danced in front of her eyes for a second before she chased it away. "How do you like it?"

He looked back at her and gave one of his oh-so-familiar good-natured shrugs. "Actually, I've enjoyed meeting all these different builders. I've learned a lot, too, and I've gotten some ideas that maybe Sam and I can use in the company." He gave a wry smile and glanced over his shoulder toward the people standing on the platform at the front of the room. "If only these meetings wouldn't run on so long. Then we could all get some work done."

"Isn't that the truth?" Kelly agreed with a little smile. Just then, she spotted one of her Warner colleagues coming her way.

"Hey, Kelly, the meeting is about to start," a short, plump blonde woman said, beckoning Kelly. "We've got a place saved."

"Thanks, Brenda," Kelly said, then turned back to Steve. "Speak of the devil," she said with a rueful smile of her own. Then she added, "Take care."

"You too, Kelly," Steve said as she walked away.

Feeling her insides churning, Kelly followed Brenda toward the front rows. Noticing a hotel employee standing nearby with a tray of donuts, Kelly sped over and grabbed two blueberry ones. Right now, she needed sugar.

"Would you park it close by, please? We'll be using it in less than an hour," Kelly said to the parking attendant.

"Yes, ma'am," he said and took the keys.

Jennifer was already standing by the hotel entry doors. "I hope Megan is here. I want to have time to stop for a salad or something. I'm starving."

"Me, too," Kelly said, following her friend through the doors and into the lobby.

"Oh, before I forget, Burt called me back around noon, and said his friend Paul appreciated the information and was going to follow it up." She wagged her head. "I feel sorry for Renee."

"So do I, but you had to tell the truth," Kelly said as they entered the elevator. "By the way, Steve came up to me before the meeting started this morning. We got to say hello."

Jennifer jerked around and stared at Kelly. Her eyes sparked with obvious delight. "Really? Well, good for Steve. He made the first move. At last!"

Kelly gave her a crooked smile. "Yeah, I had to prime the pump at first. I told him he looked like he was afraid I'd bite his head off. Then he seemed to relax."

"What else did he say?" Jennifer asked as the elevator rose.

"Ohhh, he noticed I'd changed my hair and said it looked good."

"Safe subject, hair. Anything else?"

The elevator door slid open and Kelly walked out, Jennifer behind her. "I told him I'd heard about Sam promoting him. And he said he was in charge of the joint project so Sam could stay out on the building sites. And then, the meeting started, and that was that."

Jennifer and Kelly were both silent as they walked down the hotel corridor. Finally Jennifer spoke as they neared the hotel room. "Well, at least he broke the ice. How'd you feel?"

Kelly fished out the hotel key card and swiped it at the door. "Pretty churned up inside, as you can imagine," she admitted as she pushed the hotel room door open.

Kelly glanced around for Megan as they entered. Megan's jacket and briefcase lay on the sofa, but no sign of her. "Megan? We're back. Are you in the Jacuzzi or something? We've gotta get to the game—"

Kelly's sentence stopped when Megan stepped from around the corner. At least Kelly thought it was Megan. It was hard to tell. She'd never seen Megan look like this before.

Megan was a vision in white. She wore a strapless white wedding gown that hugged her slender figure all the way to the knees, then flared out gently to the floor. Not in gathers or ruffles, just subtle, flaring curves of white satin fabric. Or, at least it looked like satin to Kelly. And . . . were those beads edging the strapless bodice? *Beads?* On no-beads Megan? Kelly could barely believe her eyes.

Megan stood grinning at both of them. "Ta-*dah*!"

"Oh, my God! You found a dress!" Kelly cried, hand to her chest. She wasn't sure, but she thought she felt her briefcase slide off her shoulder to the floor. Shock had taken over.

"Megan, you look *beautiful*!" Jennifer exclaimed, both hands to her chest. "Oh, I'm going to cry!"

"I don't believe you found a dress," Kelly said again, standing in place, unable or unwilling to move. The vision might disappear.

"Wait! Don't cry yet," Megan teased. "Wait'll I put on something else." She dashed from the room, moving almost as fast in the form-fitting dress as she did on the ball field.

Kelly turned to Jennifer, who looked like she really might cry. "She found a dress. Impossible Megan found a dress. I don't believe it. And it's . . . it's beautiful! And . . . and it has *beads*, for Pete's sake! Beads on no-bead Megan! And it's satin, too! Surely the apocalypse must be coming."

Again, Kelly was cut short by the even lovelier vision that appeared around the corner. This time, Megan wore a gauzy white veil that started at a delicate bead-enrusted crown and fell gracefully to her waist. Simple and elegant. It added a sweetness to the sophisticated and stylish gown's lines.

"Ohhhh, Megan," Kelly whispered. "It's gorgeous, and so are you."

"Now, I *am* gonna cry," Jennifer said wetly, digging in her purse. "I need tissues."

"Take a box, silly," Megan said, laughing as she handed Jennifer a tissue box. "I already teared up hearing my mom on the phone. I'd e-mailed her a photo I took on my smart-phone at the bridal shop. Well, the lady took it, but, you know."

Kelly took her briefcase and dropped it on the sofa. "*Details!* Where did you find this gorgeous gown and how come you're wearing it? It fits perfectly. Was there a seamstress there or something?"

Megan shook her head. "It just happened to be my size. I'd been to two shops in the morning, then after lunch—"

"You ate lunch after a huevos rancheros breakfast?" Jennifer said, between wiping her nose.

"Of course," Megan said with a grin. "Anyway, after lunch I drove over to this shop in Lakewood on Sheridan Avenue. It was the third on my list. And—I walked in, and there it was! Right on the mannequin in the shop."

"You're kidding!"

"Nope. I took one look and fell in love with it. Exactly

like Jennifer said might happen." Megan dropped into a deep curtsy, despite the dress. "I bow to your wisdom, oh, Great One. Doctor of Love or whatever."

"How can you bend so low in that dress?" Kelly asked in admiration.

Megan rose effortlessly from her curtsy. "Shorter legs, but super strong." She winked.

"Better not do it again," Jennifer advised. "You don't want a bead or something to pop off."

"Quiet!" Kelly barked at her friend. "Maybe she hasn't noticed the beads. You don't want her to take it back."

"I saw the beads," Megan said, gently removing the veil. Jennifer rushed over to take it from her. She placed it gently across the sofa arm. "I figured you guys would rub it in, considering all the fuss I made before. Let's just say, these beads were . . . more subtle than the others."

Kelly walked up to her friend and gently ran her finger over the beads, then fingered the smooth satin. "It truly is gorgeous, Megan. I'm so glad you walked into that shop when you did."

"So am I. The saleslady said the gown had only been put out that week. She didn't want to sell it to me at first, but I begged and pleaded with her to let me take it home. I mean, it fits me perfectly." Megan spun in a little circle.

"Like a glove," Jennifer agreed.

"Looks like the begging worked," Kelly said, kicking off her heels and slipping off her suit jacket.

"Well, it was a combination of begging and my going over to the bank and getting a cashier's check for the full amount of the dress plus veil. I raced to the bank and returned to the shop in less than an hour." Megan's smile turned sly. "Nothing speaks like hard cold cash. Or cash equivalents."

Kelly had to laugh. "Ah, yes. As an accountant, that's music to my ears. And obviously, to the saleslady as well."

Jennifer glanced at her watch. "Uhhh, folks, I hate to interrupt this fantastic fashion show and celebration. But it's after six. If we want to have time to stop for a quick dinner, we need to get moving. Kelly said eight o'clock we had to be in the gym."

"Thanks, Jen, I lost track of time," Megan said, heading toward the bedroom. "I don't want to miss dinner. I'm starving."

"You're always starving," Kelly teased, following her friend.

"Can we stop at a place that has burgers and salads, pretty please?" Megan asked as Jennifer assisted her with the back zipper. "After all, we're playing volleyball. Lots of jumping and running around."

"I'll be in the bleachers with my laptop typing in notes on today's meeting," Jennifer said, slowly unzipping the gown. "Besides, all that jumping and running will work up quite a sweat, so I want to be downwind from all of you."

Thirteen

Steve jumped up and grabbed the basketball as it swished through the net. Pushing off, he charged down the court, moving the ball in front of him as he drove for the other basket, his opponents right behind him. Reaching the basket first, Steve pivoted and sent up the shot. Hands snatched for the ball but missed. Airborne for a split second, the basketball brushed the rim and fell through the net.

Yessss! Steve pumped his fist in the air. *Sweet,* he thought as he wiped sweat from his forehead with the back of his arm. He needed that. Oh, yeah. Nothing like a pickup game of basketball to blow off steam and stress.

"Time!" his teammate Vic called, arm in the air. "They're signaling from across the gym, guys. Gotta go and play some volleyball."

"Good game, guys. Great shot, Steve," one of the other

players called as he and another dribbled the basketball back down the court.

"Thanks," Steve mumbled, wiping his forehead against his tee shirt sleeve. Sweat dripped into his eyes. It stung, but it felt good. It felt right. *Damn,* he'd missed playing ball with the guys. He used to play pickup games back in Fort Connor regularly, but ever since he'd been in Denver, his schedule had turned upside down. Hell, his whole life had turned upside down. All he did was work—until this past week.

"Monday night? Same time?" another player asked as he grabbed some towels from a bench against the gym wall.

"Sounds good," Vic said, catching a couple of towels the guy tossed to him. Handing one to Steve, Vic clapped him on the back. "Man, you were on fire tonight, Steve. Am I glad you came on board this week. We've been mowing down the competition ever since, buddy." Tall and thin, with a hint of beard edging his chin and cheeks, Vic had a quick smile. He kind of reminded Steve of a less-crazy Marty. But then, Marty wouldn't be Marty is he wasn't half crazed.

Steve wiped the towel across his face as they walked off the court. Another pickup game was starting, and they needed to get out of the way. "Yeah, I should have joined you guys sooner. Man, I needed that, especially today."

Vic wiped his arms and draped the towel around his neck. "Yeah, those meetings are gonna kill us all. At least the mayor was funny, otherwise I would have fallen asleep."

"We're not going to have enough energy left to build anything. They're sucking us dry every week." Steve wiped his arms then draped the towel over his shoulder.

Glancing around the large gymnasium located in north

Denver, Steve observed another basketball game going on at the far end of the high-ceilinged gym. In between the two basketball courts, two volleyball courts were set up. He noticed men and women clustered around the courts, warming up. Volleyballs flew over the nets in high arcing loopy serves, rocket drives, and low, net-brushing last-gasp wobbles. One woman practiced serving the white ball. Across the net from her, another player passed the ball with her outstretched forearms, draining the serve's power and speed with her skin, then sent it arcing high to teammates.

At least those two knew what they were doing, Steve decided. Unlike the other people he saw racing around the court, hitting at but mostly missing the balls as they sailed across the net. Rockets and wounded birds. Some were shot down, others slammed to the court, untouched by human hands.

Steve watched the good, the bad, and the totally clueless race around the courts, laughing, running into one another, falling on the floor, flailing at balls, and generally having a wild and crazy time. All except the real athletes on the court. They were just trying to stay out of the crazies' way.

Gorilla ball, Steve observed to himself with a crooked smile. Injuries waiting to happen. It was inevitable. Some bozo would lunge at a ball, miss, of course, but succeed in taking out a teammate. Gorilla would be oblivious to the damage he'd inflicted; meanwhile his teammate would be lying on the floor, grasping his or her injured limb and screaming in pain. Blown-out knees, broken wrists, arms, dislocated shoulders—you name it, it would happen in one of these pickup games.

"Hey, Vic, come on over and warm up," a guy from one of the volleyball courts yelled across the gym, waving at Vic.

"I'm already warmed up," Vic called back with a laugh.

"Are you gonna play with those guys?" Steve jerked his thumb toward the volleyball wannabes. "Man, you're crazy. Most of them don't know what they're doing."

"Yeah, they do look pretty bad. But, I'm quick." He laughed, then looked at Steve. "You play volleyball? We could use you, man."

"A little, but I haven't played in a while. Besides, I don't want to get—"

Steve broke off his sentence as he stared across the gym toward the volleyball courts. Someone else appeared on the courts now. Someone he recognized. *Kelly*. Dressed in her everyday running outfit of tee shirt and shorts. She was passing the ball to another girl who . . . was that Megan? *What the hell?*

"Holy crap," Steve said softly, staring at Megan pass the volleyball to Kelly. Kelly jumped up and spiked it. Damn! What was *she* doing here?

"Steve? Hey, Steve?" Vic waved his hand in front of Steve's face. "Who are you looking at? What'd you see?"

"What . . ." Steve said, noticing Vic staring into his face.

"You kinda disappeared there for a second. You were looking at someone. It must have been a girl."

Steve's gaze was pulled back to Kelly, like a magnet toward metal. "See that tall brunette over there at the right-hand court? She's passing to the shorter girl?"

Vic followed Steve's pointing finger. "Oh, yeah. You know her, or you wanta know her?" He grinned.

"She was my girlfriend back in Fort Connor."

Vic's smile disappeared. "*Was?* What happened?"

Steve watched Kelly race over to catch a high looping pass from someone else. "I screwed up. Big time. Acted like a jackass. Let's just leave it at that."

"Hey, man, we all screw up. Go over and apologize. Make up." Vic watched Kelly for a minute. "Hell, I would if I were you."

Steve's mouth twisted. "I wish it was that simple. I walked out on her."

Vic jerked his head around. "*What?* Why'd you do that?"

Steve pointed to Kelly, who jumped after a ball, tried to spike it and missed, then bent over laughing. "Look at her. Do you think I would have walked out if I'd been in my right mind?"

Vic did as he was directed, watched Kelly racing around the court, hitting the ball. "Yeah. You had to be crazy to walk out on *her*."

"Tell me about it."

"What happened, dude?"

Steve kept watching Kelly. He couldn't turn away, even though his gut was churning. "I was losing my business in Fort Connor and . . . and everything was going down the toilet . . . and I snapped. I dunno. Went a little crazy, I guess. She said something I didn't like, and I got stupid. Walked out on her. Didn't return her calls. Nothing."

Vic stared at Steve for a minute. "Yeah, I'd say that was primo jackass. How long's it been?"

"Six months."

Vic flinched. "Ouch! Why'd you wait so long?"

Steve shrugged. "It only took a few days for me to realize that I'd acted like a jerk. But by then all my friends and family were slamming me, so I . . . I just stayed down here in Denver and focused on my job. I didn't know how to fix it. After that, I heard she was mad as hell. So, I didn't even try."

Watching Kelly snag a few balls and begin to serve, Steve noticed Dave Germaine approach her. Kelly stopped serving and talked to a smiling Germaine.

"Uh-oh. That prick Germaine is moving in on your woman. We can't have that. He's an arrogant bastard in the best of times. C'mon." Vic clapped Steve on the back and began to push him toward the volleyball court.

"Hey, what're you doing?" Steve protested, drawing back. "I'm not gonna play—"

"Yeah, you are," Vic insisted, grabbing Steve by the arm and yanking him forward. "Hey, Jim, I found another player for the team," he yelled toward his friend on the opposite side of the court Kelly and Megan were playing.

"Great, bring him along," Jim yelled, beckoning them over.

"Hey, wait a minute. . . ." Steve protested.

"We don't have a minute to lose, Steve." Vic said. "You want Germaine with your woman or not?"

Steve watched Germaine grin at Kelly. "Hell, no."

"Okay, then. Experienced player, here," Vic called out and shoved Steve in Kelly's direction. Dave Germaine had already started passing balls to another player.

Steve watched as Kelly turned around and saw him walking toward her. Kelly's eyes went wide and her mouth fell open in obvious surprise. Steve stared at her for a second, then the mule that had been kicking him in the gut these last few months suddenly switched aim. That old mule kicked him upside the head this time. Steve swore he saw stars for a split second, and then . . . something clicked into place. He blinked.

Kelly watched Steve stare at her. *What the . . . hell?* Why was *he* here? She walked up closer. Close enough to smell the sweat. Steve's sweat. Something tugged at her inside. Old memories. Making love after a late morning weekend workout, sweaty and . . . and . . . *stop it!*

"What are *you* doing here?" she blurted.

Instead of going mute or hesitating, Steve shot back. "The same thing you're doing here. Playing ball."

Steve was smiling at her now, that old, familiar, easygoing smile of his.

Damn! What was he doing here? Looking all relaxed like he used to after he'd come back from a game, all sweaty and sexy at the same time. *What the . . . hell?*

Dave walked up and waved his arms, calling out. "Okay, everybody line up. Women, divide up on each side. Gotta spread you around because all of us guys need a lot of help."

Laughing comments bounced around the court like volleyballs. Dave put his hand on Kelly's shoulder. "Kelly, why don't you play middle blocker? You're tall and can block some shots."

"You hope," Kelly retorted, breaking away from the surprise encounter with Steve. This was too much. Two times in one day. Too much aggravation. Way too much.

"Hey, Steve," Megan said, walking up to him, grinning from ear to ear. "Good to see you. Gonna play with us?"

"Oh, no, he's gonna play on our side," Vic demanded, yanking up the net and beckoning Steve under. "We need a good middle blocker, too. Dude, you can play, right?" Vic teased.

Steve grinned. "We'll find out." Then he ducked under the net and joined Vic and the other players.

I don't believe this. Kelly groaned inwardly. *Right across from me. Damn!* She needed a donut. Where was sugar when you needed it?

"Hey, Dave, where can I play?" A big, hulking guy in long rapper shorts and a faded Ohio State tee shirt lumbered onto the court. Tall and muscle-bound, the guy wasn't fat, just bulky. Kelly had seen lots of guys like him in gyms and on the field over the years. Some were good athletes. Others used enthusiasm to compensate for their lack of skill. Two hundred pounds or more of uncoordinated muscle mass randomly moving, jerking, and getting in everyone else's way. Unguided missiles on the court.

"Hey, Bubba, how're you doing?" Dave said with his ingratiating smile. "Why, don't you play right here on the front line. See if you can block some shots. Watch Kelly."

"Got it," Bubba said, giving a toothy grin to Kelly.

Kelly gave him a wan smile. *Great.* Steve right across from her. Not silent, tongue-tied, hesitating Steve, but the old Steve. Steve who gave back whatever she sent him. Bantering Steve. Stress-free Steve. The Steve she used to know. The one she fell in love with.

And to her right, Bubba. He was probably a great guy, a magnificent human being, good at his job, kind to his mother and animals, but on the court . . . any court . . . a total disaster. Wreaking havoc instead of play.

Fantastic. A sexy ex-lover right in her face and a gorilla on her flank. Tonight was just getting better and better.

"Hey, Steve, we're gonna whip your butts," Megan threatened from the back row.

Steve grinned. "You the setter, Megan?" He turned to his teammates. "We're in trouble, guys."

More good-natured bantering followed until a girl came up and volunteered to referee. She tossed a ball to the server on Steve's side of the net, and the game began. Kelly settled into game mode.

The volleyball arced high over the net, dropping toward the back court. Megan positioned herself right beneath the descending ball. *"Mine!"* she called and passed the ball perfectly for someone to hit it. The guy beside Megan hit the ball and it sailed across the net.

"Got it," Vic called and whacked the ball into the net.

"No, you don't," a guy behind Kelly yelled, and they all laughed.

The front line shifted, and Megan dropped back to serve. The ball flew across the net hard and fast, obviously surprising the other team when it smashed into the floor, inside the line. Point for Dave's team.

Kelly and her teammates yelled in triumph, while Vic's team yelled catcalls. Play resumed as the volleyball flew across the net back and forth. Impossible saves kept the ball from touching the court. Back and forth. Kelly got several good hits, which felt good. Steve got three. She couldn't believe she was keeping count.

"Mine!" Bubba yelled as the ball came flying over the net in Kelly's direction. Spotting Bubba's movement from the corner of her eye, Kelly jumped out of the way as Bubba came crashing toward her. Missing the ball, of course. Gorilla ball at its finest.

"*Watch it!*" Kelly warned Bubba as he got up off the floor where he'd fallen in his lunge. "You nearly took me out!"

"Sorry. I was going for the ball," Bubba mumbled, not looking the least bit contrite.

This time it was Kelly's turn to serve, and she took a deep breath. She hoped she could send up a rocket like Megan. She could knock a baseball outta the park. She oughta be able to knock this one out. Not out, but right inside the line. Like in tennis, too much power could work against you. *Pull it in. pull it in,* Kelly reminded herself.

She tossed the ball up into the air with her left hand as she swung her right arm back and *wham*! The ball shot across the net. Just like one of Megan's rockets. The other team bobbled it, and the ball hit the floor.

More jubilation and taunts from Dave's side were greeted with jeers from Vic's team.

"We gotta step it up, guys," Vic warned beside Steve.

The volleyball flew back and forth again, Vic, Steve, Dave, Kelly, and Megan digging, setting, and spiking. Wounded birds were shot down. *Wham!* High drooping arcs had a greedy Megan under them like a crocodile waiting with open jaws for a wounded bird to drop inside. Pass, set, over the net. Volleys going back and forth, again and again.

Every now and again, Kelly had to jump out of the way of a lunging Bubba. She'd scowl and warn him, but Bubba seemed oblivious. He'd behave for a couple of returns then, bump into Kelly, or leap in front of her and totally screw up a shot she could have returned easily. Kelly was losing patience.

Bubba's efforts brought a great deal of hilarity from Vic and Steve's side of the net. The score was evening up now.

Kelly faced off with Steve once again. He grinned at her. Kelly just stared at him. Did he wink?

The other team's serve sailed over and was passed back and forth, then Megan sent a hard shot sailing low across the net. Steve's arms shot up and blocked the shot, sending the ball right into Kelly's face. *Hard.*

Kelly staggered back. The ball dropped to the floor. Score for the other side, who were all jumping up and down.

Kelly shook her head to clear it, then looked across the net at Steve. He'd stuffed her. *Damn!* She scowled at him. Instead of looking contrite, Steve grinned at her, then winked. Again.

"Oh, no, you didn't!" Kelly accused, hands on hips.

"Yeah, I did," Steve teased, grinning wider.

Kelly couldn't believe it. He was taunting her.

"Careful, Steve," Megan called from the back of the court. "You don't want to make her mad. You know what happens."

"What happens?" Dave asked Megan.

"You don't wanna know," Megan said, grinning wide. "Trust me."

Kelly pointed at Steve. "Coming back at ya," she warned.

Steve's grin got as wide as Megan's. "Bring it," he said, giving a "come on" gesture with both hands.

Kelly couldn't believe it. Steve was laughing and teasing her like nothing had happened. Like he hadn't walked out on her six months ago. Like . . . like . . . he hadn't been a total *jackass*! Her eyes narrowed on Steve, framing him in her sights. That did it. She was taking him out.

Unfortunately, someone else got in her way first. Vic hit the ball, and it flew through the air, low and fast, about two feet above the net. Perfect. Kelly was just about to jump up and spike the ball right in Steve's grinning face when a moving mass appeared in the corner of her eye.

Bubba. Lunging toward the ball—and her. Kelly's quick reflexes sent her jumping backward just in time to avoid being knocked down by the unguided missile. But Bubba's arm whacked into her shin as he crashed into the floor—once again.

"Yeow!" Kelly yelled. She rubbed the welt that was forming on her shin already. Right on the bone. A contusion for sure. Bruised bone.

"Take it easy, Bubba," Dave warned. "You're gonna hurt someone."

"Okay, okay," Bubba said automatically as he pulled himself from the floor and walked back to his position. Clearly, not about to change his behavior, no matter the consequences.

Not so fast, Kelly thought as she watched Bubba return to her flank. Time to take action. Bubba had made his last lunge.

She walked up to him and grabbed Bubba's sweat-drenched tee shirt, then yanked him toward her. "Hey, *Godzilla!*" Kelly yelled right in his face. "You get near me one more time, and I swear I'm gonna go to my car, get my Louisville Slugger, and break both your knees! *Got that?* Now, get outta my face and off my flank!" She shoved Bubba back so hard he staggered. Meanwhile, both sides of the court erupted in shouts and laughter.

"Whoa!"

"About time!"

"I warned you not to make her mad!"

"Go, Kelly!"

"Tell him, girlfriend!"

"Careful, Bubba!"

Kelly saw Steve bent over, laughing. She turned to Dave, who was wiping his eyes. "Get him outta my sight, Dave. I meant what I said."

"I'll take care of him, Kelly," Megan said, pointing to a stunned-looking Bubba. "*Yo, Bubba!* Get your butt over here with me." She jerked her thumb toward the back line.

"Okay," Bubba said and meekly trudged to the back court beside Megan.

Megan pointed at him and—in her loudest on-the-field manager voice—commanded, "I don't wanta see you move off that back line, you hear? You're looking at the back of our shirts, got it? If I see you move up, Kelly won't have to get her bat. I'll break your knees with my bare hands. Are we clear?"

Bubba just stared back at the shorter version of Kelly, barking orders up at him. He had no response. He looked too stunned to speak.

"Are we clear!" Megan bellowed as she moved closer, hands on hips.

Kelly had to smile at Megan's imitation of a famous movie marine general barking the same line of dialogue. Meanwhile, the rest of the players on both sides of the court were trying not to laugh out loud and not succeeding. Steve was bent over again, both hands on his knees this time, he was laughing so hard. Old memories floated back to tease her. Kelly grasped at them, then let them slip away. She had work to do. She had a game to win. And a score to settle.

"All right! All right! We're *clear*! Damn, Dave! Where'd you find these women? They're meaner than junkyard dogs!"

Kelly laughed out loud. Steve wiped both his eyes and looked across the net at her. "I got a feeling I'm next on your list."

"You got that right," Kelly said, trying not to smile.

"Junkyard dogs. I like it," Megan called. "Let's play ball."

"You got it," Vic called out, signaling the server at the back of their court.

The volleyball flew back and forth across the net as both teams settled down into the rhythm of play once again. Pass, set, hit, back and forth. Over the net, again and again. Serves smashing into the floor. Shots blocked. Kelly blocked and spiked everything she could reach. Some smashed to the floor in winning shots. Jumping higher and higher. Her shin would throb later. She didn't care. She'd learned to play with pain years ago.

Another shot sailed toward her side of the net, coming fast. It looked a little too high for her to spike. But just as it approached the break line it started its downward arc, just a little. It was just enough. Enough to encourage Kelly to push off from the floor straight up, higher than before, her arm swinging back and up, then coming down—hammer-like—hard and fast.

Blam! Steve's arms went up to block her shot, but it was too late. She spiked the ball right into his face. *Hard.* Steve rocked backward and stumbled.

Kelly's teammates hooted in laughter, while the other players tried not to, unsuccessfully. Vic came over as Steve regained his balance.

"You okay, buddy?" Vic asked, smiling. "She really rang your bell with that one."

"Ohhhh, yeah." Steve said, shaking his head.

Kelly watched Steve shake his head again, then turn to her and smile. His old, familiar, good-natured smile. She couldn't believe it.

"You enjoyed that, didn't you?" he called across the net.

Kelly smiled back at him. "Ohhhh, yeah."

That felt good. *Real* good.

Steve took the towel Vic handed him and wiped his face as he watched Kelly, Megan, and Jennifer walk toward the gymnasium doorway. Jennifer turned around right before the doorway and waved at him. Megan, however, turned and grinned wide and gave Steve an enthusiastic thumbs-up sign. Kelly never turned around.

Vic clapped Steve on the shoulder. "Man, she's a wildcat. You sure you want her back?" he teased.

"Ohhhh, yeah," Steve said, feeling a rush he hadn't felt in months course through his veins. "If she'll have me."

"Well, you've got a shot. That spark is still there, dude. You can tell. If it wasn't, she wouldn't have gotten so mad." Vic laughed.

Steve joined in. Vic was right. If Kelly was mad at him, it meant she still cared enough to be mad. Mad, he could deal with. He'd been afraid she'd just written him off as a total jerk. "I hope you're right."

"Megan, I can tell you're grinning. Stop it now before we get in the car," Kelly warned, only halfway serious. Her shin throbbed in pain from all the hard impacts. It needed ice, ice, and more ice. Every thirty minutes. And she needed hot water to soak in. Jacuzzi tub. Tiny jets of water massaging away tight muscles and pulled tendons. Aches and pains. Massaging away stress. Massaging away Steve.

"I'll try, but my face won't cooperate," Megan said, still grinning from ear to ear.

"I'll put a bag over her head, Kelly. You drive. Megan can grin under the bag in the backseat," Jennifer said.

"I don't want to hear teasing tonight. My shin hurts like hell, and I want to relax in that Jacuzzi. How about some wine?"

"Oooo, sounds good," Megan said. "And some food. We can order something. My treat."

"She's hungry again. I don't believe it," Jennifer said as they entered the women's locker room. "I'll order some wine. I've noticed the hotel has a nice wine list. How about a Pinot Noir? Pete and I have tasted some good ones lately."

"Order whatever you want. Let's get back to the hotel and that Jacuzzi," Kelly said, inserting the key into the locker that held their warm-up sweats and purses.

"You got it, chief," Megan gave a salute. "Food, wine, and Jacuzzi coming up. Why don't you relax in the back, and I'll drive us home while Jennifer orders room service."

Kelly pulled on her sweats. Room service. That sounded good. So did the Pinot Noir. She sensed she'd need the Jacuzzi *and* red wine to get to sleep tonight. Too much aggravation for one day. Way too much.

Fourteen

Kelly merged from the interstate exit lane into traffic flow-
ing on a major thoroughfare in northeastern Denver. A huge
exhibition building lay up ahead. Kelly joined the line of cars
turning into the exhibition center's vast parking lot, which
looked packed already. After ten minutes of winding through
rows of parked cars, Kelly found someone backing out and
quickly claimed it.

Another sunny Colorado day beckoned, tempting Kelly
to grab the mild temperatures while they lasted and take a
hike through the Poudre Canyon. Kelly resisted. Not today.
Today was for research, she reminded herself and shoved her
keys, money, and a folded paper into her jeans pockets, then
headed for the exhibition hall's front entrance.

Kelly was amazed at the steady stream of people entering
the exhibition hall. The filled parking lot indicated that hun-
dreds of people were already inside the huge building. Both

men and women of all ages were walking toward the banks of glass entry doors. Couples pushing baby strollers, children in tow. A large banner stretched above the doors announcing GUN SHOW. NATION'S LARGEST. OVER 1,000 DISPLAYS.

Pushing through the doors, Kelly paid her admission to a man wearing a Colorado Rockies baseball hat and entered the huge hall. Only to be stopped within a few feet by a woman who checked her admission ticket and inquired if she was carrying any firearm, warning that no loaded weapons were allowed within the building.

The immense building was packed. Every aisle was filled with people and vendors. Kelly scanned the hall from side to side, trying to estimate the number of aisles. Fifteen? It was hard to tell because of the number of people browsing, standing, and talking. Observing the crowd, it reminded Kelly of the Camping and RV show she had attended with Mimi and Burt last fall.

Merging into the crowds, Kelly scanned the green-cloth-draped display tables. Firearms of every description lay spread out on the tables, mounted on wooden stands, or locked inside glass cases. Rifles and handguns, camouflage hunting clothes, backpacks, hunting scopes for rifles, canteens, camping gear.

Kelly walked slowly through the aisles, trying to check the tables on each side as she went. The woman at the entrance said dealers in antique firearms were scattered throughout the hall. Spotting an old-fashioned rifle laying between the modern hunting models, Kelly examined the well-preserved piece. An 1877 Springfield, the card read. She looked for more old weapons, pistols or revolvers, but didn't see any and moved on.

Finishing that aisle, Kelly turned into another and immediately spotted another old rifle displayed amongst the modern Browning deer-hunting models. Kelly leaned over the table and admired the older rifle's gleaming wooden stock and long metallic barrel. An 1895 German hunting rifle, the card read. In excellent condition, she noticed. Farther down the table was a "European" 1842 rifle with bayonet attached. Amazingly, there was only a little bit of rust visible.

Beside it lay an antique sword with a hand-carved ivory handle labeled *The Seige of Vienna, 1683*. Kelly marveled at the sword's good condition, considering its age. Next to it was an English cutlass, dated 1804. Its inscription read: *Death to the French!* Right beside the cutlass was a collection of engravings of the French Revolution. Farther down was a 1906 U.S. Cavalry saber. And beside that was another sword labeled *The Mexican War, 1830s*.

Fascinated by the historical displays, Kelly glanced around for more vintage firearms. In the next aisle, she spotted some revolvers mounted on a red velvet display stand. At last, she thought, and waited her turn to examine them. The couple ahead of her took their time, commenting on antique weapons. Kelly noticed this vendor's displays stretched to three adjacent tables. Maybe she'd found the mother lode.

She approached the display and scanned the antique handguns. All of them were revolvers, not pistols. The gun Fred Turner had was a pistol, which used a magazine to hold cartridges that slid into the handle. Revolvers had a cylindrical chamber with bullets and were easily recognized as the guns that "cowboys" used. Unable to see the adjacent table, Kelly observed the revolvers displayed. Colt .45s and Colt .44s from the 1870s. Another from 1892. All were in excellent condition, she noticed, metal barrels gleaming, some of the handles carved in ivory.

Peering down to the next table, she saw modern carbine rifles as well as more modern handguns. Glancing around, she spotted the vendor still talking with that couple. Kelly approached and positioned herself right behind the couple who was describing their own antique gun collection to the attentive dealer. Once the couple turned to walk away, Kelly gave the vendor a bright smile.

"You've got a beautiful collection of antique firearms here," she complimented, gesturing down the tables.

"Thank you," the older man replied, then took a sip from his coffee cup.

Kelly recognized the logo of a gourmet coffee franchise and her caffeine lobe woke up from its crowd-induced slumber. Later, she thought. "I was wondering if you carried any pistols from World War Two."

"Sorry, I don't have any at the moment. Were you looking for a particular model?" he asked, clearly interested.

Digging into her back jeans pocket, Kelly withdrew a folded printout of the photo she'd taken at Fred Turner's cabin. "I'm trying to find a pistol like this one. We're looking to buy one for my father's sixty-fifth birthday." Kelly had chosen a convenient and easy fictional explanation to explain today's search.

The vendor scrutinized the photo, eyebrows furrowing. "Whose hand is that?"

"My uncle's," Kelly continued breezily. "He thought it would give perspective."

"Hmmmm, looks kind of like one of the German pistols, maybe a Mauser. Who's gun is this? Your uncle's?"

"Yes, it is. But his memory has deteriorated a lot and he can't remember much anymore." Kelly shrugged. "Anyway, my dad always wanted a pistol like my uncle Bob's. I was hoping to find one at this show. Do you have any idea who carries guns like this? This exhibition is huge, I don't know where to begin."

The vendor handed the photo printout back to Kelly. "I think John Bridger may have some Mausers along with his antique pistols." He pointed out into the sea of tables and the tide of people moving past them. "I'm not sure, but I think his table is somewhere over there, a few aisles from the other wall."

Kelly glanced out into the morass of people, filling the aisles, and sighed inwardly. "Hey, thanks, I appreciate it," she said as she stuffed the photo into her pocket. Merging back into the crowds again, Kelly made note of which aisles she'd covered, then skipped the next five, aiming for the other half of the hall.

Entering an aisle, Kelly moved faster since she didn't find any tables with antique weapons. She did see several tables of Native American turquoise jewelry and hand-carved belts next to another table filled with intricate beading comparable to what she had seen at fiber arts shows.

Coming to the end of that aisle, Kelly was about to start the next when she spotted the gourmet coffee franchise and hastened over. She needed caffeine for this time-consuming task. While she waited in line for the strong coffee, Kelly sniffed a delectable aroma. Glancing down the row of food vendors, she saw the barbeque signs. And noticed all the people sitting at tables in the food court area, enjoying barbeque, fries, corn dogs, salads, and ice cream. Kelly's stomach growled. Trying to be good, Kelly didn't give in to the cookies that sat beside the coffee register. Caffeine would have to fill her up for now. She had work to do. After she'd talked to that last dealer, she'd reward herself with a barbeque sandwich. Trying to ignore the others munching happily away, Kelly rejoined the throngs in the aisles.

Table after table of hunting rifles, scopes, handguns small and handguns large, handguns that would do Dirty Harry proud. Interspersed with tables of books. Books on guns. War histories. Biographies. Soldiers' diaries. There were even tables displaying soldiers' uniforms from past wars—World War One and Two. American uniforms. British uniforms. French uniforms. German uniforms. Japanese uniforms. Even Vietnamese uniforms. Next to that were several tables of hunting equipment, which Kelly sped by, until something caught her eye. An LED pocket light. She'd been looking for one exactly like that. Glad she'd brought her credit card with her along with some cash, Kelly paid for it and quickly returned to her search.

Another aisle, then another. More guns. More rifles. More books. And in between, a beautiful display of silk scarves. Kelly had to examine the fibers and recognized the work of some of the same vendors who had scarf displays at the fiber arts shows. Fascinating, she thought, as she continued on, slowing for a display of family wartime photos. Turning into another aisle, she passed by a table of crystal jewelry, then she spotted something up ahead. Once the crowd moved along, Kelly saw two curved antique pistols in a glass case.

Glancing down the vendor's table, she glimpsed more pistols. At last, she exulted, noticing the vendor's name displayed above the table. JOHN BRIDGER, ANTIQUE FIREARMS, it proclaimed. And rightly so, Kelly decided, admiring the dueling pistols displayed in locked cases. Antique Flintlock pistols. Another pistol from the American Revolution, circa 1780s, the display read. Pistols that Kelly had only seen pictured in Hollywood movies.

Marveling at the beautiful condition of the pieces, Kelly inched her way down the table. She saw several pistols displayed that resembled the one in the photo. Drawing closer at last, Kelly was able to lean over the table and scrutinize the vintage weapons laying there. The vendor was absorbed in conversation with another customer.

There were three rows of older pistols. Kelly looked at each, noticing the way the barrel looked, the handle. Then, she spotted it. A pistol that looked like the one in her photo. She approached that row and scrutinized the pistol, feeling her pulse race. That looks just like it, she thought, digging out the photo from her back pocket again.

She examined the photo, then the pistol on the table, then the photo. It was a match. Or, as close a match as she had found so far.

"May I help you, miss?" the older, gray-haired vendor asked with a friendly smile.

"Yes, yes, you can." Kelly returned his smile. "I'm trying to match this photo with a pistol, and I think I've found it. I didn't know what kind it was, but it must be this one." She pointed to the pistol on the table below. "The photo looks just like this German Mauser you've got here. What do you think?" She handed the photo to the vendor.

The older man examined the photo and nodded. "Yep. That's a Mauser, all right. Where'd you get this photo?"

"Off the Internet," Kelly lied again. She had a selection of plausible explanations available, depending on the questioner. She sensed this vendor might not buy her memory-deficient uncle story.

The vendor peered at her. "Whose hand is that?"

"I dunno. Some guy on the Web," she gave a dismissive wave. "I'm just trying to find a real German World War Two pistol for my uncle Harold. He's a real history buff, and he's getting kind of old. He fought in the war."

The man handed the photo back to Kelly. "Did you want to purchase the pistol yourself?"

Kelly shrugged. "I wish I could. Uncle Harold will have to buy it. I don't think I have the money." She pointed at the seven-hundred-dollar price tag on the German Mauser.

He smiled. "Actually, a gentleman told me he's planning on buying that pistol today, so it won't be available. He's building a collection."

"Do many people buy these pistols? They're kind of pricey."

"Collectors, mostly. But some people buy them from family estates. Our soldiers brought the pistols home from Europe after the war." He reached into his shirt pocket. "Take my card and give it to your uncle. He can check out my website online and contact me. If he's interested in purchasing a Mauser like that one, I can let him know when I've got one in stock. Then, we can set up an appointment. Of course, I live in another state, so he'll have to travel or wait for another gun show to come into town. But there's no guarantee a Mauser like that would be available. They're beautiful pieces." He handed her a card.

"Yes, they are." Kelly glanced at the card. "Tell me, Mr. Bridger, where do you get most of these pistols? Do people come in and sell them to you? Do you go to estate sales or something?"

"We mostly obtain these vintage pieces from private collectors. Tell your uncle I'd be happy to give him the name of a couple of other vendors who carry vintage weapons who might have one available. He can e-mail me."

Kelly examined his card. He lived in New England. "Thanks. I'll e-mail you tonight, if it's okay. My uncle doesn't go on the web." She smiled and extended her hand. "Thanks again for your help, Mr. Bridger. I really appeciate it."

"Glad to help, miss," Bridger said, returning her firm handshake.

"Mind if I take a photo of the Mauser?" Kelly thought to ask.

"You can, but I've got better photos online at my website," he said before turning to another customer.

Perfect, Kelly thought. That way, she could find out where some of those other pistols came from and maybe where they wound up. But first, hunger pangs had to be satisfied. Her coffee had run out two aisles ago, and the barbeque beckoned.

Kelly merged her car into the interstate highway traffic heading north from Denver. Since it was Saturday midafternoon and no rush hour, she should be back in Fort Connor in an hour. That should give her enough time for a short run on the river trail before she went to dinner with Curt and Jayleen.

Her cell phone's music sounded on the seat beside her. A

classic rock song, loud guitars. Staying in the right-hand lane, Kelly slowed her speed a bit and reached for her phone. Steve's number flashed on the screen. Startled, Kelly clicked on. "Hello?" she said cautiously.

"Hi. Did I get you at a bad time?" Steve's voice was deep and warm. The sound of it brought back a truckload of memories. Kelly felt her stomach twist.

"Uhhhh, no . . . I'm driving, that's all." Pausing for a second she asked, "What's up?" She hadn't expected to hear from him.

"I just called to say I'm sorry I stuffed you last night in the game."

Kelly could hear the smile in his voice, and more memories loosened from the back of her mind. She found herself smiling in response. "That's okay. I got you back."

"Yeah, you did." Steve laughed low on the other end. "You really rang it. You been working out more?"

"Way more. Lots of free weights."

"I could tell. Which gym are you going to?"

"The new one that opened up in the middle of town. It's open early in the morning till late at night. Good hours." She set the car's cruise control so she didn't have to worry about her speed.

Steve went silent on the other end. Kelly waited for him to say something. It felt so strange to talk like they used to on the phone. Six months ago. It felt awkward . . . and good, at the same time.

Finally, Steve's voice came again, low and soft. This time, Kelly heard sadness.

"Kelly . . . I'm so sorry for walking out on you like that. I know I hurt you. Bad. I . . . I didn't mean to hurt you,

Kelly, I swear I didn't. I . . . I just lost it. Went a little crazy, I don't know. I was losing everything, and I . . . I panicked . . . and I lost you . . . and everything we had."

Kelly held the line, letting the silence fill the space. She didn't know what to say. She hadn't expected this. Last night, Steve had laughed and joked. And this phone call started the same way. Joking, Kelly could handle. But suddenly Steve had turned serious. Kelly wasn't prepared for serious.

"Kelly? Are you still there?"

"Yeah . . . I'm still here," she said softly.

"I just wanted to tell you that. I didn't want you to keep thinking I was a jackass. And . . . and I'm sorry it took me so long to apologize. I . . . I wanted to. I just didn't know if you'd hear me out. I figured you'd hang up on me. But after last night, I thought I'd give it a shot."

"I'm glad you did," Kelly said quietly. "Apology accepted." She'd added that without thinking and realized she meant it. The past was over. They were in new territory now.

"Thank you."

"You're welcome." Kelly waited, wondering what Steve would say next. Now that the elephant in the room had been dealt with at last. She considered sharing some of her own feelings, but wasn't sure how to start.

After a few more seconds of silence, Steve said, "Are you driving back into Fort Connor? I thought you'd be there by now."

General questions. Familiar territory. "Megan and Jen went back this morning. But I stayed and went to a gun show at the Northeast Convention Center."

Steve waited before answering. "A gun show, huh? Should I be worried?"

Taken aback by his quip, Kelly laughed without thinking. "Not really. I didn't go to buy anything. I went to ask questions from some of the dealers there. One of Jennifer's clients was shot in the house he had for sale in Poudre Canyon. Jennifer and I actually walked in and found him dead. I took some cell phone photos of the gun because it looked really old, and I was curious why someone would kill the guy with a collector's piece."

Steve paused again, then Kelly heard his low chuckle. "Sleuthing, right?"

Kelly heard the smile in his voice and relaxed. "Well, Jayleen's friend Renee is the chief suspect, so Jayleen asked me if I could find out stuff in Denver. You know."

He laughed softly. "Yeah, I know. Well, good luck finding the bad guys, Kelly."

Surprised by his mellow reaction, Kelly replied. "Thanks, but I'm not sure who the bad guy or girl is. It may be Jayleen's friend."

"You'll figure it out." Steve paused for a second. "It feels really good talking to you, Kelly. Like this, I mean. Regular, you know."

"Yeah, I know," Kelly replied quietly. She agreed. It had felt good. Like old times. She and Steve used to talk about everything. Up until, well, the bad times. Then, Steve stopped talking.

"I've missed that," Steve said.

"So have I," Kelly let slip. It was out of her mouth before she knew it. But it was true. She *had* missed talking to Steve.

"Take care of yourself, Kelly. Bye now," Steve said, then clicked off. He was gone.

Disappointed that the call had ended, Kelly clicked off

her phone and tossed it to the seat. Then, she hit the accelerator and sped toward Fort Connor and home.

"**Hey,** buddy!" Greg's voice came over Steve's phone. "Are you coming into Fort Connor this weekend? Megan's bouncing off the walls, she's so excited. She's convinced you two are gonna get back together."

"Let's just say there's a chance," Steve said, nosing his car around the corner of Fort Connor's main north-south thoroughfare, College Avenue. "I didn't think I had a prayer before last night. Every time I talked to her at those meetings, she was all business. I thought I was dead for sure. But last night . . ." Steve smiled to himself in the car. "Well, last night I saw a spark. So, maybe I've still got a shot. But I've gotta move slowly. Carefully. I don't want Kelly to take me back. I want her to *want* me back."

"Careful, huh? Well, I heard you stuffed her last night. That doesn't sound careful to me." Greg hooted. "How'd she take it?"

"Let's just say it got her attention," Steve said with a laugh.

"Listen, you gotta come over and give us a play-by-play. Megan cracks up every time she talks about it. And who is Bubba?"

Steve laughed out loud. "Bubba is a clueless gorilla who had the bad luck to get in Kelly's way when she was trying to block shots. I'd just stuffed her, so Kelly grabbed him by the shirt and threatened to break both his knees with her bat. Poor old Bubba didn't know what he was dealing with."

Greg cackled loudly. "Oh, man, what I would have given to see that. When can you come back into town?"

"Actually I'm in town now. I promised my mom and dad I'd come for dinner. Why don't I drop over to your place later tonight?"

"Great. I'll round up everybody. We want a play-by-play for sure."

"The funniest thing was Megan channeling her inner Jack Nicholson." Steve laughed out loud. "Damn! I nearly split a gut laughing."

"Okay, this I gotta hear. Come on over as soon as you can, buddy. We'll be waiting for you."

Fifteen

"Here you go, Carl," Kelly said, placing Carl's refilled water dish on the patio. Carl, however, was far more interested in watching the movements of two chattering mountain jays who were fussing on a branch of the nearby cottonwood tree. Monday morning had brought warmer temperatures along with the bright Colorado sun. Kelly didn't need her winter jacket when she ran on the river trail earlier.

Golfers were out on the course despite patches of snow. Most of the snow had melted already, but the green closest to Kelly's cottage was shaded by huge cottonwood trees and was still snow covered. White golf balls were hard to find in white snow. Colorado golfers were a hardy lot.

Sliding the patio glass door shut, Kelly reached for the smartphone on her desk. She checked her watch and flipped through her directory for Arthur Housemann's office number. After hearing from Jennifer that Renee Turner had told

Housemann's real estate agent about her willingness to sell the canyon property, Kelly was curious what Housemann would do. Had he said anything at the office? Secretary Doris answered after two rings.

"Housemann Properties," Doris answered.

"Hi, Doris. It's Kelly. How are you?"

"I'm quite well, Kelly," Doris's cheerful voice replied. "If you want to speak with Mr. Housemann, I'll have to take a message. He's in his office with that historical writer, Mr. Eustace Freemont, right now."

Kelly retrieved her coffee mug from the kitchen counter. "Oh, I'm so glad they finally had a chance to get together. I know Eustace wanted to interview Arthur." She took a sip.

"Well, Mr. Housemann found some time in today's schedule, so he squeezed Mr. Freemont in. I must say he's a delightful person. Quite a storyteller."

"Yes, he is. He entertained Curt and Jayleen and me at dinner the other night. Tell me, Doris," Kelly switched subjects to the one she'd really called about. "Do you recall if Arthur has mentioned the canyon property anymore? Has he given up on buying it?"

"I don't recall his saying anything? Why do you ask?"

Kelly fished around for the most likely sounding lie she could think of. "I was with a group of people this past weekend and one of then was a real estate agent. She mentioned she'd heard that Fred Turner's wife, Renee, indicated she would sell the property if someone was interested. I immediately thought of Arthur. I mean, he told me how much he loved the land up there. Maybe there's a way for the sale to go through after all."

"Hmmmph. I wouldn't put much faith in anything that woman says," Doris said in a cold voice.

Her response surprised Kelly. "You mean the real estate agent? I don't even remember her name—"

"No, I mean Renee Turner." Doris cut her off in uncharacteristic fashion. "I wouldn't believe a word she says. Excuse me, Kelly, there's another call coming in. Do you want to leave a message?"

"No, no, that's all right. Good-bye, Doris," Kelly said, then heard Doris click off.

That was a surprise, Kelly thought. *What was up with Doris?* That was so out of character for the mild-mannered secretary. Clearly, Doris didn't care for Renee Turner.

Kelly shoved her phone in her jeans pocket, grabbed her briefcase and knitting bag, and headed out her front door. Today would be a good day to work at the shop. She could set up in the café, then take knitting breaks. She could use some relaxation after the past weekend.

A brisk breeze whipped her hair into her face, and Kelly hurried across the driveway and into the melted garden behind the café. Snow still lay in clumps and layers in the shadier sections of the garden, while it had melted away in the open sunny areas. The flagstone path that wound through greenery was mostly clear.

Another blast of chilly breeze caused her to shiver in her thick red knitted sweater. This was the warmest one she had. Kelly raced up the wooden front steps to the café, wishing she'd worn her jacket. Old Man Winter wasn't ready to leave yet.

The warmth of Pete's café enveloped her the moment

Kelly stepped inside. Along with the enticing breakfast aromas. She would be good this time, she vowed, as she waved at Julie. "Is this table free?" Kelly asked, spotting one of her favorite spots to work. A smaller table sat right beside a window with a view of the garden and the foothills, the Rockies glistening white behind them.

"It's got your name on it, Kelly," Julie said as she brought a mug and coffeepot over. "Here you go. Would you like breakfast?" she asked as she poured Eduardo's brew into the tall mug.

"Some fruit would be nice, thanks," Kelly said as she dropped her briefcase and bag on the adjoining chair. Settling into the cozy spot by the window, Kelly took a deep drink of coffee. *Ahhhh.* She was ready for those accounts.

"Hey, Kelly, I was getting ready to call you," Burt said as he walked over to her table. "I'm glad I spotted you. Do you have a few minutes?"

Kelly gave him a grin. "For you, Burt, anytime."

Burt sat in the chair across from her and placed his coffee mug in front of him. Kelly sensed he had information to share, and she shoved the encroaching financial accounts back into a corner of her mind.

"I wanted to update you on what's happened since I told Paul about Jennifer's phone call the other day. I had a call from him late Sunday."

"Did Peterson's men question Housemann's real estate agent? Did she confirm what she told Jennifer?"

Burt nodded. "Yes, she did, and Peterson and my friend Paul went over to question Renee Turner again. They didn't call her, they simply showed up on her doorstep yesterday."

Kelly remembered Renee Turner saying her attorney had

advised her not to speak to the police without him being present. "I'll bet she told them to come back when she had her lawyer. I remember Renee talked to Jayleen and me right after she'd been to her attorney's office."

"As a matter of fact, she didn't send them away," Burt said, then took a sip of his coffee. "Paul said she looked very nervous, but when Peterson told her they knew she'd made the offer to sell the canyon property right after her husband's death, she looked kind of scared. That's when she started talking."

Kelly sipped the dark brew. "That wasn't smart. It sounds like Renee needs all the protections an attorney can give. Did she admit making the offer?"

"Absolutely. But then, it got interesting. Peterson started asking her about Arthur Housemann and how she knew him. And Renee started acting nervous and began to pace around her living room." Burt cradled his coffee mug in both his hands. "Apparently Peterson had heard from someone he'd interviewed that Renee Turner and Arthur Housemann had an affair years ago." He paused, obviously waiting for Kelly's reaction. It came swiftly.

Her eyes popped wide. "*What?* You're kidding!" She hadn't expected that.

"Nope. Apparently Peterson heard the rumor from several different people in northern Colorado."

"Did Renee admit it?"

"Not at first, according to Paul. But you know Peterson. He kept on circling around and around Renee Turner and asking her more questions and giving out more details from the other sources, and finally she admitted it. Paul said she put her head in her hand and started to cry."

"Oh, brother. Not good."

"That's probably why Peterson went to interview House-mann the first time. He wanted to get a read on him in person. Now, it looks like Renee wanted to get control of the land so she could sell it to her old lover."

"She's looking guiltier and guiltier, isn't she?" Kelly shook her head. "I have to say she's a convincing liar then. She had me giving her the benefit of the doubt after I met her here in the café with Jayleen."

Burt took a long drink of coffee before answering. "Well, she may be telling the truth after all. Because this investigation has gotten more complicated."

"What? Have you interviewed Housemann yet? What did he say?"

"They'll be questioning Arthur Housemann very soon, I promise. Now they have a reason other than an old lover connection." Burt gave a little smile but didn't say anything else.

Her curiosity about to burst, Kelly prodded. "What is it, Burt? You're teasing me deliberately, I can tell. Tell me. You know I have zero patience."

Burt chuckled. "Sorry, Kelly. I couldn't resist. Peterson planned to question Housemann simply to verify his former relationship with Renee Turner. But then, Deputy Don reported in. You remember I told you Deputy Don was going to ask Turner's recluse neighbor some more questions."

"Oh, yeah. Benjamin Shaggy Hair. What did Deputy Don find out? He's a really good cop."

"You bet he is. Apparently Don called Peterson late yesterday and told him he'd had a talk with Benjamin. According to Don, Benjamin doesn't really like uniformed cops, so he clams up when a uniform tries to question him. Don's known Benjamin for over fifteen years. So, Don figured Benjamin might not have told Peterson's guys everything he knew. And it turns out, Deputy Don was right."

Kelly smiled. "He usually is. He's helped solve three cases so far." She held up her coffee mug. "To Deputy Don, kudos. What did he find out?"

"Well, Benjamin told Don that he did see other cars at Turner's property that Saturday morning. He knows Turner's and Renee's trucks by sight. Then he described Jennifer's car. But he said he'd seen two other cars up there that morning. One of them was a medium-sized black car, which he glimpsed there before, but he didn't see who drove. Peterson thinks it might belong to another real estate agent who was showing the property." He took a deep drink of coffee.

"Makes sense. What about the other car?"

"It was a silver Lincoln Town Car. Benjamin said he recognized it, because the man who owned it has been up at the property several times. In fact, Benjamin spoke with him."

Kelly held still. Arthur Housemann drove a silver Lincoln Town Car. "Oh . . . my . . . Lord," she breathed, shocked at what she heard. "I don't believe it. Housemann drives one like that. Maybe it's someone else."

Burt shook his head. "Apparently Housemann identified himself to Benjamin when they talked. According to Don, Benjamin liked Housemann because he said he wanted to keep the land intact and preserve the natural setting. Benjamin was afraid any new owner would cut down the trees and build some mega-mansion right on the river."

Kelly had seen those eyesores. Fortunately, not too many were in the Poudre Canyon. But other canyon settings in

Colorado had more than a few "status" properties where the owners decided to trumpet their wealth. Of course, now with the recession, Jennifer said more than one of those properties were for sale at greatly reduced prices.

"Oh, no, what was Housmann doing there on Saturday?"

"That's what Peterson intends to find out. Especially after Benjamin mentioned Turner and Housemann had an argument." Burt turned the coffee mug between his hands. "Apparently Benjamin heard voices shouting outside the cabin, so he went over to see what was going on. Kind of hid himself in the bushes, so he couldn't be seen."

"He was hiding behind those bushes when I spotted him. He appeared to be listening to Jennifer's phone call to the police."

Burt nodded. "Well, according to Benjamin, Turner and Housemann were shouting at each other outside the cabin. He said they yelled at each other, then Turner went inside. Benjamin said Turner acted like he didn't want to talk to Housemann, but Housemann followed Turner into the cabin."

Oh, brother, Kelly thought grimly. That didn't sound good. "Were they arguing about the property? I know that Turner cheated Housemann out of a parcel once before."

Burt nodded. "Peterson had learned about that. Apparently Benjamin heard only a few words, like 'cheating me' and 'leave her out of this.'"

Kelly closed her eyes. "Oh, no. That's gotta be Renee they were arguing about. Now that bad blood comment makes sense." She released a long sigh. "I understand why you said this investigation is getting more involved. That's for sure. When's Peterson going to question Housemann again? I'll make sure I don't show up to discuss financial statements."

Burt gave a crooked smile. "Paul sounded pretty anxious last night. Don't worry. I'll keep you posted, Kelly, as soon as I hear anything. And thanks again for your help."

"What help? I didn't do anything."

"Yes, you did. You convinced Jennifer to call me. She told me so. If she hadn't, Peterson might never have learned of that offer Renee made to Housemann." He gave her a fatherly smile. "I made sure I told my friend Paul, and I'm sure he told Peterson."

Kelly felt a little glow of pleasure inside from Burt's praise. She'd made a difference. She liked that. It felt good. "Sherlock Flynn, on the job." She gave a mock salute. Then, her smile faded. "I can't help feeling bad though. Who would have thought Arthur Housemann would be involved? I simply cannot picture him shooting Fred Turner, Burt." She looked Burt in the eye. "Housemann is a good, decent man. An honorable businessman in a business that doesn't have that many of them. I cannot believe he'd kill someone." She looked out into the café, saw Jennifer clearing a table across the room. Julie pouring coffee for a customer.

"I know the feeling, Kelly. But we're all human. And we're all susceptible to our emotions. That's why crimes of passion are so prevalent. Trouble boils over between two people and sometimes that toxic brew explodes. Violently." He took another sip of coffee.

"I don't know, Burt. It doesn't feel right."

"Murder never feels right, Kelly." Burt drained his coffee. "By the way, you mentioned you were going to that Denver gun show to show some of the dealers the photo of that pistol. Did you learn anything?"

"Well, yes and no. One of the dealers had a pistol exactly

like the one in the photo. It's an old German Mauser from the war. He also promised he'd e-mail me the names of some other dealers who might have a Mauser. And he said he might know of a collector."

"That's interesting, Kelly, but it doesn't really matter where the gun came from, you know. Just who used it."

Kelly shrugged. "I know. But I can't shake this feeling that the gun has a story behind it. There's a reason the killer used that gun. I don't know. I'm just going on my instinct, that's all."

Burt reached over and patted her on the arm. "You're got great instincts, Kelly. Keep following them. You always find something."

"I only hope I don't find out Arthur Housemann is a secret gun collector," she said with a rueful smile.

Kelly trailed her fingers along the spring yarns bunched on the maple table in the middle of Lambspun's central yarn room. There were soft skeins of hand-dyed merino wool and silk in shades of violet, purple, and pink. Skeins of deep blue and jade green hand-dyed bamboo and silk. Soft, soft.

Drifting over to the woven baskets stacked on a metal stand, Kelly indulged her fingers again. Fluffy yarns of turquoise and green kid mohair. Larger shawl balls of pastel pinks, greens, and coral kid mohair. Below that were luscious balls of hand-dyed soy silk in coral pink. Kelly always thought it fascinating how the spun vegetable fiber could match the sheen and feel of real spun silk.

Next, bins of pastel yellows and blue cotton twill beckoned

with its distinctive feel. Beside that, bins with tidy stacked skeins of multicolored wool and cotton. Durable. Dependable. And hanging on the wall were the Lambspun spinners' loops of spun merino and silk all the colors of spring—early green grass to deep emerald, azure blue to rich sapphire, light peach to red salmon, and rose pink that traveled all the way through strawberry to vibrant raspberry red. Kelly caressed each loop of spun froth.

She glanced into the main knitting room and saw Lizzie sitting alone at the table, working on an azure blue baby blanket. Surprised that Lizzie was without her constant companion Eustace, Kelly decided this was a good time to catch up on Lizzie's romantic adventures. It would be a welcome antidote to the depressing conversation she'd had with Burt earlier.

Only the pull of her clients' financial worksheets could keep Kelly from worrying about the disturbing news regarding Arthur Housemann and Renee Turner. But when she took a lunch break a short while ago, those worries came roaring back. Now, she needed a pleasant distraction.

"Hi, Lizzie, I'm surprised to find you without Eustace," Kelly said as she dropped her things to the long table. "Is he out interviewing?" Kelly already knew the answer, since she'd spoken with Doris that morning.

Lizzie's bright blue gaze looked up, her cheeks coloring. "Indeed he is, Kelly. In fact, he's interviewing your client Arthur Housemann today."

Kelly settled into her chair and pulled out the multicolored unraveled silk yarn and her half-finished scarf. "I'm glad to hear it, Lizzie. Arthur Housemann has a long career in real estate investment. I'm sure he'll be a fountain of information and stories for Eustace," Kelly said to herself as she picked up her knitting stitches where she'd left off.

Lizzie beamed. "Oh, I hope so. Eustace says he's gotten so many wonderful stories the book will wind up longer than he'd thought. He's quite pleased." She returned her attention to the spring yarn she was working in quick, sure stitches.

"Is that another baby blanket for one of your nieces or nephews?"

"Actually, this blanket is for Eustace," Lizzie said, color rising even more on her cheeks and face. "He loves this shade of blue and has commented many times on how pretty it is. He says it reminds him of the bluebonnets that grew near the house where he grew up in Texas."

Making a blanket for Eustace. Kelly decided to let that pass and asked something else that intrigued her. "I really enjoyed dinner with you and Eustace and Curt and Jayleen on Saturday night."

"Yes, wasn't that lovely? Curt is such a gracious host. And Jayleen's chili is simply scrumptious. Eustace kept raving about it the rest of the evening."

That opened the door for Kelly's curiosity to walk through. "He's such a charming storyteller. His stories about some of those old cowboys were priceless. I was sorry when you two had to leave." She paused. "Curt said Eustace has taken a room in one of the Old Town hotels."

Lizzie's cheeks flamed. "Yes . . . yes, he did. Curt had extended his hospitality for nearly a month. Eustace didn't want to presume any more."

"Oh, that makes sense," Kelly said quickly, keeping her

smile inside. "Everyone likes some privacy. It's hard living in someone else's home."

Lizzie tucked her chin. "Yes, indeed," she said softly.

Her instincts about Eustace's recent need for privacy confirmed, Kelly quickly changed the subject. "Those stories of Eustace's early years were fascinating, too. I didn't know he acted as a young man."

"Oh, yes," Lizzie said quickly. "He was quite the thespian it seems."

Kelly remembered something else she was curious about. This was a good time to ask about Hilda. "I've been meaning to ask, Lizzie. How is Hilda doing? I haven't seen her in such a long time. Connie said Hilda's arthritis is giving her a really hard time. Her knees, as I recall."

Lizzie's smile disappeared and a look of concern claimed her cheerful face. "Oh, my, yes. It's gotten so painful for Hilda to climb stairs and get in and out of cars, she no longer goes out as much as she used to. Poor thing. She's only getting out to church nowadays." Lizzie wagged her silvery head sadly.

"That's awful," Kelly looked up in concern. "Isn't her doctor doing something for her?"

"Well, he's done about all he can do. He's given her a cortisone shot but that only lasts for about two months with Hilda. And the specialist says he cannot give those shots more frequently then six months. She's hoping that when she's allowed to have another shot, maybe she can come over to the shop for a few weeks before her knees protest too much."

Kelly pictured big, bossy Hilda confined at home, knitting away, listening to her favorite music. "What about surgery?"

"Hilda says she doesn't want it. I've tried to persuade her, but she refuses." Lizzie wagged her head.

"Poor Hilda, she must be bored to death. At least she has her knitting. And her reading."

"Yes, indeed, and she's grown fond of some of the dramas and comedies on the public television channels. I introduced her to some of the ones Eustace and I enjoy watching. Sometimes, we've watched them with Hilda, too."

That surprised Kelly, she couldn't resist following up. "So, Hilda has met Eustace? I was wondering if you'd had the chance to introduce them."

Lizzie looked up, totally surprised. "Why, of course. Hilda was delighted to meet Eustace. She had read several of his histories. I'd completely forgotten." Lizzie smiled. "They've had some fascinating discussions about American history. It's enjoyable to listen to them. I was never much of a history buff, but I really enjoy listening to Hilda and Eustace. And I think those little discussions help Hilda deal with her confinement."

Well, I'll be, Kelly thought. All this time, she'd thought Hilda might be miffed at Lizzie's having a "gentleman caller." Not at all.

Sixteen

Kelly tabbed through the accounting spreadsheet that filled her computer screen. Entering new numbers, watching the spreadsheet automatically adjust totals at the bottom of columns and the ends of rows. She moved her cursor over the spreadsheet, changed a date and watched the totals and subtotals change again.

Clicking once more to save the spreadsheet to its file, Kelly reached for her coffee mug and shook it. Empty. Pushing back her desk chair, Kelly headed for the coffeemaker on her kitchen counter. She poured the last of the pot into her mug, then stuck it in the microwave to warm it even hotter. Surely her taste buds must be fried after all these years.

Watching Carl sniff the last of the snow patches in her backyard, Kelly made a mental note to bring out the beach towel she kept near the patio door in winter. Melting snow meant mud, and four big dog feet carried a lot of mud. Carl wasn't crazy about having his feet cleaned whenever he came in from his outside playtimes, but he stoically put up with it.

Kelly retrieved her mug from the microwave and took a deep sip of extra hot coffee. *Now, that's more like it.* Fortified, she returned to her desk and computer, ready to tackle the next spreadsheet. Then she noticed the messenger icon indicating she had e-mail. Deciding that she had time to indulge a minor distraction, she clicked and watched as her e-mail program flashed on the screen.

Peering at the name, she didn't recognize it. Then, she saw the subject line. "Per your request for German pistol." That had to be the dealer from the Denver gun show who promised he'd check his files for her. She clicked on the subject line, and the e-mail message appeared on her screen.

Kelly Flynn—I checked my files and found three other dealers that often have German Mauser pistols like the one in your photo. Good luck on your hunt. J. Bridger.

Kelly read the three dealer names printed below Bridger's message. Next to each name was a website address or a phone number. Indulging her curiosity, Kelly started clicking on the websites.

The first dealer, named Belzer, liver in Michigan. Kelly browsed through his website, which had several pages of weapons pictured. Most of them were old Western Colt revolvers or early 1800s dueling pistols. None of them matched the German Mauser. Kelly clicked on the "contact me" button, which brought her to Belzer's e-mail program. Kelly wrote a polite request for information on the vintage World War Two pistol and attached the digital photo from her files, then sent it off. Clicking on the second website, Kelly searched the photos of firearms. Not finding a matching pistol on that website, either, she sent off an identical e-mail and photo to that dealer in Ohio.

Returning to the gun show dealer's e-mail, Kelly scribbled down the third man's name and phone number. Faber from Texas. Kelly picked up her cell phone and was about to call the dealer when the phone rang in her hand. Burt's name and number flashed on the screen.

"Hey, Kelly, I bet I got you in the middle of client work, right?"

"That's okay, Burt. I was taking a break. What's up?" She leaned back in her desk chair and sipped her coffee. Checking her watch, she noticed it was past lunchtime. No wonder she was getting hungry. "Are you over at the shop? I could run over and you could join me for lunch. I'm getting hungry."

Burt chuckled. "I'd love to, Kelly, but I'm in the midst of running shop errands right now. But, I wanted to let you know what I heard from county cop Paul. He called me a little while ago. Turns out he and Peterson went over to see Housemann first thing yesterday morning. They were questioning him while we were talking about it in the café."

Kelly jerked her chair upright. "Really? What did they find out? Did Housemann admit his affair with Renee Turner?"

"He sure did. Paul said he looked really nervous, too. But he turned white as a sheet when Peterson said someone saw him up at Turner's cabin that Saturday morning."

Kelly's stomach started to twist, worrying about Housemann. "Oh, brother . . . what'd he say?"

"Paul said he admitted it and didn't try to deny it. He

told Peterson everything. Apparently he'd gone up to the cabin because he'd learned from his real estate agent that there was another offer on the table. His agent had talked with Turner's assistant that morning and found out. Once Housemann heard that, he said he figured Turner was trying to cheat him out of a deal again, so he decided he'd go up to the canyon and confront Turner. He wanted to find out about this other buyer. You know, Birmingham."

"Yeah, the one who disappeared into the mist."

"Anyway, that's why he went. Then Peterson asked him about the argument. Again, telling Housemann they have a witness who saw Housemann and Turner yelling at each other, and Housemann following Turner into the cabin. Paul said when Housemann heard that, he just sank into his chair, looking like the air went out of him. Then he admitted he'd had an argument with Turner that got ugly. But he swore that Fred Turner was alive when he drove away."

Kelly let everything Burt said sift through her head. She felt so sorry for Arthur Housemann. Police had a witness to prove Housemann had a fight with Turner right before his death. But Housemann had no way to prove he wasn't complicit. No witness to confirm that Turner was still alive when Housemann drove off. Renee Turner swore that Turner was already dead when she arrived, which was only minutes before Kelly and Jennifer stumbled in on Turner's dead body. Kelly's stomach twisted again. Her client, good and decent Arthur Housemann, was looking guiltier by the minute.

"Wow, Burt, it's looking really bad for Housemann, isn't it? I feel so . . . so sorry for him."

"Yeah. Paul said Housemann begged Peterson to try and keep the news quiet about his earlier affair with Renee Turner.

He said the affair nearly destroyed his marriage years ago and said he broke it off when his wife threatened to walk out on him and take the kids." Kelly heard a long sigh on the other end of the phone. "He swore he hadn't been with Renee since."

"Oh, that is so sad, Burt," Kelly said, leaning her arms on her desk.

"Yeah, it is, Kelly. And that's why a detective's job is so hard on you. Take it from me. You hear all these sad stories from people who've committed crimes, and you want to believe them, but the facts tell another story."

"Does Paul think Housemann killed Turner? Does Peterson?"

"Paul didn't say one way or the other, Kelly. He's not like Dan, who gives you his gut response right away."

"What's your gut response so far?"

Burt let out a long sigh. "I can't tell, Kelly. I have to be in front of someone, look into their eyes, watch how they react before I get a gut reading. I can't listen to the rundown on the phone and come up with anything. Right now, it looks like either Renee Turner or Arthur Housemann could have killed Turner. Apparently, Peterson told Housemann that both he and Renee were the only ones seen at the cabin during the time when Turner was still alive. You and Jennifer arrived just as Renee drove off, and Turner was dead by then."

Burt was right. Facts were facts and often told another story. No matter how much we might like them not to. And the facts showed that Housemann and Renee Turner were the only ones who came to see Fred Turner before she and Jennifer arrived at the cabin and found Turner dead.

From the back of Kelly's mind, that niggling little thought buzzed again. *What about the British guy, Birmingham?* He'd made the appointment that brought Fred Turner to the cabin that Saturday morning. What if he showed up in between Housemann and Renee?

Her logical side tried to dismiss the idea of mysterious client Birmingham. It had proved a dead end. It led nowhere, Burt said. But every time she tried, those little buzzing thoughts kept nagging at her.

She'd give it one last try. She knew Burt had dismissed Birmingham long ago, but she ventured anyway. "Do you think there's any possibility that guy Birmingham might have come up to the cabin between Housemann's and Renee's visits? What if he was someone from Turner's past? Someone who was cheated by Turner and finally decided to get even."

"That's a good theory, Kelly, except we've got Benjamin as a witness. And he said he saw Housemann's car, Turner's and Renee's trucks, and Jennifer's car. And a smaller black one that probably belonged to a real estate agent because it had been there before. And Birmingham's message said he was anxious to see the property. That sounds like he hadn't seen it before. So, it couldn't be him."

"Yeah, I remember about the cars, but there are a lot of black cars on the road, Burt. And it doesn't sound like shaggy Benjamin really eyeballed the car. Maybe two different black cars drove up that day. A real estate agent and Birmingham. What if?"

"You're grasping at straws, Kelly."

Kelly expelled a breath. "Yeah, I know, but Birmingham

keeps popping into the back of my head, Burt. Plus, that old German war pistol keeps bothering me. It's connected somehow. I can feel it."

"Well, for the record, Paul said Housemann was asked if he collected guns, and he said he didn't. In fact, Housemann said he'd never owned a gun."

"Well, that's something, I guess."

"Yeah, but not much. You know how easy it is to get guns. Who knows where it came from? Either Housemann or Renee found a gun somewhere."

"Unfortunately, that would mean one of them decided to kill Fred Turner, which is premeditated murder. Murder in the first degree."

"You got it, Sherlock. Listen, I'm pulling into a shopping center right now. I'll talk to you later, Kelly. Bye."

Kelly clicked off and tossed the phone to her desk. She felt awful now. The noose was tightening around both Arthur Housemann and Renee Turner. Which one would be left to swing in the wind?

Her stomach growled then, and Kelly suddenly got an idea. An urge, actually. She grabbed her briefcase and shoved the financial reports she was working on plus her notes inside. Then she went to the kitchen, riffled the cabinets until she found a power energy bar, and shoved that into her briefcase as well. Finding her keys beside her purse, she tossed on her jacket, swung her briefcase over her shoulder and headed out the cottage door.

She wanted to see Arthur Housemann. Wanted to talk with him, even about accounting issues, something, anything. She just wanted to be in the same room with him. See if she could get a read on what was going on with House-mann. They hadn't had a face-to-face meeting since right before Fred Turner's death.

Sliding into her car, Kelly turned the key and revved the engine. She wasn't in her usual business suit, but she didn't care. What she did care about was the man she'd worked with for a year. Was he still the good, decent honorable businessman she knew? Or had he turned into a cold-blooded killer overnight?

Kelly smoothed her knitted sweater over her jeans, hitched her briefcase higher on her shoulder and pushed through the door to Housemann's office. Secretary Doris looked up at her entry. Kelly noticed Doris looked a little surprised at Kelly's attire but said nothing. Kelly also noticed Doris's usual smile was missing.

"Hi, Doris," Kelly said cheerily. "I know I don't have an appointment, but I was going over these reports and I wanted to ask Arthur some questions if I can. Is he in?" She already noticed Housemann's office door ajar, a sure sign that he was there.

"Yes, he is, Kelly. He's cancelled most of his other appointments, but I'm sure he'll make time for you. You two haven't been able to get together for a while." She picked up the phone and pressed a button. "Mr. Housemann, Kelly is here. She wondered if you have a few moments to look at some reports. All right, I'll send her in."

Kelly noticed that Doris's normally cheerful demeanor was missing, and an expression of concern replaced it. Even the older woman's voice sounded hesitant.

"Thank you, Doris. I appreciate it," Kelly said, sending her a warm smile. Doris gave a weak smile in return. Clearly, Doris was perturbed by visits from Detective Peterson and fellow officers. The quiet real estate investment office wasn't used to visitors like that.

Kelly knocked lightly on the partially open door, waiting for a response. Housemann's door was usually open and inviting. Housemann's entire office seemed to reflect the recent upheaval.

"Come in, Kelly," Housemann's voice called.

Kelly took a deep breath, slipped back into professional mode, and strode inside. Her relationship with Arthur Housemann had always been about business. Now, she was about to venture into personal territory. She would need to tread carefully. Everything that was happening in Housemann's life was none of her business, and he would be shocked that she knew as much as she did.

"Arthur, I'm so glad you had a moment to see me," she said, forcing a bright smile. "I promise I won't take much of your time. I simply wanted you to look over these figures so you'll know where we're headed this month. I think you'll be pleased." She pulled the portfolio from her briefcase.

Housemann looked up and gave her a little smile. "Sit down, Kelly. It's good to see you. I'm sorry I've been hard to reach lately."

"I understand, sir," she said, handing him the portfolio. "Business pressures."

"I wish it were all business," he said, smile evaporating as he spread the portfolio on his desk and started to read.

Kelly watched him survey the columns of figures and her written notes. "You'll be glad to see that your careful planning has paid off, Arthur. Rental rates have risen and vacancy rates are way down. Profits are going up and I fully expect that to continue, given the increased demand for rental housing. The present economic environment has forced many people to leave their homes and become renters."

Housemann nodded as he turned the pages, perusing the pages. "Good work, Kelly. You're keeping an eagle eye on each market segment, I see from your notes. Excellent analysis, too, I must say." He glanced at her from over the top of his reading glasses. "I'm going to depend on that eagle eye of yours over these next few months as I start to sell some of these properties."

Kelly didn't have to feign her surprise. "Sell them? But these are investment properties. I thought you planned to hold them for at least ten to fifteen years."

"Plans change, Kelly," Housemann said as he removed his glasses and sat back in his chair. "I don't want to sell them. God knows I don't. But I may be forced to."

Kelly didn't have to guess. She could feel the regret coming across from Housemann. He had to mean the impending legal issues. Lawyers cost money. A lot of money, especially if a criminal trial was involved. Kelly debated how best to venture into this forbidden territory and decided caution was the best policy, even though it was not her nature.

"Do you anticipate a sudden expenditure of some sort, Arthur? We were making future predictions in January, and you were still committed to keeping all the investment properties. Have you learned something new?"

Housemann glanced to Kelly, then toward the large windows that surrounded his corner desk. They looked out on Fort Connor's northeastern views. North toward Wyoming, east toward the interstate and the farmlands stretching toward Kansas and Nebraska.

"Yes, I have. But it has nothing to do with business, I'm afraid. Business problems are easier to solve."

"I'm sorry, sir. I shouldn't have asked. I certainly hope everyone in your family is all right." Kelly watched Housemann swing his eyeglasses by the earpiece as he stared out the window.

"Yes . . . yes, they are. So far."

Kelly let the cryptic comment hang in the air for a few seconds, then she had to say something. "Arthur, forgive my asking, but has something happened? You look like you're worrying about something."

Housemann glanced back to Kelly and observed her for a moment. "I guess I am, Kelly. I spent yesterday afternoon in my attorney's office. Stan Winston. I may be incurring some large legal fees soon, and I'll need to pay for them. That's why we'll be forced to sell some of the properties."

Kelly felt that cold return to her gut. Arthur Housemann was preparing himself to be charged in Fred Turner's death. Still, she had to ask. "Are you in some kind of trouble, Arthur?"

"I'm afraid so, Kelly." He sank back into his chair as he looked out at her. "Yesterday morning two detectives from the Larimer County Police Department came to the office to question me. It seems they learned that I had driven up to Fred Turner's canyon property the day of his death." He looked back toward the window again. "I had heard from my agent that Turner was communicating with another buyer for the property, and we were about to finalize the contract between us. I immediately assumed that Turner was trying to cheat me out of a deal like he had once before. So, I drove up to confront him." Housemann closed his eyes and rested his head against the high-backed leather chair. "Looking back now, I realize it was a rash and foolhardy thing to do. I allowed my feelings for Turner to cloud my thinking. As soon as I arrived, Turner came out of the cabin and started yelling at me. Well, my temper got the better of me, and I confronted him right there with my accusations. Unfortunately, I must have been yelling, too, because the same person who recognized my car also heard some of our argument."

Regret hung over Housemann like a cloud; Kelly could almost see it. She certainly could feel it. Her stomach twisted. She felt so bad that Arthur Housemann's old relationship with Turner had come back from the past to ensnare him. "Do you think the police actually suspect you of Fred Turner's murder?" Kelly didn't have to feign her disbelief in the idea.

Housemann looked over at Kelly sadly. "I'm afraid they do, Kelly. Even though I know that Fred Turner was still alive when I drove away from the canyon, I have no way to prove it. There are no witnesses. And others arrived at the cabin within an hour. And they testified that they found Turner dead. I believe it was Turner's real estate agent who found him."

Kelly turned away and stared out the window this time. She didn't want him to see the discomfort she was feeling. "Arthur, they cannot be serious about accusing you. You've been an upstanding member of the community and business leader for a lifetime here in Fort Connor. I cannot believe they would think you're guilty."

She and Arthur Housemann locked gazes for a moment. Kelly felt his anguish briefly come across in a sharp stab. And something else. Disbelief and panic.

Arthur Housemann was innocent. She could feel it coming through as strongly as she saw the sunbeam slice across his desk.

"Unfortunately there are only two suspects in the case. Me and Turner's wife, Renee. Apparently the Turners were in the midst of a bitter divorce. She also went up to the canyon that morning. Detective Peterson told me Renee Turner claims she found her husband dead on the floor and drove off in a panic, right before the real estate agent arrived. The good detective also informed me that Rene Turner and I were both under suspicion."

Despair darted through Housemann's eyes, which caused Kelly to throw some of her newfound caution out the window. "What about that other buyer? Have the police found out who he is? Who knows? Maybe Fred Turner had an enemy from the past who decided to settle a score."

Amazingly, Arthur Housemann found a smile. It was a small one, but it gladdened Kelly's heart to see it. "I really wish that was a possibility, Kelly. But Detective Peterson told me they could find no trace of the man other than his recorded phone message to Fred Turner."

Kelly watched him stare out the window again. She wished she could offer some hope, no matter how small. But she had nothing to offer, other than her sincere feelings. "I'm so sorry this is happening to you, Arthur. I wish there was something I could do to help."

Housemann found his smile again. "There is something

you can do, Kelly. You can use that sharp analytical mind of yours and prioritize my investment properties and list them in the order of sales. Which I should sell first and so on."

"You can depend on it, Arthur," she said fervently. "I'll get started right away."

Housemann sat back in his chair and folded his glasses. "I know I can also depend on your discretion, Kelly. Everything I've shared with you today, I've shared in total confidence. I know you would never breach the confidentiality of our meetings."

Kelly looked Arthur Housemann straight in the eyes. "Absolutely. You have my word on it, Arthur."

And she meant it. This was one conversation that Kelly would never reveal to Burt.

Seventeen

"**Hey,** Jen, can I have a refill, please?" Kelly held out her own mega mug from her cozy spot beside the café window.

Jennifer wiped the table beside Kelly's. "You were here bright and early this morning. Do you have some financial reports due? I notice a lot of income statements spread out. Not that I'm nosy or anything." She poured a long black stream of coffee into Kelly's mug. Steam wafted off the top.

This smaller table was right beside a large window with a view of the mountains and was the perfect size for Kelly's laptop computer and reports.

"Actually, I'm doing an extra project for Arthur Housemann. Analyzing his investment properties." Kelly left the description there and took a sip of the scalding hot brew.

Jennifer gave a mock cringe, watching her. "I do not understand how you don't burn yourself doing that."

"Experience, plus caffeine deadens the pain. Like anesthesia," Kelly teased as she moved the cursor on the screen.

"Riiiight," Jennifer replied as she turned toward her other tables in the alcove. "Let me know if you want more food to absorb all that anesthesia."

Kelly returned to examining the income statement on the table beside her. She was transferring figures to the new spreadsheet she'd created to compare Housemann investment properties' revenues and expenses. She entered another amount from the income statement to the spreadsheet. Then she heard the familiar sound of her e-mail program alerting her to a new message.

Taking another sip of hot, hot coffee, Kelly indulged herself in a long stretch as she glanced around the half-full café. It was a good morning to come over to the café to work. The sky was varying shades of gray as storm clouds rose over the Rockies and blew into Fort Connor from the west. Kelly studied the dark clouds that gathered over the foothills now. They looked like snow clouds to her.

Great. More snow. Kelly was tired of snow. But it was March, after all. It didn't matter if everyone was tired of snow. It was coming anyway. She took a sip of coffee and clicked into her e-mail program. At least after she'd finished working, she could reward herself with a knitting break in the shop.

An e-mail message from "Belzer" appeared on her screen. Subject line read: *World War Two pistol*. Kelly clicked on the subject line and the message appeared. The Michigan dealer replied that he wished he did have a pistol like that. But he didn't. He did suggest two more dealers for Kelly to contact.

Kelly accessed her original message to him and created

two new e-mails with the new addresses, then sent them off. One to Vermont and the other to Idaho. She was about to exit the program when another message came in. This one was from the Ohio dealer. Clicking on that, Kelly read that this dealer had had a few pistols like that over the years, but they weren't often available. Collectors usually bought them before he could get to them. The Ohio dealer, Capris, wished her luck in her search but offered no other suggestions.

She leaned back in the café chair and watched the storm clouds multiply and grow more ominous. *Why was she spending time searching for that old war pistol?* She had other work to do that could actually help Arthur Housemann.

Then that feeling nudged her inside again. Something about the gun was important. Kelly didn't know why, but she sensed she was supposed to keep searching. Then she remembered the third dealer listed in Bridger's original e-mail. The one that had no website, only a phone number listed. Kelly forgot to call him.

Paging back through her received messages, Kelly found the gun dealer John Bridger's e-mail, clicked on, and copied down Joe Faber's phone number. No street address was listed, simply San Antonio, Texas, as his location. Kelly dug her phone from her jeans pocket and punched in Faber's number, sipping her coffee while she listened to the ringing.

She kept waiting for an answering machine to come on, but a man's voice sounded instead. "Joe Faber here. What can I do fer you?"

Kelly heard the distinct twang of the Texas hill country in Faber's voice. "Mr. Faber, this is Kelly Flynn here in Colorado. I got your name and number from John Bridger at the Denver gun show last weekend."

Faber's voice brightened. "Oh, yes, I know John real well. What can I help you with, Miss Flynn? Are you looking for a certain type of weapon? I've got several types of firearms. Don't have a website yet, I'm afraid, if you tell me what you like, I'll gladly fax some pictures to you. Got myself a good fax machine. I can only manage one or two pieces of this technology at a time. You know what I mean?"

Kelly had to smile at Faber's chatty phone persona. "I do, indeed, Mr. Faber. What's your fax number?"

He rattled it off, and Kelly supplied her fax number.

"All right, Miz Flynn, send your photo through, and I'll see if I have anything like it. And, call me Joe."

"Okay, Joe, I'll fax you the photo this morning. The gun I'm looking for is an older pistol from World War Two, a German Mauser."

"Oh, they're beautiful pieces."

"Yes, and I'm wondering if you sold any of those Mausers to collectors or . . . or other people. I'm looking for one as a gift to my uncle," Kelly grasped at the most ordinary situation she could think of and lie about on the spot. "Uncle Bill fought in the war and—"

"As did my daddy. Brave men. The greatest generation says it all."

"Yes, sir, I agree," Kelly replied, picking up Faber's Texas rhythm. "Anyway, Uncle Bill brought home a pistol from overseas after the war—"

"Like a lot of our soldiers did."

"And . . . and it was misplaced and lost when he moved into a retirement home here in Colorado. You see, my uncle is ninety years old, and his memory is failing. I wanted to find a pistol exactly like his. Uncle Bill felt like that pistol was a part of his past, and he really misses it."

"I understand, Miz Flynn. So, you're looking for a German Mauser like the one he lost, right?"

"Yes, sir, I am. I'm trying to find one exactly like that one if possible."

"I wish I had some of those older pistols in stock, Miz Flynn, but I don't right now. Most of those Mausers are owned by private collectors. Fine workmanship in those pieces. But I keep files on all my customers and contacts, so I'll be glad to go through those files for you and see what I can find."

Encouraged by Faber's helpfulness, Kelly expressed her gratitude. "Thank you so much, Mr. Faber . . . uh, Joe. I really appreciate it. I'll get this fax off to you as soon as I can get to the machine. And I'd be interested if any of those Mausers were sold to people in Colorado. Maybe . . . maybe my uncle might like to know so he could talk to them. He really likes to reminisce nowadays."

"I certainly understand, Miz Flynn. I can check on those addresses for you, too. Send that fax anytime. I work outta my home. Have all my weapons under lock and key in storage units in my garage. My files are in there, too. So give me a little time to go through them."

"Of course, Joe. That's fine. Again, I really appreciate your help. Bye-bye now." Kelly heard Joe's cheerful farewell and clicked off, picturing the San Antonio, Texas, garage, filled with firearms and files.

Kelly was about to return to the income statements and computer spreadsheet when she noticed Jayleen enter the café from the other door. She also noticed the wind whipping through the trees, sending them swaying as the sky darkened. That could be a sign of rain. That's Colorado for you. Snow one moment. Rain the next. March in Colorado.

"Hey, Kelly, I was hoping to find you here," Jayleen said as she walked up to the table. Pulling out a wooden chair, Jayleen straddled it backward in her usual fashion and dropped her Stetson to the adjacent chair.

Making a mental note to remember to fax the photo to Joe Faber, Kelly looked at her friend and recognized Jayleen's worried expression. "What's up? Did the cops talk to Renee again?"

Jayleen shook her head. "On, no. Her lawyer railed on her pretty good when he heard that she'd talked to Peterson without him." Jayleen frowned. "But it's too late now. Renee's already given Peterson enough to charge her. *Damn fool!*"

Kelly watched her friend's expression change. It had gone from anger to a look of resignation. Good Lord! Just like Arthur Housemann, it appeared that Renee Turner believed she would be charged in her husband's death. Arthur and Renee couldn't both be charged. *Could they?*

"Has Peterson contacted Renee's lawyer?"

Jayleen shrugged disconsolately. "Not that I've heard. But I wouldn't be surprised if he did. After everything that Renee told him. She looks guilty as hell. And there's nobody else in the picture. Cops never found hide nor hair of the British guy. So, it's all on Renee's doorstep."

Kelly kept her mouth shut. For a moment. "How's Renee holding up?"

"Not good. She's just hiding inside her ranch house with the dogs. Damn shame. I wish there was something I could do, but I don't think anybody can help her now. Except her lawyer."

Grasping for something to say, Kelly ventured, "Well, John Skinner has a good reputation, from what I've heard. She's in good hands, at least."

"I know . . . I know. But my gut keeps nagging me. Renee is no killer, I would stake my life on it. I still have this feeling that there's someone else out there who wanted Fred Turner dead and was willing to do it. And whoever he is, he's damn clever. Because he's covered up his tracks so well, nobody can find him."

Jayleen's gut feeling matched Kelly's own. Both of them suspected there was someone else "out there" who killed Fred Turner. Both she and Jayleen sensed it. *Did that mean something?* Or, were they both just victims of wishful thinking because they didn't want to see people they cared about be charged. In Jayleen's case, it was Renee. And for Kelly, it was Arthur Housemann.

"Well, I agree with you, Jayleen. I've had the same kind of feeling that someone else wanted Turner dead. But police have absolutely no connection to anyone. Birmingham may have been an innocent buyer, but we'll never know. He disappeared into the mist. It's really strange."

"Yeah, I've been beating every bush I can find to see if anything flies out, but no luck. Hell, I even caught up with the deputy who patrols our canyons. You remember him, don't you?"

"Heck yes. He came riding to the rescue when I was holding off a killer," Kelly said, curious as to what he told Jayleen. "What'd Deputy Don say? Did you learn anything new?"

"All Don said was that several cars or trucks were seen at the property the day Turner was killed. But he wouldn't give any details. I've gotten to know Don over the years, and I got the feeling there was something he wasn't saying. He never mentioned Renee or anyone else."

Kelly figured Don was keeping quiet about Arthur Housemann's involvement and the other cars that were spotted. "Old Deputy Don is a cagey old bird. I don't think you'll pry any information out of him he doesn't want to give."

Jayleen gave a crooked smile. "You got that right, Kelly. He did start talking about the previous owners of the property, though. I suspect Don was just trying to change the subject. Apparently that piece of land has been owned by one family for over a hundred years."

That caught Kelly's attention. A little buzz went off inside. "Who's the family, did he say? Are they from Colorado?"

"He thinks they're from another state. He only met the husband and wife once, over ten years ago when he saw a little RV parked at the place. Don said he went over to see if it was someone camping and trespassing at the same time. He met the couple, and they told him they used to come more often when their kids were little. He forgot what state they were from. But he did remember that they said their family had owned the land since 1898." Jayleen wagged her head. "*Whooooeee!* That's saying something. People don't usually hold land for that long anymore. I wonder what made them sell it?"

Kelly wondered, too. And that little buzzer inside her head got more insistent. There was something about the former owners she needed to find out. "I agree, Jayleen. That's really exceptional now to have family properties that can sit idle. Maybe it was this nasty recession that forced the family to sell."

"Probably." Jayleen glanced at her watch. "Well, I've gotta get back on my horse and ride. Lotta errands to run before I head back home."

Kelly stared out the window toward the front gate. "I don't see your horse," she teased.

Jayleen grinned. "Well, you and Steve come up this summer and we'll go riding—" Jayleen stopped short and slapped her own cheek. "*Damnation!* I've been tryin' to be good and not mention him. I'm sorry I slipped, Kelly."

Amused rather than discomfited at Jayleen's slip-up, Kelly grinned at her friend. "Don't worry about it, Jayleen. Nobody's died. It's okay to talk about Steve. In fact, he and Megan and I were playing in a pickup volleyball game in Denver last week."

Jayleen brightened immediately, her contrite expression disappearing in an instant. "Well, I'll be damned. That's good news!"

"It was only a volleyball game, Jayleen," Kelly explained patiently. "It was organized by some of the developers in that joint project we're all working on in Thornton. I was on Warner's team."

Jayleen swung her leg over the chair, then grabbed her hat. "It's good that Thornton funded that project. It's been a lifeline for several smaller builders, Curt says. Listen, you've gotta come over for dinner again, maybe next week. How's that?"

"Sounds good, Jayleen, I'd love to," Kelly promised.

"See you soon," Jayleen said and walked toward the hallway that led to the knitting shop.

Kelly noticed Jennifer approach a nearby table that had just emptied and load dirty dishes on her tray.

"Hey, Jen, I've got a question when you've got a minute," Kelly called.

Jennifer balanced all the dishes on her tray and raised it to her shoulder as she walked over to Kelly's table. "What do you need? Food for that caffeine, maybe?"

"No, I'm good. I've got a request. Could you check the real estate property records and find the names of the previous owners of Fred Turner's canyon property, please? I learned that the same family had owned it for over a hundred years. Isn't that great?"

"Wow, I didn't know that. Of course, we agents don't do the title searches anymore, so I had no clue who owned it before. Where'd you hear it from?"

"Jayleen, who heard it from Deputy Don. You remember him? He patrols the canyons for the county police. He told Jayleen that he met the owners years ago. They're from out of state. And they told him the land had been in their family since 1898."

"That's fascinating. Now, you've got me curious. I'll be leaving for the office after lunch, so I'll look it up then," Jennifer said as she turned away.

"Thanks, Jen. I appreciate it." Kelly took another sip of coffee, then glanced at the storm clouds gathering. No longer approaching, the sky had darkened completely now. Kelly peered at the flagstones outside. Were those raindrops? Watching the wind shift the tree branches, she saw more droplets appear on the stones, then more.

Watching the rain sprinkle the garden in a light shower, Kelly sipped her coffee. Until her conscience started nagging her. Back to work. She'd only begun her analysis of Arthur Housemann's properties. She'd better get busy. But first, she needed to ask Mimi if she could use Lambspun's fax machine.

"Hello, dear," Lizzie chirped as Kelly walked into the main knitting room. "Have you finished all that accounting? Eustace and I saw you bent over your computer, so we sat in the corner of the café and didn't bother you."

Kelly dropped her knitting bag and briefcase to the table. "I didn't mean to scare you folks away. I was simply burrowed into the numbers." she said as she pulled out a chair across from Eustace and Lizzie. Eustace was assembling his papers and note cards into tidy neat piles.

"I completely understand, Kelly," he said, slipping a rubber band around a thick bunch of white cards. "When I'm deep into research and writing about one of these historical figures, I am simply oblivious to everything else around me."

Kelly pulled out her almost-finished sari silk scarf, running her fingers across the nubbly uneven texture. The silk felt warm to the touch almost.

"How's the book coming, Eustace? Have you finished all your interviews yet?" Kelly picked up her stitches where she'd left off.

"Ohhhh, it's coming along splendidly," Eustace declared, peering at her from over the top of his eyeglasses. "I have one more developer to interview in Denver tomorrow. Everyone's been kind enough to provide me with their e-mail addresses, so if I have further questions, then I can simply e-mail them."

Lizzie rearranged the baby blue afghan she was knitting on her lap, patting the soft yarn. "He's been writing feverishly," Lizzie observed. "I don't know if I can wait until the book is published before I can read it. Eustace has told me some fascinating stories about these men," Lizzie said, eyes bright.

Eustace looked over at her and smiled. "Don't you worry, Lizzie. I shall make sure you have a copy of the manuscript to read, once I've finished. You'll get to read it before my publisher."

Lizzie beamed. "Ohhhh, Eustace, that's wonderful." The afghan dropped to her lap as she placed both hands to her breast. "I am honored. Would it be all right if Hilda read it after me?"

"Of course, my dear, of course," Eustace said, patting her hand again.

Kelly was enjoying watching the two of them together, simply enjoying the pleasure of each other's company. Wasn't that what relationships were about? Enjoying someone's company so much, you wanted to see them again and again? Kelly was about to let that thought filter through her mind, when Mimi walked into the room holding three skeins of pink yarn.

"Well, hello, everyone. I haven't had a chance to talk to you today, Kelly. You've been in the café working. I'm glad you're taking a break." Mimi proceeded to arrange the bubblegum pink yarns into one of the wall bins.

"Well, the numbers were starting to make my eyes cross, so that's a sure sign I needed a break," Kelly said, starting another row. She noticed that she was almost to the end of the two small balls of sari silk.

"Speaking of taking a break, Lizzie and I are going to take

advantage of the break in the clouds and go for a walk." Eustace snapped his laptop computer shut and slid it into his old-fashioned teacher's briefcase, complete with double handles on top. It reminded Kelly of her old history professor's briefcase in college.

"But isn't it still sprinkling?" Mimi asked, glancing over her shoulder toward the wood-paned windows.

Kelly observed the sunshine outside. "March in Colorado, folks," she said with a smile. "You should move here permanently, Eustace. We have fascinating weather." She couldn't resist teasing.

Lizzie's cheeks flamed pink as she pushed her knitting back into its upholstered tapestry bag. Mimi caught Kelly's glance and gave her a wink.

"I think that's an excellent suggestion." Mimi picked up the thread Kelly dropped. "I've gotten so used to seeing you here at the knitting table, Eustace. We'll all be bereft if you leave."

"Well, I'm certainly tempted, I must admit," Eustace said as he helped Lizzie from her chair. "There are many more charms than the weather," he added with a smile to Mimi and Kelly. "May we leave our things here, Mimi? We'll be walking along the river trail for a while."

Mimi gave a dismissive wave of her hand. "Of course, you can. They're totally safe here at the table. Take your time, you two."

"Enjoy," Kelly added as Eustace and Lizzie headed toward the front door.

"Aren't they the cutest couple you've ever seen?" Mimi cooed when they left.

"They're adorable. Do you think Eustace is serious about staying here in Colorado?" Kelly wrapped the scarf around her neck and checked the length. It was a little short. Drat.

"I certainly hope he is. Lizzie would be heartbroken if he left," Mimi said, straightening the magazines that were strewn across the table.

Kelly held up what was left of her sari silk yarn. "Do you have any more of this yarn, Mimi? Can we order it? My scarf is shorter than I like it."

"I'm afraid not, Kelly. Those yarns are really one of a kind. Someone's beautiful silk sari was unraveled to make each individual skein. Maybe two saris. It was a special purchase, and I haven't found any more like it. You could always check online, though."

Kelly frowned. "But if it's from another country, who knows how long it could take to get it."

Mimi scrutinized the scarf around Kelly's neck. "Well, you could always finish up the yarn and bind off the scarf. Then you could add some really pretty fringe. Some complimentary or maybe even a contrasting color. The sari silk has so many colors imbedded in it that you could choose just about anything. Simply make the fringe longer than you would normally, and voila! Your scarf becomes longer, too."

"Hmmmm." Kelly rubbed her thumbs across the rough and smooth texture. "That's a really good idea, Mimi. I think I'll start looking at fringe yarns. Mother Mimi to the rescue as always."

"That's my job." Mimi smiled.

"By the way, did you know that Eustace has rented a hotel room at that historic Old Town hotel?" Kelly asked slyly.

Mimi's eyes lit up. "Why, no, I didn't. That's . . . that's nice to hear."

"Yes, and convenient, too." Kelly couldn't resist as she returned to her stitches.

Mimi laughed softly as she gathered the magazines.

Eighteen

"**Hey,** I'm glad to catch you here," Jennifer said as she walked into Lambspun's central yarn room, knitting bag over her arm. "This is the second morning in a row you've been over here early. What's the matter? Is the cottage giving you claustrophobia?"

"No, I'm simply in an antsy mood," Kelly replied as she fingered a multicolored ribbon yarn. "Maybe it's an early bout of spring fever. I don't like sitting in one place and working for a long time anymore."

"Are you looking for a yarn for another project? It looks like you've finished your scarf."

Kelly lifted the edge of her sari silk scarf, which she'd draped around her neck. "Yeah, but I ran out of this special yarn. So it's a little short. Mimi suggested some long fringe would work." She moved to another bin and stroked the bamboo and cotton yarns bulging from the bin. Blues, greens, reds, and yellows all mixed together.

"That's a good idea. Any of those colors would look great with the sari silk. You can't go wrong."

"Decisions, decisions," Kelly pondered as she held up one skein then another beside the scarf.

Jennifer walked through the archway into the knitting room. "Well, decide later. I've only got a few minutes on café break, and I wanted to show you the county records printout for Turner's Poudre Canyon property."

All thoughts of fringe forgotten, Kelly followed Jennifer, who had already settled into a chair at the table and taken out her knitting and a portfolio from her bag. Kelly pulled out a chair beside her and noticed Jennifer's coral top was finished. She was binding off the edges.

"Was Deputy Don right? Was it one family who owned the place all those years?"

Jennifer handed Kelly a computer printout. "Indeed, he was. Here's the legal record of everyone who's owned the property or anyone who's ever had a claim against it."

"You mean like a lien holder or a creditor?"

"Exactly." Jennifer pointed to the top of the page. "See, there's Fred Turner's company. Turner Properties Inc. They're the recorded owners of the property now. But look beneath. A woman named Claire McAllister was the previous owner. And before her, it was Benjamin McAllister, then Catherine McAllister, and on down. They all have the same last name, so they have to be from the same family. I can't tell you, Kelly, how rare that is. Most properties have pages of owners. Some only a few. But it's hard to find land that hasn't changed hands several times to several different owners."

Kelly leaned forward and perused the small-print legalese. "Claire McAllister, San Antonio, Texas. Did you ever hear Turner speak of her or her family?"

"Never. Turner was all about selling the property. He specialized in quick turnarounds. He got this property on a defaulted loan, so he got it below market price like he usually did. That way he could maximize his profits when he turned around and sold it."

"I wonder if he cheated them out of it," Kelly said soberly.

"Well, that's certainly a possibility, given his track record. Here, you can keep it." Jennifer handed her the printout, then picked up her knitted top where she left off. "I can tell you're sleuthing, Kelly. What're you looking for?"

Kelly folded the paper and shoved it into her open briefcase on the table. "I don't know, exactly. I was curious. Jayleen asked me to start poking around into Turner's death. She's still convinced her friend Renee is innocent." Kelly took a sip from her mug of rapidly cooling coffee. "But I have to admit, poor Renee keeps looking guiltier and guiltier."

"But you're still poking around. I know you, Kelly. You don't take time to sleuth around unless you've found something. So, Sherlock, what clues have you found?"

Kelly had to smile. Jennifer could read her too well. It was hard to hide anything from her. "I haven't found anything substantial, really. All I have are suspicions."

"Like?"

"Well, like the British guy, Birmingham, for instance. I wonder why he was so hot to see the property but then never showed up." Kelly paused dramatically. "Or, did he? What if he did show up before Renee Turner came?"

Jennifer glanced up over her knitting, her fingers still

moving in the familiar rhythmic motions. "Even if that's true, there's no way to prove it, Kelly. Burt has told me they found absolutely no connection to Birmingham. No trace on the phone, either."

"And that's another thing. Why did he use one of those disposable phones rather than his own cell phone? I mean, practically everybody has a cell phone now. That's suspicious, right there."

"Spoken like a true-blue techie. First, not everyone has a cell phone. Or, maybe he's visiting this country. Lots of travelers purposely leave their cell phones at home because of expensive roaming fees. They buy disposable phones instead when they visit another country."

"I know you're right, but that Birmingham guy keeps nagging me. Something about him doesn't fit. I'm beginning to wonder if he was connected to the property somehow, especially since it's been held in one family so long."

"True, but he's still a blind alley, Kelly. What about that gun? Didn't you go to the gun show to find another one like it or something?"

"I went to ask the dealers if they had a pistol like that and maybe records of who they sold it to. Unfortunately, none of the dealers at the show had anything available that looked like that pistol we saw. But they all agree with Curt that it's probably a World War Two weapon and in the hands of a private collector."

Jennifer gave her a sympathetic look. "Another blind alley. Clues aren't panning out, are they?"

"Not yet." Kelly drained her mug. "But I'm waiting to hear from another dealer I found. Maybe he remembers someone."

"You know, Kelly, I hate to point this out, but I know you've already thought about it. Even if some dealer does give you a name of someone who bought a similar pistol, it doesn't really mean a thing. You know that."

Kelly closed her eyes and leaned back in her chair. "I know, I know, I know," she chanted disconsolately. "I've really got nothing substantial. But I've still got this feeling the gun is important somehow. That's why I keep beating the bushes, like Jayleen said. Hoping something useful will fly out."

Jennifer glanced at her watch and shoved her knitted top back into her bag. "Well, if anything flies out, grab one of those knitted shawls and catch it before it gets away. Meanwhile, I've gotta get back to the café. Break's over."

Kelly pushed back her chair. "I'll be over in a few minutes. Let me buy the yarn for the fringe. I've got to get back to work, too. Housemann's accounts are calling through the fiber distraction."

Kelly picked up a forgotten morsel of her cheeseburger on the lunch plate. Too good. Way too good. She wiped her fingers on a napkin and returned to the income statements spread out on the café table. This table was larger and located along the other café wall, looking out onto the garden and pond, shrubbery, and the tall cottonwood trees that would spread their shade over most of the patio garden by May.

"Fill-up, Kelly?" Julie asked, coffeepot in hand.

"Always, Julie. Thanks." She held out her mug. "Tell Eduardo those cheeseburgers are deadly. It's a good thing I don't eat lunch over here all the time. They're addictive."

"I'll tell him," Julie said as she continued to the next table of lingering lunch customers.

Kelly sipped her coffee and checked the columns of figures on the property she was analyzing. Running her eye down a column, she heard her cell phone's music. A 1980s rock classic. She checked the screen and saw "Unknown" listed.

"Kelly Flynn here," she said, then took a sip of coffee.

"Miz Flynn, this here is Joe Faber from Texas. How're you doing? I hope I didn't get you at a bad time."

"Not at all, Joe. I'm glad to hear from you. Don't tell me you went through your files that soon?"

"Yes, ma'am, I did. We had one of those early spring thunderstorms that soaked us all yesterday afternoon. So I went into the garage and pulled out my files. I've been needin' to do it for quite a while. And I found the person who has a pistol like the one you're looking for."

Kelly perked up. She was expecting the dealer to tell her he hadn't found anything that matched. "Really? Why . . . that's great, Joe! Is it a World War Two pistol like my uncle's?"

"Yes, ma'am. It's a German Mauser and looks exactly like the one in your photo. Let's see, I made some notes on a card," he paused. "An elderly woman brought one in about ten years ago. She wanted a valuation on the pistol, but she didn't want to sell it. She said her husband had brought it home from Germany after the war. He hid it in his army duffel bag, she said." Joe chuckled. "I recall her now. Nice-lookin' older lady. I tried real hard to buy it off of her, but she wouldn't sell it. I understand. Sentimental value and all."

That was ten years ago, Kelly thought. Maybe the woman

sold it to someone else during these years. "Did you get the woman's name by chance?"

"Sure did. Her name's Claire McAllister. And she lives in Dallas."

Kelly held still for several seconds, the phone pressed to her ear. Meanwhile, her pulse speeded up. "Did you say 'Dallas'?"

"Yes, ma'am. Don't have a phone number, but I've got the address here, if you'd like it."

"Yes, yes, I would, Joe." Kelly grabbed her pen.

"That's Claire McAllister at 3340 Galveston Lane, Dallas, Texas. Sorry, but I don't have a zip for ya."

"That's okay, Joe," Kelly said, scribbling the address on the back of one of the Housemann properties' income statements. "You're great to do that search for me. I really appreciate it."

"Sure thing, Miz Flynn. And don't forget, if that McAllister lady doesn't want to sell you her pistol, you call me back, and I'll see where else we can find you a German Mauser, okay?"

"Thank you so much, Joe, you've really helped me out. Thank you again. I'm going to find this woman's phone number and give her a call."

"How you gonna do that without the number?"

"I'll search some phonebook websites online. If she doesn't have an unlisted number, I'll be able to find it somehow." Kelly said, already anxious to start searching. "Thank you, again, Joe, and I wish you a lot of success in your business."

"Well, thank you kindly, Miz Flynn. We can always use more of that success. Bye-bye now."

Kelly moved the cursor on her laptop to minimize the accounting spreadsheets that filled her screen. Instead, she immediately got onto the Internet and found her favorite search engine. She had to find out if the Claire McAllister who had owned the Poudre Canyon property was the same Claire McAllister who owned the pistol that killed Fred Turner. There had to be a connection. It was simply too much of a coincidence. Turner foreclosed on their family property, and he wound up shot by a pistol like the Mauser Claire McAllister owned.

Maybe the woman moved from San Antonio to Dallas, Kelly thought as she input *Claire McAllister, Dallas, TX* into the search screen and clicked. Nothing. Several McAllisters showed up on the screen, but none of them were the right one. No Claire McAllister.

Next, Kelly went to a phonebook search site and chose Dallas, Texas, as her search area. Once again, she input Claire McAllister and let it search. Once again, a list of McAllisters appeared on the screen, but none of them were Claire. Next, she input the street address Joe Faber had given her. After a few seconds, names came up. None of them were McAllister.

Darn it! Kelly sipped her coffee and stared out into the afternoon sunshine bathing the garden, melting all of yesterday's short snow. There had to be a connection. San Antonio Claire had to be the Dallas Claire. She *had* to be. Deputy Don described the woman who owned the canyon property as "older." And about that same time, Joe Farber described the woman who showed up with the old war pistol as an elderly woman. The same name, the same state, and the same age. That had to be too much of a coincidence.

It was ten years ago when Claire McAllister went to see Joe Faber. Ten years was a long time. She could have lived at the address then moved. Kelly clicked on several sites that might yield information, but to no avail. No links to McAllisters of Dallas or San Antonio or anywhere else in Texas appeared. Did she move out of state? If Claire still lived in Texas, she obviously had an unlisted phone number.

Drat! Another dead end. Frustrated, Kelly stared at the search engine screen. She *knew* those two Claire McAllisters were the same person. She could feel it. But how would she find her? Kelly stared at the address, 3340 Galveston Lane, Dallas, Texas, and suddenly got an idea.

She scanned her smartphone's directory and clicked Jennifer's number. After two rings, Jennifer picked up.

"Hey, what's up?"

"Are you at your office?"

"Yeah, I'm on floor duty. Taking care of any potential clients who walk in the door. Problem is, there's not a soul in sight. No one comes in during the week. Do you know any funny stories you could entertain me with, so I won't fall asleep?"

"No, but I've got a real estate search that you could help me with. That oughta keep you awake."

"Don't tell me you're interested in mountain property again?"

"Nope. Not for me. I've been searching all the phonebook and search sites I can find online, but no luck. I'm trying to track down Claire McAllister."

A pause before answering. "Why, Kelly? Do you seriously think she has some connection to Fred Turner's death? Come on! She's supposed to be an old woman."

"Yeah, I know, but I just heard from that dealer, Joe Faber, in San Antonio, Texas. And he says a woman came to him ten years ago and showed him a pistol like the one we saw in Fred Turner's hand. And that woman's name was Claire McAllister." This time, Kelly paused.

"Whoa . . . you're kidding."

"Nope. He said she didn't want to sell it because her husband had brought it back from the war."

"Kelly . . . you can't be serious. Do you really think an elderly woman flew here from Texas to kill Fred Turner with her husband's old war pistol? Are you *crazy*?"

"I don't know what I think, Jen. But I recognize a too-good-to-be-believed coincidence when I see it. This woman knows something. I can feel it. I just want to talk with her, but I need your help to find her phone number. I've checked online phonebooks, search engines, whatever, but I can't find Claire McAllister together with that address, let alone a phone number."

"Okay, okay," Jennifer relented. "Let me check the real estate property records in Dallas. What's the address?"

Kelly rattled off the address Joe gave her. "I figured you'd know how to access some real estate websites I couldn't."

She sat and sipped her coffee, watching the wet leaves sparkle in the glint of sunbeams outside. Meanwhile, the sound of Jennifer's keyboard clicked in the background.

"Okay, I'm into the Dallas, Texas, property records, so let's see who's living at 3340 Galveston Lane, shall we?"

Kelly felt her pulse speed up as she listened to Jennifer's keystrokes over the phone. She waited a full minute, then she had to ask. "What'd you find?"

"Well, I found the owners of the property at 3340 Galveston Lane, but their name is Turnbull. William and Patricia Turnbull. No McAllisters listed."

Kelly's momentary excitement of the chase evaporated. Nothing. No fox at the end of the hunt. Not even a field mouse. She remembered the Turnbull name from one of the searches, but there was no phone number. "Check to see if Claire McAllister was a former owner."

"Okay," Jennifer said and clicked away. After a minute she spoke. "Nope. The former owners were named Sampson. And they owned it for fifteen years."

"Damn," she said softly into the phone.

"I'm sorry, Kelly. It was a good hunch, but not all hunches pan out."

That was true, but Kelly's hunches or gut feelings or instincts always panned out. Her instinct was always on to something. She'd learned to trust it implicitly over the years. "I know what you're saying, but I can't shake this feeling. There's a connection there. I know it."

"You know, maybe the older woman died since she sold the property. And these people bought her Dallas house. Who knows?"

"Yeah, yeah, that's possible——" Then another idea hit her. "Or, *maybe*, Claire McAllister is the elderly mother of William or Patricia Turnbull. Maybe she's living with them." That brought a little buzz. Something resonated inside. She was back on the hunt.

"That's always a possibility."

"Are those Turnbull names listed anyway else? Do you see any middle initials anywhere?"

"Let's see . . . William and Patricia . . . scrolling down . . . nothing. Ooops. William P. Turnbull, so Bill's out. Let's see if Patricia is listed anywhere else."

Kelly waited another full minute, until Jennifer spoke again. "Well, I'll be damned. . . ."

Kelly's heart skipped a beat. "What'd you find?"

"Patricia M. Turnbull. It's not much, Sherlock, but it's something."

"Thanks, Jen, I'll talk to you later." Kelly clicked off. She needed to go back to her cottage. She needed privacy to follow this scent.

She gathered up the Housemann income statements into her portfolio and shoved it and her laptop back into her briefcase. Dropping a generous tip onto the table, Kelly slipped on her jacket, shouldered her briefcase, and stuck her mug into her jacket pocket. She needed a free hand for her phone.

Speeding down the wooden steps to the café garden patio, Kelly clicked on Burt's number. Mimi had already told her Burt was out on errands this afternoon. Three rings and he picked up.

"Hey, Kelly, how're you doing?"

"I'm okay. But I wanted to bounce an idea off you. Are you in the midst of a store or something? I can call you back." She brushed a wet hanging branch out of her way as she walked along the garden's flagstone path.

"Actually, this is a good time, Kelly. I'm driving from one shopping center to another. Shoot. What's on your mind?"

Kelly wound through the parked cars, making sure no one was nearby as she headed toward her cottage. "This may sound weird, but bear with me, okay?"

"Don't I always?" Burt said with a chuckle.

He certainly did. Kelly gave Burt credit for more patience than anyone she'd ever met. "Yes, and thanks for that. Okay, here goes. Apparently Deputy Don told Jayleen that the previous owners of Turner's canyon property—which he foreclosed on, by the way—had owned the land for over a hundred years."

"Wow, that's a long time."

"Yeah, it is. So, I was curious, and asked Jennifer to check the land records. Turns out the woman who owned it before Turner got his hands on it was Claire McAllister from Texas. Deputy Don said he'd met Mrs. McAllister and her husband about ten years ago up in the canyon, and they told him how long the property had been in their family."

"That's really nice, Kelly. But what does this have to do with anything?"

"Well, today I heard from one of those gun dealers I've been contacting. I'd told them all I wanted to find a World War Two German Mauser pistol, and the last guy called back from Texas. He remembered someone coming to see him ten years ago who had a Mauser pistol like that. It was an elderly woman who wanted a valuation only, because she didn't want to sell the pistol. Her name was Claire McAllister."

Kelly heard a long pause on the other end of the phone. Finally, Burt spoke. "Well, that *is* interesting, Kelly, but I don't know if it means much."

"I think it means something. Fred Turner cheated Claire McAllister out of her family property. She was bound to be mad."

"Surely you're not suggesting that elderly woman came up here from Texas to kill Fred Turner."

This time, Kelly paused. "No, not exactly, but I *am* wondering if British Birmingham might be related to the McAllisters. He called up out of the blue right before the property was going under contract and made an appointment with Turner for that Saturday morning in the canyon. Then, Turner is killed. I'm just saying that it's too much of a coincidence. And coincidences make me suspicious." She unlocked her cottage front door and stepped inside.

"Well, you're right on that point. I'll run it past Paul and see what he says. But don't be surprised if he doesn't think it's worth pursuing. It's pretty far out there, Kelly."

Kelly dropped her bag and briefcase on the dining table. "I know I may be grasping at straws, Burt, but Birmingham keeps bothering me."

Burt chuckled. "Well, I understand that, Kelly. Gotta run. I'll talk to you tomorrow."

Kelly dropped her phone onto her desk and headed into the kitchen. She wanted more coffee, yet she didn't want to go back to the café. There was something she wanted to do, and she needed privacy.

Quickly dropping a packet of her favorite brew into her coffeemaker, Kelly filled it with water and let it go. Soon, the aroma would waft through the room. Meanwhile, Kelly couldn't wait a minute longer. She had to call Patricia Turnbull and find out if her hunch was right. Was she related to Claire McAllister? As for the war pistol, Kelly figured she'd pose again as a buyer so she could ask questions without seeming too nosy. She hoped.

Riffling through her briefcase, Kelly found the income statement where she'd scribbled Claire McAllister's address and the Turnbulls' information. Now, she had to find the phone number. This time, she touched the Internet browser sign on her smartphone and the search engine appeared. When she accessed the phonebook website, she entered both Turnbull names and complete Dallas address.

She clicked and held her breath, hoping to see a phone number appear at last. In an instant, it appeared. *Yesss!* Kelly pumped her fist in excitement and settled into her desk chair. Copying the number into her phone screen, she clicked and waited for the rings. Then, she took a deep breath, and called up her imaginary shopper persona.

A woman's voice answered after four rings. "Turnbull residence."

Kelly took a deep breath. "Hello? I'm looking for a Claire McAllister. Do I have the wrong number?"

"Uh . . . uh, no. Claire McAllister did live here for several years. Who's calling, please?" The woman sounded concerned.

"My name's Barbara Smith, and I'm calling from Denver, Colorado. I hope I didn't disturb you, Mrs. Turnbull."

"No, no, it's all right. Claire McAllister was my mother. But she passed away last year. Why were you calling exactly?"

"Oh, I'm so sorry, Mrs. Turnbull," Kelly said, in complete sincerity. She didn't expect to hear that. "I . . . I was given your mother's name by a Texas firearms dealer. You see, I'm looking for a World War Two German Mauser pistol for my uncle, and Joe Faber in San Antonio said he recalled your mother had one. I simply called to see if she might be interested in selling it."

"Oh, I see. You must be talking about my father's old German war pistol. Yes, Mama kept that with her all these years."

Kelly noticed the tinge of nostalgia in her voice and decided to follow up on it. "I understand completely, Mrs.

Turnbull. Would you by any chance be interested in selling the pistol? My uncle fought in that war, and he's in the hospital now with cancer."

"Dreadful disease. That's what took Mama."

"I'm so sorry—"

"I'm afraid we won't be parting with the pistol, Miss Smith. We want to keep it in the family. I'm sure you understand."

Kelly felt her gut twist. The Turnbulls still had the gun. It couldn't be the one that killed Fred Turner. Her hunch was wrong. Dead wrong.

"I understand, Mrs. Turnbull. It's a family piece. I can imagine you have it displayed prominently."

"Well, we plan to. My brother has it right now. He took it after Mama's death. He and my mother were quite close."

Kelly's pulse skipped a beat this time. And her hunch picked itself up off the ground. "Oh, really? Is your brother in Texas, too? Is his name McAllister?" she couldn't help asking.

There was a slight pause on the other end of the phone. "I'm sorry we can't help you, Miss Smith. You have a good day." The phone line went dead. Patricia Turnbull hung up on her.

"*Damn!*" Kelly mentally kicked herself for pushing the woman. Now, she couldn't get any more information out of her. Kelly could hear it in the suspicious tone in Patricia Turnbull's voice. Right before she hung up.

Kelly tossed her phone onto the desk and sprang from her chair, totally frustrated with herself. *Why did she do that?* She knew better than to push someone. Now, she'd never find out who Patricia Turnbull's brother was. Or where he was, either. He might be in Texas, and he might live in Europe for all Kelly knew. Stupid, stupid, *stupid*.

She slammed three cabinet doors as she located a clean coffee mug, venting her frustration. At least the coffee was ready. She filled her mug, took a sip, and started pacing the cottage's small living room.

Housemann's investment properties were sitting in her briefcase, waiting for her to return to her analysis. Her laptop sat on her desk, waiting for her to return to the familiar spreadsheets. Work awaited. And waited.

Kelly kept on pacing. She was so aggravated with herself, she didn't think she could sit still and do the financial analysis right now. Right now, she wanted answers, and she wasn't getting them. In fact, she might never get the answers she wanted. Kelly wasn't used to that. And she didn't like it.

After another two laps around her living room, her cell phone rang. Grateful for the distraction, she snatched it from her desk and tried not to growl. "Kelly Flynn here."

"Hey, Kelly," Megan's cheerful voice sounded. "Lisa and I thought we'd go over to the batting cages and hit some balls. The guys may come, too. We'll probably have to wear snow boots and winter jackets, but, what the hey? Spring's coming!"

Kelly released a huge breath. "Bless you, Megan. I really, really need to hit something right now. You're a lifesaver."

"Those accounts getting to you? I know mine are."

"Oh, yeah," Kelly lied. She didn't feel like explaining. "And I'm tired of being cooped up inside all winter."

"It'll be muddy and messy—"

"I don't care if we have to wear waders. Let's get outside and hit some balls!"

Nineteen

Kelly stepped inside the knitting shop foyer. Morning sunlight shone through the skylight above, illuminating the bright spring yarns scattered across the cabinets and shelves along the wall. An antique dry sink bulged with newly spun silk and mohair—lime green, raspberry, blueberry, lemon yellow. A cabinet door stretched wide, revealing more bundles and skeins spilling forth.

She stroked the silk and mohair first, then the bamboo and cotton. Then the soy silk. Soft, soft. Maybe she would start one of those short sleeve tops Jennifer was knitting.

"Hey, Kelly, how're you doing?" Burt said as he rounded the corner into the foyer.

"Hanging in there, Burt," she replied, shifting her briefcase strap higher on her shoulder. "I'm trying to work up enthusiasm for hours of financial analysis, so I thought the yarns would help soften my resistance."

Burt cocked his head. "That doesn't sound like you, Kelly. You always get right to work, no matter what. Something's bothering you. What's up?"

Burt could see right through her, exactly like Jennifer. Kelly gave him a little smile. "Boy, you and Jennifer. I can't hide anything from you guys."

"I knew something was up. Do you have a minute to talk? There's nobody at the table." Burt gestured toward the knitting room.

"It's nothing, really, Burt," Kelly said as she followed him to the long table and dropped her briefcase and bag. "It's simply the residue of frustration." She settled into a chair. "I called Claire McAllister yesterday afternoon."

Burt pulled out a chair beside her, clearly interested. "Really? Well, whatever you learned, you don't look too happy."

"I talked to her daughter, Patricia Turnbull. Claire McAllister lived with her in Dallas before she died last year from cancer."

"I'm sorry to hear that," Burt said. "And I'm sorry your hunch didn't pan out, Kelly. It must be the first time."

"Actually, it did. I told Patricia Turnbull I was looking for a World War Two German Mauser, and a San Antonio dealer gave me her mother's name and address. And it turns out her mother was the same Claire McAllister who owned the pistol."

Burt's bushy brows shot up. "No kidding?"

Kelly nodded. "She said they didn't want to sell it, then she mentioned that her brother took the pistol after his mom's death. So, naturally, I couldn't resist asking her where her brother lived and his name." Kelly gave Burt a wry smile. "Well, she must not have liked my questions, because she hung up on me."

Burt stared at Kelly for a moment, then started to laugh softly. *"No!"* he teased. "She hung up in the midst of your interrogation? The nerve of her. Clearly she didn't know who she was dealing with."

"Yeah, I know," Kelly admitted. "I came on too strong, I guess."

"You think?" Burt teased again, sounding all the world like Steve when she was relating past missteps.

Kelly shrugged good-naturedly. "I couldn't help it, Burt. You know how I get when I'm on the hunt. I was convinced the pistol was still in Texas and was about to throw in the towel when she suddenly mentioned her brother took the gun after Mom died. Well, you know how suspicious that sounded. And you know me."

"Oh, yeah. You jumped right over the phone. I'm sure Patricia Turnbull thought you were going to show up in her kitchen." He laughed harder.

"You know I've got to follow up on that, Burt. That brother could be British Birmingham."

Burt looked at her with what Kelly recognized as his patient expression. "And he could be an auto mechanic in Toledo, Ohio. Give it up, Kelly. There's no connection to follow. Birmingham was simply a client who didn't show up. Or, who showed up, saw police cars, and skedaddled back down the canyon and far away."

Kelly released a long sigh. "Yeah, but why did her brother take the pistol?"

Burt shrugged. "Who knows? Maybe he wanted to get a valuation. Maybe he wants to mount it in a fancy case. It's okay, Sherlock. You can give it up. Not all clues pan out."

Kelly knew Burt was speaking the truth . . . as he knew

it. Not all hunches panned out. But Kelly also knew that *hers* did. In her four years of poking her nose into murder investigations, Kelly did so because her instinct told her to. She had a hunch, a feeling about something, and she simply had to follow up on it. Kelly couldn't stop herself any more than she could stop breathing. She had to keep searching until she found answers to the puzzle.

Knowing Burt understood her frustration and was trying to make her feel better, Kelly gave him a little smile. "I know. But I don't like running into brick walls, Burt. I like answers."

"Well, to be honest, the answer to this puzzle may have been right in front of us all along. Peterson and his guys have found two suspects, and each one had a stormy past relationship with Fred Turner. One of them is the killer. Or, maybe they worked together and both are guilty."

Kelly's smile vanished. That answer didn't sit well with her. It never had. Every time she pictured Arthur Housemann shooting Fred Turner, Kelly got a funny feeling inside. Kind of like static on the radio. It didn't fit.

Renee Turner, however, was different. Kelly didn't really feel anything when she tried to picture Renee shooting Turner. Maybe that was because she didn't really know Renee. She'd met her, sure. But she'd also met some charming and completely believable liars these last few years. People who could lie right to your face, and you'd never know it. They acted and looked and sounded completely sincere.

"I hear you, Burt, but I don't like that possibility. I was so hoping I could search out this Birmingham and discover he was the villain in this story." She let out a resigned sigh.

Burt reached over and gave her arm a fatherly pat. "I know

you did. But sometimes, the guilty person is right under our nose and in front of our eyes."

"Yeah, I know," she admitted reluctantly.

"Tell you what. I've got to go up front and help Mimi before she starts classes, but I can stop in the café first." Burt pushed back his chair. "You look like you could use some coffee. Why don't you set up your computer and work right here in the midst of the yarns, Kelly."

Kelly had to smile. "That sounds like an offer I can't refuse. Thanks, Burt."

"Oh, yes . . . Eustace and Lizzie should be coming in soon. When they do, would you ask him to put the date on the title page, please? Eustace autographed my copy of his book, *Cowboys and Heroes of the Old West.*" Burt pointed toward the middle of the long table. "I left it there so I wouldn't forget to add the date."

"Sure, Burt. I'll ask him as soon as they come in. They've gotten into a regular schedule, like an old married couple," Kelly joked as she pulled her laptop from her briefcase.

"Hey, watch it with those comments about old married couples," Burt teased. "Mimi and I are coming up on our first anniversary."

"That calls for a party," she said as he walked away. Kelly fired up her computer and dug out her portfolio, ready to return to her financial analysis. Talking with Burt always made her feel better.

Reaching across the table, Kelly picked up Eustace's history book and placed it beside her portfolio. That way she wouldn't forget Burt's request, even if she was sucked into the spreadsheets and the "financial zone."

Hefting the book, Kelly felt its weight. *That's a whole lot of cowboys in there*, she thought as she flipped through the pages, picking up on names she'd heard since childhood. Wyatt Earp. Wild Bill Hickok. Kelly turned past the table of contents to the title page and saw Eustace's autograph. It looked like it had been written in ink pen, instead of ballpoint. That fit, she thought as she read the inscription.

To Burt Parker, a modern-day marshal of the New West. Thank you for your many years of service protecting the citizens of the community of Fort Connor, Colorado. Eustace M. Freemont.

What a nice thing to say, Kelly thought with a smile, as she flipped the page, past the Acknowledgments, to the Table of Contents. . . .

Kelly held still, the next page in her hand. Something stopped her. *What was it?* Something she saw. She flipped back to the Acknowledgments page and let her eye read rather than skim the words written there.

There are so many great researchers who have proceeded me in this work, and I stand on their shoulders. But before I list each and every one who has spent his or her lifetime researching our rich Western history in these United States, I want to thank one special person in my life. The woman who first ignited that spark, that love of history within me . . . my mother, Claire McAllister. She has been a lifelong student of American history and made sure I learned the stories of our great country early on, practically in the cradle. When other children were hearing childhood favorites like "Little Red Riding Hood" or Peter and the Wolf, my mother told me stories of Colonial patriots and Civil War heroes. Unfortunately, my mother passed away at the time this book was published, but she did live long enough to read and enjoy my first historical work, Outlaws and Villains of the Old West. *She may be gone, but her presence is with me still.*

As for the many historians whose works have inspired me, I will have to list them alphabetically so as not to infer preference. . . .

Another paragraph followed listing one author's name after another, but Kelly didn't bother to read it. She kept staring at the name in the first paragraph. *Claire McAllister.* Eustace Freemont's mother.

Oh . . . my . . . God . . . Kelly took in her breath. *Eustace.* Eustace is Claire McAllister's son. He's Patricia Turnbull's brother. He's been right here in northern Colorado all this time. And . . . he brought his mother's pistol with him.

Kelly stared out into the yarn bins across from her, stared at the spring colors while her mind raced. Eustace came here to kill Fred Turner. He must have. Otherwise, why would Eustace bring the pistol? He had the perfect excuse to be here and gain access to Fred Turner. As an author he would gain Turner's trust in their interviews. No one would ever suspect such a mild-mannered scholar like Eustace of plotting violence.

But that's exactly what Eustace did. He posed as a British property buyer to lure Fred Turner into the canyon that morning. Turner would have been surprised when Eustace suddenly appeared, but he wouldn't have felt threatened. After all, he trusted scholarly Eustace, which is exactly what Eustace depended on. How else could he walk up behind Turner and smash a rock into his head?

Kelly's pulse raced almost as fast as her thoughts. That was Eustace's car neighbor Benjamin saw at the property. The police thought it was another real estate agent who'd come to see the property. Nothing about Eustace's movements had ever aroused suspicion. All the time he was interviewing Turner, Eustace was planning the crime. Planning his murder. Sweet-natured, polite, and sociable Eustace was in reality a cold-blooded killer.

Kelly sank back into her chair, letting the book lay open on the table. Eustace had stayed in Fort Connor, conducting interviews and writing his new book. Had that all been a ruse so he could keep an eye on the police investigation?

Lizzie's smiling rosy-cheeked face appeared in Kelly's mind next. Oh, no . . . poor Lizzie. Had Eustace been using her as a diversion to give him cover to hang around the knitting shop and keep an eye on the investigation? Poor Lizzie.

Kelly glanced up and saw Burt walking through the central yarn room, two mugs of coffee in hand, heading her way.

"Here you go. This ought to perk you up, Kelly." He set a mug next to her laptop.

"Something else just perked me up," she said as she turned Eustace's book around and slid it across the table for Burt. "You have to read the Acknowledgments."

Burt fished his reading glasses from his shirt pocket. "Is there someone I know in there?"

"Ohhhh, yeah." Kelly watched Burt peer at her quizzically, then leaned over the book and began to read. After a couple of minutes, she watched Burt's expression change.

"I'll be damned," he said softly, then glanced at Kelly. "Are Eustace and Lizzie here yet?"

"Nope. But they should arrive any minute. And when they do, I think you and I need to have a serious talk with Eustace. What do you think?"

"Ohhhh, yeah," Burt echoed Kelly's earlier reply. "Let me ask Mimi if she can distract Lizzie. Maybe have her help with a class, while you and I invite Eustace for coffee."

The sound of tires on gravel caught Kelly's attention, and

she glanced out the wood-trimmed windows to the driveway in front of the shop. She glimpsed a small black car approaching the shop. She wasn't sure, but it looked like Eustace was driving.

"A small black car, exactly like neighbor Benjamin observed," she said, pointing outside. "My money's on Eustace and Lizzie."

"I agree. Let me go talk with Mimi. You stay here and act normal. I'll be back in a couple of minutes," Burt said as he turned away.

"Sure," Kelly replied, not really sure if she even knew what was normal anymore. Her life had changed so much these last few months, she felt like she was constantly checking her balance. Trying to find true north on her internal compass.

The tinkling doorbell sounded in the foyer, and—sure enough—Lizzie and Eustace appeared, walking side by side toward the knitting room. Kelly felt her stomach clench. *Damn*. Why did it have to be Eustace?

"My goodness," Lizzie chirped when she entered. "You're here bright and early, dear. I see you've already started to work."

"Good morning, Kelly," Eustace said as he set his professor's briefcase on the table. "I believe this is the first time you've ever arrived before Lizzie and me."

"Well, I have a great deal of work to do for one of my clients. Analyzing investment properties takes time," she said, pulling out a sheaf of income statements from her portfolio. "I thought these warm and fuzzy surroundings would help me get through all of it."

Eustace helped Lizzie remove her coat, then helped her

seat herself comfortably. "Thank you, Eustace," Lizzie said, sending him a dazzling smile.

"My pleasure, dear," Eustace replied as he slipped off his suit jacket and arranged it on the back of his chair.

Kelly's gut tightened, watching them go through these small but loving actions with each other. She felt awful.

Just as Eustace settled into his chair, Burt walked into the room. He gave Eustace a smile. "Morning, Eustace. Would you mind writing the date on the cover page of my book, please? It's going in a special place in my library." Burt reached over and closed the volume, then slid it across the table toward Eustace.

"Why, certainly, Burt. I'd be happy to," Eustace said as he slipped a fountain pen from his tailored shirt pocket.

Kelly watched him turn to the cover page and write the date at the top. Just then, Mimi hurried into the room, looking slightly flustered.

"Oh, thank goodness you're here, Lizzie. I could really use your help with my class this morning. They'll be arriving any minute. Do you think you could help me?"

Lizzie set aside the new turquoise afghan she'd started. "Why, of course, Mimi. I'd be happy to," she said and pushed back her chair.

Eustace quickly rose to assist her. "You go and help Mimi. I'll be right here, starting that new chapter I mentioned." Lizzie sent him a bright smile in answer, then followed Mimi into the central yarn room.

"Thanks, Eustace. I appreciate it," Burt said, holding up the autographed book. "Why don't we go into the café and chat for a few minutes. Kelly, you come along, too."

"Sure, I can always use more coffee," Kelly said and rose from her chair.

Eustace hesitated a moment. "I really should return to my writing. Perhaps, closer to lunchtime?"

"Why don't we do it now?" Burt suggested with a small smile. "It's quieter there, and customers will start to come into the shop pretty soon."

Eustace glanced from Burt to Kelly and back, his eyes widening. "Of course. After you, please."

Kelly followed Burt through the central yarn room and down the hallway leading to the café, Eustace bringing up the rear. Burt chose the small table farthest away from the other customers. Kelly spotted Jennifer and tried to catch her eye but couldn't.

"Would you like some coffee, Eustace?" Burt asked as he sat down at the table. Kelly settled into a chair beside him.

"No, no, thank you. I've had enough caffeine for the day," Eustace said, as he sat across from them.

Burt folded his big hands together on the table in the manner Kelly recognized as his serious talking pose. She leaned her arms on the table and tried to look relaxed. In fact, her pulse was racing.

How best to approach Eustace? Dance around the edges? Go straight to the point?

"I thought we should have a little private chat with you, Eustace, because some information has come to our attention that has caused both of us concern."

Eustace looked at Burt, his pale blue eyes wide. "Really? What is it?"

Burt placed Eustace's book on the table and turned to the

Acknowledgments page, then angled the book toward Eustace. "You mention your mother, Claire McAllister. Was that her maiden name?"

"Why, yes, it was. Mother kept her maiden name after her marriage to my father, Ralph Freemont. She was ahead of her time for her day," Eustace said with a little smile.

"I wondered if she was the same Claire McAllister that was listed on the court records as the previous owner of Fred Turner's Poudre Canyon property."

Eustace's smile vanished quickly. "What?" he asked with a startled expression.

"A search of the court records and title records revealed that the property Fred Turner was selling had been owned for over a hundred years by members of the same family. Their last name was McAllister. And Claire McAllister of Texas was the last owner before Turner. I wondered if that was your mother."

Eustace glanced from Burt to Kelly again. Kelly thought she spotted apprehension before his gaze darted away. "Why, yes . . . yes, she was. Why do you ask?"

Burt leaned back in his chair, assuming what Kelly recognized as his relaxed pose, arms crossed over his chest. "I was wondering why you'd never mentioned it. I mean, you interviewed Fred Turner. In fact, you are putting him in your book. It seemed strange that you never mentioned that Turner bought that property from your mother."

Eustace averted his gaze this time, looking into the café instead. "It didn't seem relevant. The sale had happened over a year ago. I was there to interview a successful investor, not hash over past history."

"I see. Well, it made me curious when Kelly told me

about the connection. Especially after hearing what else she learned. You want to tell him, Kelly?"

Eustace turned his wide-eyed stare to Kelly. This time Kelly glimpsed panic in his eyes, and her heart squeezed. She'd grown fond of Eustace as had everyone. *Damn*. She hated to have to do this. She took a deep drink of coffee first.

"No one but the police know that I was with Jennifer when we walked into Turner's cabin that Saturday morning and found him dead. . . ."

"Ohhhh . . . I'm so sorry, my dear. . . ." Eustace said softly, looking genuinely contrite.

Kelly took another drink of caffeine to bolster her courage. She hated doing this. "Well, I noticed an unusual gun beside Turner's hand so I took a photo with my cell phone camera. I showed the photo to Burt, and he said the gun looked like a vintage weapon, perhaps from World War Two."

She spotted a flash of recognition go off in Eustace's eyes and she continued. "The pistol intrigued me, so I checked a gun show and found the names of dealers who carried vintage weapons. I sent them the photo, and a dealer in San Antonio, Texas, called me. He said an elderly woman had brought in a gun like that, a German Mauser, several years ago. She didn't want to sell it, but he wrote down her name and address in Texas. It was Claire McAllister, 3340 Galveston Lane, Dallas, Texas." Kelly paused, watching Eustace's reaction.

Eustace's eyes went huge, and he stared at Kelly for several seconds. Then, he stared down at his hands, which were folded on the table. He said nothing so Kelly continued.

"Naturally, that made me very curious since I'd learned the previous landowner had the same name. So, I located the phone number for Claire McAllister's address in Dallas and called. I spoke with her daughter, Patricia Turnbull, and she told me her mother had died. Mrs. Turnbull also said she no longer had the Mauser pistol. Her brother had taken it." She paused and watched Burt wave away Julie, who was approaching with her ever-present coffeepot.

"Do you have another brother, Eustace?" Burt asked in a quiet voice.

Eustace shook his head without looking up. He kept staring at his hands. "No, no, I don't."

"Could you show me the pistol, Eustace? Do you have it back at your hotel room?" Burt continued.

Again, Eustace shook his head without looking up. "No, no, I don't."

Kelly felt an intense desire to cut this painful interrogation short. She leaned over the table, getting her head close to Eustace's, then whispered. "It was you who set up the Saturday morning appointment with Fred Turner in the Canyon, wasn't it? You posed as Birmingham, a British man, to disguise your identity from Turner's assistant, didn't you?"

Eustace kept his head bowed, his hands clenched now, knuckles bled white. "Yes, yes, it was me," he said in a tight whisper. "I knew I had to disguise my voice because I'd already spoken with Turner's assistant, Anita. It was the only way I knew to get Turner somewhere alone, where he could pay for what he did to our family. My mother died of a broken heart because of him."

Kelly and Burt exchanged glances. Then, Burt leaned forward over the table again. "Why don't you start at the beginning of this story, Eustace," Burt suggested in a gentle tone.

Slowly Eustace raised his head, and Kelly saw the panic was gone from his eyes. It was replaced by a steady determined gaze. "As you wish. This horrible tragedy began over a year ago, when I was hospitalized with a severe hip fracture," he said in a firm voice. "It took over six months to heal and I was in extensive rehabilitation therapy for another six months afterward. Consequently, my sister Patricia had to handle all of my mother's financial affairs. My mother's advanced age of ninety-seven required her to have constant care, especially after she slipped and broke her arm. My sister had to place Mother in a nursing home near Dallas where they are frightfully expensive. Consequently, my mother's savings and small investments were gone through quickly. My sister was at her wit's end. I had just undergone surgery and was barely conscious because of the pain." Eustace's face tightened with the memory.

"Patricia didn't know what to do to pay my mother's bills, and I was unable to counsel her. She was alone, as well, because her husband, Bill, had died two years before. So she did the only thing she could think of. She tried to take out a loan and use the Colorado property as collateral. Her plan was to repay the loan after I was totally recuperated. Unfortunately, in this terrible economic environment, she could not find any reputable bank to lend her the money. Finally, in desperation, Patricia sought out private lenders in Colorado and hoped they'd be interested." Eustace shook his head. "And that viper Fred Turner offered to lend Patricia the money. She was so distracted and overwhelmed by all the bills by that time, Patricia did not go over the loan documents carefully. Turner had craftily inserted a clause demanding a balloon payment at the end of the year. He had not included interest in the previous payments and put everything due in that last huge payment." His hands clasped tightly again.

"Of course, my sister was unable to come up with that larger amount of money when it was due. That was when Fred Turner exercised his rights under the loan document to seize the canyon property as collateral for the remainder of the loan. Of course, my sister protested, but to no avail. Turner promptly paid her a check for the amount of loan payments made. And our land was lost. Stolen by that thief, Turner."

Eustace took a deep breath. "Of course, I was horrified when I learned what my sister had done. And when I was finally released from rehabilitative therapy, I went to see my mother, who was no longer in the nursing home. She was in a hospital. Dying of a broken heart. The doctors said her heart was simply giving out, but I knew better. It was broken. Like every McAllister before her, my mother had been entrusted with the family land where our great-great-grandfather had homesteaded. And it was gone."

Kelly couldn't stop herself. She had to ask. Eustace's story was heartbreaking to hear. "Did you contact Fred Turner? Did you offer to buy the land back?"

Eustace's face hardened. "Indeed, I did. I offered to pay him the assessed market value for the property. He had gotten the land significantly under value. But that was his plan all along, I'm certain of it. Now, that I've researched his track record, I can tell that Turner planned to cheat my family out of our land and then sell it at a significant profit to himself."

"I'm so sorry, Eustace," Kelly said softly, wanting to offer some consolation, but she didn't have the words. There were no words to make Eustace feel better. Loss of a loved one and loss of his family's land. A double loss.

This conversation was not going as Kelly thought it would. Eustace appeared more desperate than cold-blooded.

"Is that when you decided to come to Colorado?" Burt asked, his calm, reasoned tone reminded Kelly that the man across from them had indeed been victimized, but he also killed a man.

"After Mother's funeral. That was when I decided to come to Colorado," Eustace said, voice quieter now. "I was already starting to write this book, and that provided me the perfect opportunity to spend time with Fred Turner."

When he didn't continue right away, Burt ventured, "And seek your revenge for what Turner did to your family."

Eustace looked at Burt, then Kelly with a calm blue-eyed gaze. "Revenge? Oh, no. My mother had made me promise on her deathbed that I would not let Fred Turner get away with stealing our land. I swore to her that Turner would never enjoy the profits from that swindled land. After Mother's funeral, I decided to take a page from one of my books. *Cowboys and Heroes of the Old West*. I decided to administer some frontier justice."

Kelly sat, riveted by Eustace's calm reasoning of his decision to commit murder. He was a compelling storyteller, for sure. Kelly was almost sucked into his tale. Almost.

"Is that why you used your mother's gun?" she asked.

"Precisely. It was fitting that the gun my mother had always had for her protection should be used to eliminate Turner."

"And there was no way to trace it," Burt offered.

"Correct," Eustace said, as if he were confirming a date in history.

Kelly and Burt both sat quietly for several seconds. Then

Burt pushed back from the table. "Eustace, you need to tell this story to the county police who are investigating Turner's death. Detective Ed Peterson is in charge. I'll take you down to the department and stay with you, if you'd like."

Eustace released a huge breath, and his shoulders, which had been hunched, relaxed. He slouched over the table and seemed smaller to Kelly. Air leaking from a balloon.

"Yes . . . I suppose I must. May I take my briefcase, please? I don't want to let the computer out of my sight. My entire manuscript is there."

Amazingly, Eustace looked more concerned about losing his manuscript than potentially losing his freedom. "I'll put it in Mimi's office, Eustace," Kelly offered. "We'll take care of it." Remembering something else, she asked, "Do you have an attorney you'd like to call? If not, I know of a very fine young attorney here in town, Marty Harrington."

Eustace gave Kelly a little smile. "Why, thank you, Kelly. I would appreciate it. I suppose I do need legal counsel."

"I can recommend Marty as well," Burt said as he rose from his chair. "Would you like to call him now? That way, he can meet us at the department."

"Yes, I suppose I should." Eustace said, voice even quieter.

Kelly dug out her cell phone and ran through the directory until she found Marty's number. "Here, Eustace, use my phone. There's his number."

Eustace accepted the offered phone, then looked back at Kelly. "Could you do me one more favor, Kelly? Could you speak with Lizzie and explain why I'm not waiting for her at the table."

Kelly's heart squeezed. "Eustace, I . . . I don't think I

can. . . ." she whispered. "It's going to break her heart. I can't do it."

Eustace's eyes saddened. "I understand."

"I'll speak with Lizzie when I come back, Eustace," Burt said gently. "Meanwhile, I'll have Mimi give her a plausible reason why you're not here. Then I'll explain it to her the best I can. But Lizzie will want to hear from you. You know that, don't you?"

Eustace glanced away. "Ah, yes . . . I know. Lizzie is the one part of this drama I hadn't counted on. I hadn't planned on losing my heart when I came here. Life has a way of playing tricks on us, doesn't it?"

"Yes, it does, Eustace. Yes, it does," Burt said sadly.

Twenty

Curt leaned back in his kitchen chair and sipped his coffee, while Jayleen hunched over the circular oak table, turning a coffee mug in her hands. Neither said a word, and Kelly didn't, either. There wasn't much to say.

"Lord have mercy, that is one sorry tale," Jayleen said at last. "I cannot believe kindly old Eustace could do such a thing."

"All of us are capable of murder, Jayleen, if we've got enough reason," Curt said somberly. His face seemed to have more creases visible than Kelly was used to seeing. Sadness, most probably. "And Eustace had more reason than most, I admit. That doesn't excuse what he did, but I can sure understand why he did it."

"Frontier justice," Jayleen said as she wagged her head. "Whoooeeee . . . little old Eustace. It's still hard to picture."

"I know, Jayleen. I was stunned when I found those connections," Kelly said, holding the mug closer to her chest, warming herself with it.

Jayleen quirked a smile at her. "Looks like your sleuthing paid off again, Kelly. We've gotta start calling you Sherlock from now on."

Kelly held up her hand. "That's okay. Burt's been calling me that for quite a while now. And if it's all the same to you folks, I'd really appreciate your not giving me any credit for solving this murder. Let Detective Peterson and the county cops take all the credit, please."

"Why's that, Kelly?" Curt asked. "You should be proud you found the truth that everyone else missed. I know you. That took a lot of digging and searching to find the answers."

Her fatherly mentor and business advisor's words of praise felt good, bringing the warmth of appreciation inside. "I *am* glad I found the truth, Curt. But I don't want Lizzie to find out the prominent role I played in Eustace's undoing, so to speak."

"Well, I understand that," Curt said, nodding. "I surely am sorry that Lizzie had to fall head over heels for Eustace. It's such a shame."

"I know, and I feel guilty, somehow. I feel like I'm the one who split them up and broke Lizzie's heart. They were already a couple. Eustace was planning to move here, I heard him say so."

"Kelly, that's crazy talk. You didn't break Lizzie's heart. Eustace did. Sweet little Lizzie fell for that old charmer." Jayleen took a sip of coffee. "How's Lizzie doing, by the way? Have you talked with her?"

278

Kelly shook her head. "I haven't. Eustace asked me to before Burt took him off to the police department, but I told him I couldn't do it. I didn't want to be the one to tell her. Burt did, bless his heart."

"How'd she take it?" Curt peered over his coffee mug.

Kelly sat back in her chair, cradling the mug again. "Burt said he'd talk with her this afternoon, then call me." She glanced at her watch. "But I haven't heard from him yet."

"Well, I know someone who is gonna be real grateful you did start sleuthing around and dig up the truth. My friend Renee. I plan to tell her the truth, Kelly."

"That's okay, Jayleen. Go ahead and tell Renee. And tell her I'm glad it turned out the way it did. For her and for Arthur Housemann." She sipped her coffee.

That was the only bright side to this tragedy. Good people who were innocent did not wind up being accused of murder—or having their pasts exposed to public scrutiny. The harsh glare of sensational publicity could destroy families.

Kelly's phone rang, and she dug it out of her jeans pocket. Burt's name and number flashed on the screen. "Hey, Burt, I was hoping to hear from you."

"Sorry, it's taken me so long, but I had to wait until Peterson came in and Marty showed up before I left Eustace alone. Then I went over to see Lizzie."

Kelly could hear the fatigue in Burt's voice. "I bet you're exhausted. Listen, I'm here with Curt and Jayleen at Curt's place. Do you care if I put you on speakerphone so you won't have to keep repeating this story?"

"Sure, Kelly. I'd actually appreciate it."

Kelly chose the speakerphone option and touched the screen, then set her smartphone in the middle of Curt's kitchen table. "Go ahead, Burt. You're on. You said Marty showed up, so he's taking the case, right?"

"Yes, he is, and I'm glad. Marty will take good care of Eustace." Burt's voice sounded more distant as it came over the speakerphone. Curt and Jayleen both leaned over the kitchen table, staring at the little phone.

"I'll bet Detective Peterson was surprised when you told him what Kelly found out," Jayleen said.

"Ohhhh, yeah." Burt's smile was evident in his voice. "He's seriously thinking of offering you a job, Kelly, if you ever get tired of accounting."

Kelly laughed. "Tell him I appreciate the compliment, but I work better as a free agent. Poking into whatever interests me."

"Did Eustace tell the police everything he told you and Kelly?" Curt probed.

"He sure did, and it looks like he's not going to contest the charges. At least, that's what he said to Marty while I was still there."

Kelly wasn't surprised. Eustace was a reasonable man, and he could see when the deck was stacked against him. He'd heard all the information Kelly had gathered. He knew the connections. "What kind of sentence do you think he'll receive, Burt?"

"Well, that's where Marty's skill will come into play. He told me he'd try to get Eustace sent to a minimum security prison where he could work in the library or something and continue writing his history books."

"Lord have mercy, that would certainly make more sense," Jayleen offered.

"I think so, too, folks. Let's hope the judge agrees."

Kelly took another sip of coffee before mentioning the one topic they were all dreading. "How did Lizzie take it, Burt? You said you'd talk with her."

"Yes . . . yes, I did." Kelly heard a big sigh. "I've gotta tell you, that was one of the hardest conversations I've ever had with a close family member connected to a crime."

"I can imagine," Curt added. "Bless you for tackling it. She must have been pretty broken up."

"Oh, yes. She . . . she was trying not to break down, but the tears were trickling down her face the whole time we talked. Thank God Mimi was there with us. She had her arm around Lizzie the whole time."

Kelly and the others sat silent for a full minute. Finally, Kelly had to ask. "Is Eustace going to talk with her?"

"Yes, he is. The administrative judge set a reasonable bail, and Eustace was able to arrange it. Marty was going to take him back to his hotel, so he could begin to get his affairs in order. They're going to charge him in a couple of days and take him into custody. So, he and Lizzie will have a little time together. She's anxious to see him."

"Lordy, Lordy," Jayleen chanted, wagging her head.

"I know, Jayleen. It's a sad, sad story. I never expected it to end this way."

"None of us did, Burt," Kelly said sadly. "It almost makes me not want to do any more sleuthing. I feel terrible right now."

"Don't do that to yourself, Kelly. You're not to blame. Eustace was the one who decided to seek revenge. We need you to keep poking into crimes. You're too good at it to stop."

Both Jayleen and Curt echoed Burt's encouragement.

Kelly, however, didn't say anything. Words seemed so inadequate when it came to feelings.

Greg lifted his beer bottle and saluted Kelly. "Sherlock Flynn strikes again. Congrats, Kelly. I never would have suspected that nice old dude would plan such a devious crime."

"I'm just glad Eustace has Marty for defense counsel," Lisa said, leaning over their coffee table and scooping up cheese dip.

"Marty'll take care of him," Megan said, patting her fiancé's knee.

"I'll do my best," Marty said as he turned an empty Fat Tire bottle on his other knee.

Kelly settled back into the comfy cushions of Greg and Lisa's sofa and sipped her ale. "I want to make sure Lizzie is all right. I spoke with Mimi on the way here, and she told me Lizzie was planning on meeting Eustace at his hotel tonight."

"I sure hope he's there when Lizzie arrives," Greg said, then popped a cheese puff into his mouth.

"Is there a chance Eustace would make a break for it?" Megan asked, wide-eyed.

Marty shook his head. "Naw. Eustace is a straight arrow. I'd be willing to bet he's never done anything illegal in his entire life until now. They ran a check and not even so much as a traffic ticket came up."

Greg dug out his cell phone and started entering a text message.

"Who're you texting?" Lisa asked, then sipped her dark beer.

"Steve. He said to keep him posted on what's happening up here. I'm gonna tell him Sherlock solved another case." His fingertips moved rapidly.

Kelly wasn't sure what Steve's reaction would be. Six months ago, Steve got angry whenever she spent time investigating a case. But then a week or so ago, he'd sounded really mellow and wished her luck when they talked on the phone.

"He's probably not interested," she said, trying to sound nonchalant, then took a long drink.

"Don't be so sure of that," Greg replied without looking up. "By the way, guys, I asked Steve if he could play ball with us this summer."

"Fantastic!" Megan said, exuberant. "Did you tell him practice starts next week? Marty and I have scheduled the whole wedding around the fall season."

"Sure did." Greg shoved his phone back into his jeans pocket. "He said he probably couldn't handle practice regularly, but he could be a pinch hitter whenever he could make it up here."

"*All right!*" Marty declared, pumping his fist. "The big bat is back."

"That's great," Lisa chimed in. "It'll kinda be like old times." She darted a glance Kelly's way.

Kelly didn't say anything. She wasn't expecting to hear that. It *would* be like old times . . . kind of. But it would be different, too. She and Steve were in new territory now. What would it be like? The future was out there . . . waiting.

Greg looked over at Kelly. "You two aren't gonna act weird with each other, are you?" he demanded. "We just wanta play ball. Nothing else. You okay with that?"

Surprised by Greg's direct question, Kelly answered spontaneously. "Sure. Don't worry, guys. Steve and I aren't gonna 'get weird.' Remember, we played a whole volleyball game last week right across from each other. No weirdness." She took a long drink of ale, hoping she'd satisfied her friends' curiosity.

"Except you got him good, we hear," Marty teased. "Spiked it right in his face."

"Bet it felt good," Lisa joked.

"Sure did. Plus, he'd just stuffed me, so I had to return the favor." Kelly said with a sly smile.

Soft laughter bounced around Lisa and Greg's coffee table, which was filled with bowls of nuts, cheese puffs, chips, and dips. Kelly felt something inside relax, some little muscle that had been tight for a long time. Good friends always made her feel better. No matter what was happening in her life.

"What I'd pay money for would be to see Megan giving Bubba his marching orders," Greg said. "Man, I wish I could have seen that. Steve said she channeled her inner Jack Nicholson."

"I think even the Marines would be proud," Kelly joked and joined her friends' laughter as it filled the room.

Kelly backed her red car out of Lisa and Greg's driveway and drove down the darkened residential street. She clicked on her smartphone and watched it flash brightly in the dark car as she drove along. Once connected, she saw the familiar blinking green light associated with received messages. When she pulled to a traffic light, Kelly touched the screen and waited for the first message. It was a voice mail. She was surprised to hear her client Arthur Housemann's voice. He sounded like he used to, before the legal problems started.

"Kelly. I had a call from Renee Turner. She'd learned about your involvement in solving this gruesome murder. Apparently, Renee's friend Jayleen said you kept on digging until you found the truth. Kelly . . . I am amazed you went to all that trouble and time to investigate this convoluted business. I cannot thank you enough. I'm . . . I'm simply overwhelmed by your efforts. And grateful. Please call me tomorrow when you have the chance. And I hope you have some time Monday morning to come over to the office, so I can express my appreciation in person. Thank you so very much for getting involved in this messy business. You have literally saved both Renee Turner and me from a horrendous fate. And our families. Bless you. Rest assured, I will express my gratitude with something more tangible than words, my dear. Take care, Kelly."

Kelly was stunned by the emotion she heard in Arthur Housemann's voice. She drove quietly and let his words sift through her mind in the quiet night. No music on the radio, simply the hum of traffic. Now, she knew why she was driven to keep searching for answers. People's lives depended on it. Innocent people. She'd made a difference in their lives. That made Kelly feel really good.

Finally she touched the last message. It was from Steve. A text message rather than a voice mail. She waited until another traffic light to read it.

Heard from Greg that you solved another murder. Figured it out when the cops couldn't. Congratulations, Kelly. You made a real difference. I'm proud of you.

Kelly read the message twice, surprised how good Steve's comments made her feel. As good as Arthur Housemann's praise. Maybe more, for some reason.

A blaring horn behind her reminded Kelly she was holding up traffic. The light had changed. She tossed her smartphone to the adjacent seat and turned the corner, returning her attention to her driving, where it belonged.

She wished Steve had left a voice mail like Housemann had. It would have been nice to hear his voice again.

Sweet Summer Tee

This is a quick and simple tee for the warm summer breezes. This pattern was adapted by Stetson Weddle. Courtesy of Lambspun of Colorado, Fort Collins, Colorado

LEVEL: INTERMEDIATE

Sizes:	S	M	L	XL
Bust at underarm (in)	34	36	39	41
Length (in)	23	24	25	26

* Length is easily adjusted between the bottom edge and the armhole. Changes in length or width change the amount of yarn required.

MATERIALS:

Bulky yarn or any combination of yarns to obtain gauge.

Sizes:	S	M	L	XL
Yardage:	540	630	720	850

Needles:

US Size 9—16-inch circular needle (for neck ribbing)
US Size 9—32-inch circular needle (for ribbing)
US Size 11—32-inch circular needle (or size necessary to obtain gauge)

Additional Supplies:

Stitch holders
Tapestry needle

SWEET SUMMER TEE

GAUGE:

3 sts = 1 inch, using US Size 11 needle

PATTERN STITCHES:

Sweet Summer Tee can be knit using any of the following pattern stitches without altering the finished sizes (be sure to CO an even number of stitches):

Stockinette st: (RS) k, (WS) p

Moss st: (RS) *k1, p1* repeat from * to * to the end of row (WS) *p1, k1* repeat from * to * to the end of row

Irish moss st: Rows 1 & 2: *k1, p1* repeat from * to * to the end of row Rows 3 & 4: *p1, k1* repeat from * to * to the end of row

Garter st: Knit every row

Random garter and stockinette st: Insert rows of purl stitches in the stockinette st fabric as follows:

Row 1: Knit across

Row 2: Purl across

Row 3: K

Rows 4-6: P

Row 7: K

Rows 8-10: K

Rows 11-13: K

Rows 14-16: P

Row 17: K

Row 18: P

Rows 19-20: K

INSTRUCTIONS:

Back: With smaller needles, CO 52 (54, 58, 62) sts. Work in k1, p1 rib for ½" ending on a WS row. Change to larger needles and work in pattern stitch until work measures 14 (14½, 15, 15½) inches or desired length from the beginning to the armhole, ending on WS row.

Armhole Shaping: Continue in your pattern and *at the same time,* shape armhole as follows: For Small and Medium: BO 2 sts at beginning of next 2 rows.

Next row (RS): SSK, work to last 2 sts, k2tog.

Next row (WS): Work in pattern stitch.

Repeat last two rows 2 times more.

For Large and X-Large: BO 2 sts at beginning of next 4 rows.

Next row (RS): SSK, work to last 2 sts, k2tog.

Next row (WS): Work in pattern. Repeat last two rows once more. [42 (44, 48, 50) sts remain.]

Continue for All Sizes: Continue in pattern stitch until armhole measures 8 (9, 9½, 9¾) inches, ending on WS row.

Neck Shaping: Next Row (RS): Work 14 (14, 16, 16) sts in pattern stitch, join 2nd ball of yarn and BO center 14 (16, 16, 18) sts. Work remaining 14 (14, 16, 16) sts in pattern stitch. Work both sides at once. Next Row (WS): For Small and Medium: Work one row of each shoulder in pattern stitch. For Large, X-Large: Dec 1 St at each neck edge.

Next Row (RS): Continue for All Sizes: Dec 1 st at each neck edge. Next Row (WS): BO remaining 13 (13, 14, 14) sts on each shoulder.

Front: Work same as back, including armhole shaping, until armhole measures 6½ (7, 7½, 7¾) inches, ending on a WS row.

Neck Shaping: Next Row (RS): Work 18 (18, 18, 19) sts in pattern stitch; join a 2nd ball of yarn and BO center 6 (8, 10, 12) sts; work remaining 18 (18, 18, 19) sts in pattern stitch. From this point, you will work both shoulders at once, as follows:

Next Row (WS): Work in pattern stitch. BO 2 sts at each neck edge, once.

Next Row (RS): Dec 1 st at each neck edge.

Next Row (WS): Work in pattern stitch.

Repeat last two rows 2 (2, 1, 1) times more, until 13 (13, 14, 14) sts remain on each side. Continue in pattern stitch until front measures the same as the back. BO remaining sts.

Sleeves: With smaller needles CO 40 (42, 44, 49) sts. Work in k1, p1 rib for ½". Change to larger needles and work in pattern stitch until work measures 1½ (1½, 2, 2) inches from beginning, ending on WS row.

Sleeve Cap Shaping: Continue in pattern, and *at the same time,* shape sleeve cap as follows: BO 2 sts at the beginning of the next 2 (2, 4, 4) rows.

Next Row (RS) (Dec): Ssk, work in pattern to last 2 sts, k2tog.

Repeat dec row every 4th row 2 (2, 1, 1) times more, until 28 (32, 34, 35) sts remain. BO 2 sts at the beginning of next 10 (10, 10, 12) rows.

BO remaining 10 (10, 10, 13) sts.

Finishing: Sew front to back at shoulders. Set-in and sew sleeves to body. Sew side and sleeve seams.

Neckband: With smaller, 16-inch circular needles, and RS facing, pick-up and knit 62 (64, 68, 70) sts around the neck. Join in the round and work in k1, p1 ribbing for 4 rows.

Next Row: BO in rib pattern.

Sew in all loose ends.

Yummy Chocolate Cake

2 cups sugar

1¾ cups flour (add +/- tablespoon extra for altitude)

¾ cup cocoa

1½ teaspoons baking soda

1½ teaspoons baking powder

1 teaspoon salt

2 eggs

1 cup whole milk

½ cup vegetable oil

2 teaspoons vanilla

1 cup boiling water

Heat oven to 350 degrees F. Grease three cake pans.

Stir together sugar, flour, cocoa, baking soda, baking powder, and salt. Then add eggs, milk, oil, and vanilla. Beat on medium speed for 2 minutes. Stir in boiling water. Pour batter into cake pans.

Bake 30 to 35 minutes, until knife comes out clean. Cool cake in pans on wire racks for 10 minutes before removing from pans. Continue to cool cake layers on racks.

Frosting

1 stick butter, melted

⅔ cup cocoa

3 cups powdered sugar

⅓ cup milk

YUMMY CHOCOLATE CAKE

1 teaspoon vanilla
1 pint whipping cream, whipped frothy with vanilla and sugar to taste

Beat together butter, cocoa, powdered sugar, milk, and vanilla until thickened. Add whipped cream as you see fit. You know what to do next—frost the cake! Now, enjoy!

Turn the page for a preview of
Maggie Sefton's next Knitting Mystery . . .

Cast On, Kill Off

Available in hardcover
from Berkley Prime Crime!

Kelly Flynn looked at her reflection in the seamstress's three-way mirror. The royal blue taffeta fabric shimmered under the bright spotlights shining down from the ceiling. Kelly turned to her left and admired the lines of the bridesmaid gown. Her friend, Megan, had used her own bridal gown's strapless design to model the bridesmaids' gowns, except they weren't floor length. The skirts flared gently past the knee instead. Megan had also chosen strong vibrant colors for the dresses. Kelly's was royal blue, Lisa's was lemon yellow, and Jennifer's was shamrock green. Megan's sister Janet, who was the matron of honor, was wearing her favorite—fire engine red. Kelly had laughed when Megan told her she wanted "a bold rainbow," not those pale pastels she saw so often.

Not bad, Kelly thought to herself, admiring the fabric's shimmer as she turned to the right. She had to admit Megan had a good eye for color. The royal blue set off Kelly's dark hair and fair skin perfectly.

"How does it feel, Kelly?" the seamstress, Zoe Yeager, asked from the floor, where she sat cross-legged, dressmaker pins in her hand.

"It feels great, Zoe. You did a wonderful job," Kelly said, feeling the fabric's crisp texture beneath her fingers.

"You look gorgeous, Kelly," Megan said from the corner of the room, where she sat making calls on her cell phone. Only three and a half weeks before Megan and her boyfriend Marty's wedding, and all the intricate plans had to fall into place. "I told you that color would look fabulous on you," Megan said as she paged through her bridal schedule book.

"Right as usual, Color Genius," Kelly bantered. "I bow to your expertise."

Zoe laughed from her spot on the floor as she ran her fingers over the hemline. "I swear, Megan, you and your friends make me laugh, especially Jennifer. She is hilarious."

"Well, that's Jennifer's specialty, making us laugh," Kelly added.

"Stand straight and don't move for a minute, Kelly. I want to give this hem a final check." Zoe scooted backward on the floor, leaned over, and peered at the bottom of the dress. "Okay, now turn in a circle slowly," she instructed.

Kelly did as she was told while Zoe scrutinized her handiwork. Kelly observed a slight blue smudge on the side of Zoe's face which she hadn't noticed before. Zoe's medium-length brown hair had obscured it.

"Looks good," Zoe decreed, rising from the floor. "Let me help you take it off, and I'll put this one on the finished rack along with Lisa's and Jennifer's."

Kelly allowed Zoe to unzip the dress and help her step out of it, hoping nothing would happen to the gorgeous creation once she was in charge of its safekeeping.

Zoe shook the fabric and examined it inside. Now that Zoe was closer, Kelly could see the middle-aged woman's face better. There was definitely a blue bruise along Zoe's jawline that hadn't been there before. "What happened, Zoe? Did you fall down or something?" Kelly asked, concerned. "You've got a bad bruise on your face."

Zoe looked slightly startled, then color began to stain her cheeks. "Uh, no . . . I . . . I'm just clumsy. I tripped over my back porch steps, that's all." She reached for a satin-covered hanger. "Here, let me put this away in the work closet." And she hastened from the room, taking the royal blue creation with her.

Megan approached, holding Kelly's slacks and short-sleeve top. Early September, and it still felt like summer outside.

"Don't ask her anything else, Kelly," Megan whispered when she was closer. "Those bruises are from her husband Oscar. Mimi told me Zoe had confessed to her about her husband's abuse a year ago. Mimi tried to get her to leave him, but Zoe hasn't so far." Megan glanced over her shoulder to the doorway. "I cannot understand why women stay in those relationships, Kelly." A familiar scowl darkened Megan's pretty features.

Kelly slipped on her crisp slacks. "I think it's because they're scared, Megan. Scared of what will happen if they try to leave, especially if there are young children at home."

Megan's scowl evaporated and was replaced by a contrite expression. "You're right, Kelly. I know you are, but there are shelters here in town for women to escape to with their children. I just wish Zoe would think about going. She doesn't even have children."

"I'd like to think so, too, Megan," Kelly said, slipping the lightweight top over her head. "It seems everyone has a breaking point, when they decide *enough*."

Zoe came around the corner of the fitting room, a gauzy bit of ribbons and tiny silk flowers in her hand. "Here, Kelly, let's take a look with the headpiece. I finished this one yesterday."

Kelly took the delicate confection and fingered the tiny seed pearls and blue and white silk flowers that adorned the taffeta-wrapped headband. "This is so pretty, Zoe. Simply exquisite."

Zoe beamed. "Thank you, Kelly. I love working with those silky flowers. They turn out so nicely. Try it on and let's take a look."

Kelly did as directed, adjusting the headpiece's small combs into her hair. Gazing at her reflection, she almost didn't recognize herself. Kelly never wore ribbons or flowery things. But the way Zoe had arranged them, they were very flattering.

"I look like I should be going to a fairy tale ball in some castle, rather than poring over financial statements," she teased.

"Well, wait until Steve sees you in this dress," Megan said slyly. "He may invite you to one of those fancy Denver charity balls."

Kelly deliberately didn't look at Megan. She already knew what Megan was doing. Smiling. Now that Kelly was working in Denver several days a week, she and Steve had lunch or dinner together whenever they were both in town. Consequently, Megan had made it a point to offer frequent suggestions as to other recreational activities Kelly and Steve could pursue. "Suggestions," Megan always claimed. Planting seeds, Kelly surmised.

Once Steve started driving up to Fort Connor this past spring and summer to play baseball on his old team, Kelly and Steve had a chance to be in each other's company on a regular basis. *Familiar ground.* It had made it easier for them to move to the next step of having dinner together. Of course, Megan and the rest of the gang were careful to maintain a relaxed environment. No expectations, Kelly had told them.

Now that she and Steve had gotten past their sudden and dramatic breakup last year, Kelly figured both of them needed simply to be friends right now, while they figured out what came next. *What did the future hold in store?* She didn't know. All Kelly knew was she enjoyed having Steve back in her life. After all, they'd started out as friends before they became lovers once before. Maybe they could again.

Right now, they were two friends who really enjoyed each other's company. They talked on the phone every day, even when Steve was traveling on business for the Denver company where he worked. Having watched his own small architect and builder business go belly-up in the recession that followed the recent housing debacle, Steve threw his energy and creativity into Sam Kaufman's construction company. Sam appreciated Steve's efforts and encouraged him to follow up on new ideas. Steve had jumped at the chance.

Zoe glanced from Megan to Kelly and back again, a smile tweaking her lips. "Who's Steve? Kelly's boyfriend?"

Kelly didn't even have time to answer. Megan did it for

her. "He was for over two years. Then they split up last year. All of us are hoping they'll get back together." She flashed that Cheshire cat smile Kelly had seen frequently these past six months.

"I haven't heard a word from Kelly," Zoe teased. "Why's Megan answering for you?"

Kelly pretended to continue admiring the pretty headband. "Because she does it so well. Megan's got an overactive imagination."

"It's not my imagination," Megan retorted. "We've all seen you two whenever you're together. You're a matched set."

Kelly had to laugh at that, and so did Zoe. Removing the delicate headband, she returned it to the seamstress. "She makes it sound like we're bookends. Now I know what I'm going to give you and Marty for a wedding present. A set of monstrosity bookends. Maybe two huge moose heads or something."

"Please, don't. Marty would probably fall in love with them, and we'd have them on the living room bookshelves." Megan rolled her eyes.

"You are so funny, Megan," Zoe said, chuckling. "Let me put this away and check my daytimer. Now that Kelly's gown is completed, we've finished everything with three weeks to spare."

"Wonderful job, Zoe," Megan said as the seamstress headed for the curtained doorway that led to a workroom in the rear of the small shop located in a neighborhood strip mall.

Kelly checked the mirror and fluffed her shoulder-length

hair. "You're right on track, Megan. I hate to sound like an anal accountant, but I am. Planning makes all the difference."

Megan drew her cell phone from her pants pocket as she returned to her chair in the corner. "You're preaching to the choir on that one, Kelly. I couldn't have done it without my lists. Which reminds me that I have to check on those caterers again."

"And that reminds me I have to finish up one of my clients' financial statements. I've got an appointment with him tomorrow."

"When will you be in Denver again?" Megan looked up from her cell phone screen.

"Later this week, and no, Steve won't be there," Kelly teased. "He's visiting some specialty building firms at a conference in Oregon."

"Too bad." Megan shot her a wicked grin before she spoke into the phone. "Hello, this is Megan Smith. Is Kevin there? I need to change my wedding reception estimate again."

Kelly felt sorry for caterer Kevin. Megan had been increasing the guest list estimate every week for a month. Kelly grabbed her shoulder bag and started for the door. The sooner she finished those financial statements, the sooner she could take a break at Lambspun, the knitting and fiber shop close to her cottage. She had been buried in work for several days for her Fort Collins real estate investor client, Arthur Housemann, and her Denver developer client, Don Warner.

Letting her mind return to matters financial brought another thought from the back of her mind. She needed to pay Zoe for the dress. Kelly was always scrupulous in paying small business owners by check. That way, they kept the entire amount rather than pay credit card fees. It was a small thing, but could make a real difference to a small business owner like Zoe Yeager. Her sewing business had grown substantially thanks to Zoe's creative designs. Small business success stories always made the accountant lobe in Kelly's brain buzz. Only the strongest and best survived, especially in a recession environment.

Kelly changed direction and walked through the curtained doorway that led to Zoe's workshop. She was about to turn the corner into the lighted area when Zoe's sharp voice held her in place.

"Don't give me excuses. I told you I needed that gown finished by tonight!"

Kelly didn't hear anyone reply, so she assumed Zoe was on the phone.

"I don't care how late you have to stay up. Just finish it tonight, do you hear? Or I'll take it out of your wages. You can bring it to the shop on your way to work tomorrow morning. And don't call me again. I'm busy."

Kelly quickly turned and retreated into the outer dressing room once again, not wanting to disturb what was obviously a heated conversation. She was also surprised at Zoe's tone of voice. It was sharp and dictatorial. Ugly. Whenever Kelly saw her, Zoe was always so pleasant and cheerful. Kelly couldn't help wondering whom Zoe was talking to.

Megan was clicking off her phone call, so Kelly approached and lowered her voice. "Zoe is in the midst of a phone call. I can't wait, so would you ask her to please mail me a bill, and I'll send a check right away? I need to finish some financial statements."

"No problem. She needs to send bills to Lisa and Jennifer, too," Megan said, running her finger down the smartphone's screen.

"You can add it to one of your to-do lists," Kelly said as she left.

New in the "terrific"* Knitting Mysteries
from national bestselling author

Maggie Sefton

Dropped Dead Stitch

A KNITTING MYSTERY

Kelly's friend Jennifer is a top-notch knitter—and a bit of a party girl. But she's always stayed one step ahead of trouble, until the night a stranger follows her home. As Jennifer recovers from the encounter, she leans on Kelly and her close-knit group of friends for support.

A ranch retreat in the mountains, stitching and talking, is exactly what Jennifer and the gang need. But they're all in for a shock—because the owner of the ranch turns out to be Jennifer's attacker. When the man is found dead a few days later, Jennifer is the most likely suspect. Now, Kelly has to pick up the stitches before things get out of hand.

**The Mystery Reader*

penguin.com

Don't miss any of the
Prime Crime mysteries featuring Kelly Flynn
and her eclectic knitting circle

FROM NATIONAL BESTSELLING AUTHOR
MAGGIE SEFTON

penguin.com

M395AS0112